A
SWATCH
OF
MURDER

A
SWATCH
OF
MURDER

SUMMER PRESCOTT

LEVEL
BEST BOOKS

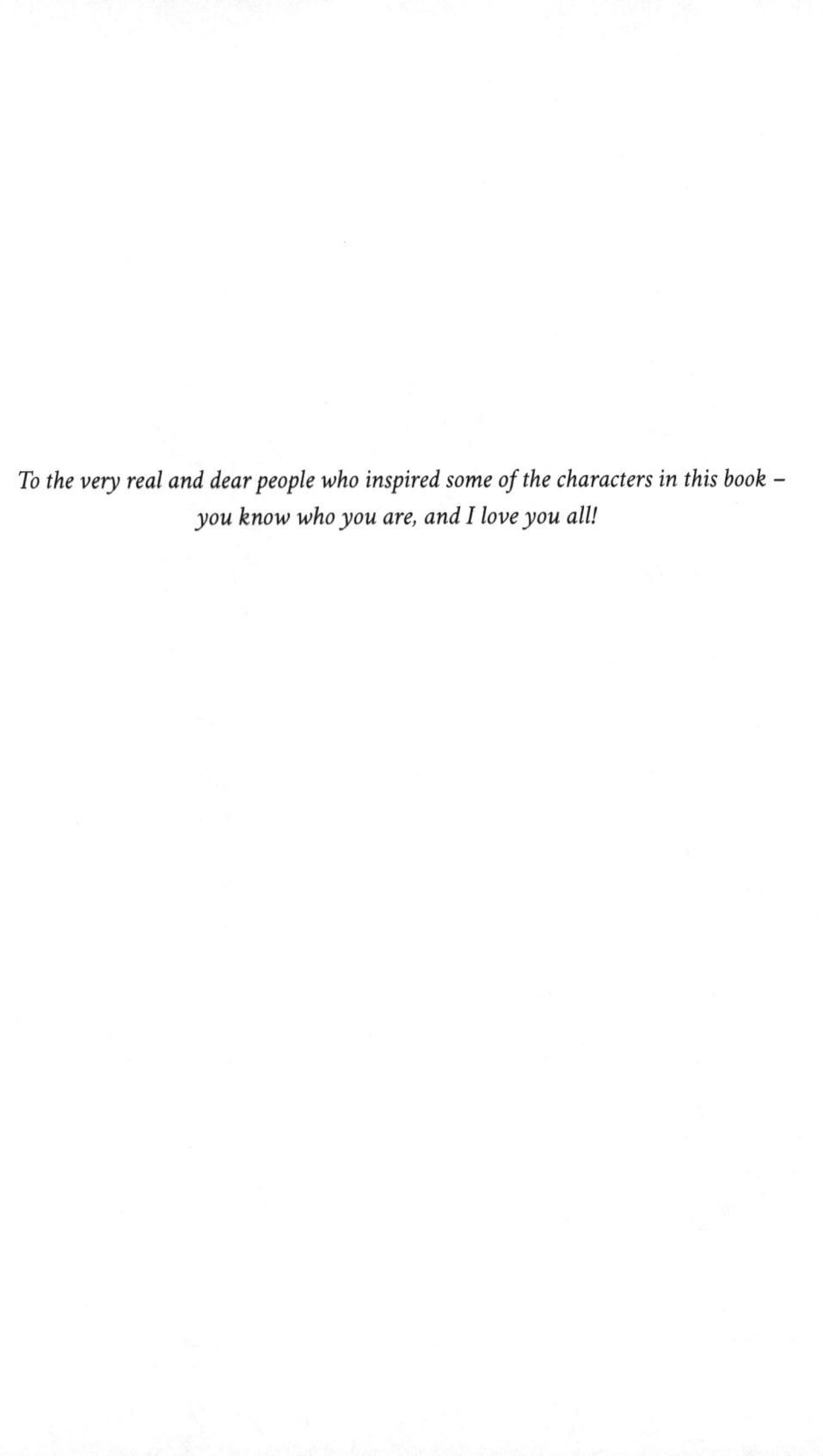

To the very real and dear people who inspired some of the characters in this book –
you know who you are, and I love you all!

Praise for A Swatch of Murder

"I absolutely loved this book. The characters and the descriptions made me feel as if I were a part of the book. I truly did not want it to end. This is a read not to be missed! My congrats to the author. I only wish I'd written it—It's bound to be a huge hit!!!"—Dianne Harman, *USA Today* bestselling author and Amazon All-Star

"*A Swatch for Murder* by Summer Prescott, is a cute whodunit that follows the quirky decorator Sari Samson on her journey to unravel a murder mystery filled with whimsical characters and surprising twists!"—*USA Today* bestselling author Tonya Kappes

Chapter One

I never dreamed that doing a guest room makeover would land me, Sari Samson, in jail, but then again, stranger things have happened. I'd done everything right that fateful April morning. I have a specific routine, you see. It's not superstition, exactly. Some of the things I do without fail are quite practical, like examining my checklist to make sure I have all the tools that I'll need. Other things are a bit more...quirky.

My long, wavy black hair goes up in a bun, but I pull down a few tendrils so that I don't look severe. A black skirt or a pair of black trousers is a must—a vain attempt to try to minimize the sand in the bottom of my hourglass—with a feminine, but not girlie, top, appropriate for the season. In this case, that meant a to-die-for lime-green cashmere V-neck sweater. I wear low kitten heels, so that I don't trip and die while walking through a client's home, and I wear exactly four rings, two bracelets, and a scarf rather than a necklace.

I labor under the assumption that if something works, use it. Over and over. Why deviate when you find a sure thing? My makeup is the same, no matter what the season, because, through some sort of genetic curse, I don't tan. Like, ever. I stay the same pasty porcelain color year-round.

I prepped, psyched myself up, and was adequately caffeinated when I stepped out of my car into a lovely central Illinois afternoon, trotted up the steps, and rang Sally Edgerton's doorbell with a confident smile, just in case she had security cameras focused on me. The darling of the local art scene answered the door, resplendent in a flowy, emerald-green caftan that made her bottle-red hair positively glow. Her eyeliner had wings so perfect that I wondered if her face might take flight, and the faintest wisp of her expensive perfume wafted out to greet me. The fifty-something beauty was a romance author who, along with her live-in boyfriend—a professor at the University—hosted art shows featuring local artists in her mid-century modern home. To say that she was eccentric was a vast understatement, but she was endearing eccentric rather than scary eccentric, I was relieved to discover, and her irreverent personality charmed me instantly. She's known for speaking her mind with glorious abandon, and I envy her ability to come up with a pithy comment at a moment's notice. I'm more of the 'think of the perfect burn twenty minutes after the event' type.

Sally had gotten my name from a past client, whom I struggled to remember, and was hopping with excitement at the thought of her guest room makeover. I stepped in the front door and was immediately transported to mid-century wonderland. She had blended vintage and contemporary pieces with an exquisite eye for balance, using a brilliant palette of blues, greens, and touches of a retro shade of burnt orange that really made the cooler colors sing.

There was a bold green and blue Chihuly chandelier in the foyer that made the light coming through the windows play on the pale grey walls in waves of color that reminded me of the ocean. Priceless works of art graced those walls, which I'm assuming were painted neutrally in order to showcase the collection and were flanked by framed fingerpaint masterpieces produced by Sally's grandchildren. The entire effect was stunning and cohesive, and I had to wonder why she'd bothered to call me. She took me through the grand vaulted foyer with its magnificent beams and soaring windows, through the expansive living room and formal dining room, into the kitchen, where she had a tray of tea and cookies waiting.

Clients always want to feed me. Always. As someone who sells my services for a living, I fully realize the value in bonding over a plate of Toll House magic, but as a woman who watches her waistline steadily expanding, I sometimes wish they'd feed me carrots and celery.

But I had a job to do, so I dutifully sat down while Sally bustled about—a perfect hostess, though she'd adamantly deny it—and enjoyed being regaled with tales of book signings gone wrong and scandalous tidbits about the local social scene. Sally's wicked sense of humor and stories about people whom I only knew through articles and talk shows kept me chuckling, and I was able to control myself enough to only consume *one* of her melt-in-your-mouth cookies, though I still planned to skip lunch, just to be safe. I took bites so miniscule that a mouse could have swallowed them, which enabled me to make that sucker last all the way through the bonding ritual.

Once it was evident that teatime was coming to a close, and I could finally get to work, I uttered my usual info-gathering request—take me to your closet. Sally stared at me as though I'd lost my mind, which is a pretty typical reaction to my initial directive.

"But, honey, we're doing the guest room, not the closet," she protested.

I let her in on a little trade secret. I always check out the client's closet to see what styles and colors they like. If they dress like Lauren Bacall, then we'll most likely be going with a classic, muted palette and clean lines. If everything is frilly and ultra-feminine, I might involve lace, softer fabrics, and a bit of pastel. The closets don't define the design, they just point me in a general direction.

"Well, aren't you just clever!" Sally clapped her hands together in delight and led me into the master bedroom, her caftan skimming the floor and flowing behind her in silky waves.

Her closet scared the dickens out of me. It was a riot of color, with exotic fabrics and bold styles. It was as if a bowl of fruit, a Hawaiian holiday, and a Pride parade had been scooped up and deposited neatly in the custom-designed room.

"What's it saying to you?" she whispered, as I took it all in.

I manufactured what I hoped to be a convincing smile. "It boldly flings open the door to all sorts of possibilities."

Sally put a hand to her heart and beamed. "Oh, that's wonderful."

I took a breath and nodded, not quite meeting her eyes. "Let's go see the guest room."

She led me down the hall, which was also graced with bold and colorful paintings—these were from exclusively local artists—and I stopped to take a look at some of the more arresting pieces. I asked her if she had designed the rest of the house herself, and she blushed and admitted that she had.

"I'm sorry, Sally, but if you don't mind my asking…why, if you're so good at putting a room together, have you hired me?"

"Because, honestly, I have a vision for this room that my beloved just cannot get on board with." Sally sighed, leading me into the guest room, which looked a bit…generic.

It wasn't a *bad* design. It just had the depth and personality of a hotel room on the off-ramp of a highway.

"What's your vision?" I braced myself for her reply.

"Well, I wanted to do this room in my favorite color." She hesitated.

"Which is?"

"Pink." She announced with a smile, as though even the very word made her happy.

"Well, that shouldn't be a problem," I assured her. "We can certainly incorporate some pink into the room without making it seem too over the top for your…uh…beloved."

I asked her to be more specific, and she started gushing about flamingos and strawberry stripes and heart wallpaper. I had to call a timeout.

"Sally, when I said we could incorporate some pink into the room, I really meant that we could give it a hint of pink. A whisper, if you will. What you're describing is more of a shout."

"Yes! Beautiful! I love that! I want a shout of pink." She nodded vigorously.

I tried again.

"Sally, sweetie, this is your guest room, correct?"

"Yes, absolutely."

"It's not polite to shout at your guests, even when it's with color." I stifled the mirth that had bubbled up within me at the thought of a shout of pink.

She immediately looked deflated.

"Look," I confided, leaning in conspiratorially. "Pink is one of my favorite colors, too." It wasn't a lie. I actually love pink in all its wonderful forms and pinkness. "I guarantee that I can give you a room with enough pink to make you happy, and a subtlety that will make your beloved and your guests comfortable. You just have to trust me."

Sally stared at me, her thickly mascaraed lashes beating like butterfly wings, her hazel eyes grave. Then she nodded.

"I like you, Sari Samson. I will trust you with my pink room," she promised, holding up her pinkie for a pinkie swear.

I locked my pinkie with hers, and we shook on it.

"Perfect. Now, if you have something else to do…" I made a shooing motion toward the door. "I'm going to be doing the boring side of things. I'll be taking photos of the room, measuring everything, and doing a couple of rough sketches, just for my use."

"Ohhhh…" Her eyes went wide. "This is where the magic begins. Okay, I'll leave you to it."

She put her hands together under her chin in a namaste and bowed, backing out the door.

"Just let me know if you need cookies or tea or anything," she called out on her way down the hall.

Once I was certain that she was out of earshot, I allowed myself the brief giggle that I'd been repressing. Sally Edgerton was a hoot, and I now had the task of creating a pink oasis that wouldn't be objectionable to most humans. Challenge accepted.

I had just finished measuring for new drapes when a figure across the street caught my eye. A technician of some sort emerged from between two houses, carrying a clipboard, and looking down at it as he walked toward a white van, which was parked almost directly across from the guest room window. I didn't take the time to examine either the man, or his van. I had to maintain my focus in order to give Sally the guest room of her dreams. A good reference from her could generate a huge amount of future business for me, so there was quite a bit at stake with this particular job. I didn't even notice whether or not the man with the clipboard was cute, which made me seriously wonder if my bestie Charla was right…maybe I was working too hard.

I measured the guest room closet, where I was planning to install a bed and breakfast type mini-kitchenette with a microwave and coffee maker, and was making notes about that part of the project when all heck broke loose.

Sirens wailed, miles away, and as they got closer, they slowed, blaring directly into the room. A firetruck came blazing around the corner, pulling up in front of the house two doors down from Sally's and across the street. Then came an ambulance, and after, a flood of police cars.

"Oh dear." Sally came into the guest room to get a better view of what was happening across the street. She hurried to the window and shoved the yards of beige sheers aside. "I hope Cliff is okay."

"Cliff?" I asked, making notes in my notebook about cabinet faces for the kitchenette. A light driftwood finish would be perfect.

"My neighbor, Cliff Bennett. He's been looking a bit peaked lately." Sally frowned, peering out and craning her neck to catch a better angle.

"Is he elderly?" I didn't really know what else to say.

"In this neighborhood, pretty much everyone is elderly." Sally hadn't moved from the window. "I'm the baby of the bunch, but they all think I'm crazy, so no one messes with me," she snickered.

Suddenly, she gasped, her hands going to her throat.

"What?"

"Look." She pointed.

I glanced out the window and saw the coroner's van parking in her neighbor's driveway.

"Oh, yikes, that's never a good sign." I was a bit embarrassed about how much the sight of that van piqued my curiosity.

I watch crime shows regularly and was well aware that the appearance of the coroner might mean foul play. Intrigue pushed past my shame in a heartbeat, and I found myself plotting ways to check out the drama that was unfolding across the street. Perhaps if I left right away, I might be able to edge a bit closer to the scene on the way to my car.

"Well, I think I have all I need for now. I'll get started on your design and give you a call when I have it pulled together. Sound good?" I sidled toward the door.

"Oh, sure, I'll see you out." Sally waved a hand toward the hall, understand-

6

ably distracted by the events playing out across the street.

Before she turned away from the window, I noticed something on one of the built-in bookshelves and picked it up, rubbing the well-worn strip of leather that had grown soft with age.

"Oh, that's Buster's," Sally murmured when she saw me holding the dog's collar.

"I didn't know you have a dog," I said, unwitting clod that I am.

"*Did* have," Sally corrected. "He passed last summer. He was the sweetest boy."

"Oh, I'm so sorry." I could feel my face turning scarlet as my heart sunk down to the vicinity of my toes, but then I had an inspiration.

I like to make a special gift for each client—something personal and meaningful that becomes a part of their décor. Choosing Sally's special gift would be easy.

"May I borrow this?" I held up the collar.

She cocked a well-groomed eyebrow at me in surprise.

"For inspiration," I hastily amended.

"We must follow where the muse leads." She nodded, looking a bit confused. "But I will definitely need that back from you, so please don't lose it. It's precious to me." She tucked her lower lip between her teeth.

"I understand. I have a fur-baby too," I said softly.

She foisted a bag of Toll House cookies on me before she'd let me leave, and out the door I went. I took furtive glances toward the neighbors' house from behind my sunglasses when I left Sally's beautiful home and spent extra time getting my bag settled in the trunk, my eyes glued to the buzz of activity across the street.

A distinguished-looking older gentleman with mussed hair and wrinkled clothing came out of the house and stood in the driveway, arms folded, staring into space. Another man, whom I assumed must be the first guy's son or something, came and put an arm around him, which the elder man instantly shrugged off. There were two paramedics, who exited right behind the two men and got back into their ambulance, looking solemn. They turned the flashing lights off and pulled slowly out of the driveway. The ambulance departed as it had arrived…empty. The old man stared after it, watching it until it disappeared around the corner. I shuffled around some flooring sample boards when they passed, so that I didn't have to make awkward eye contact with the EMTs, and when I looked up again, I was startled to see a policeman walking toward me.

Heart in my throat, I quite irrationally wondered if I was in trouble. My body pulsed with that special surge of adrenaline that everyone gets when they look in the rearview mirror and see a patrol car.

"Ma'am, we're gonna need you to clear the area, please. We're going to be cordoning off the entire cul-de-sac." The officer motioned down the street.

"Oh…uh, okay. Umm…sorry about that, I was just leaving," I stammered, feeling the heat rise in my face.

While I was glad to escape the long arm of the law unscathed, I wanted to stomp my foot in frustration. How on earth was I going to find out what had happened to cause such a hoopla? I mean, sure, I could watch it on the news, but it was much more exciting to watch the events unfold in person. I practically dove into my car, thanking my lucky stars that curiosity might kill the cat, but at least for now, it wasn't illegal.

Chapter Two

I heard Foo, my gorgeous and terribly demanding little Shih Tzu, before I saw him, as is always the case when I pull the car into the garage, and frankly, with the collar of a departed beloved pet in my purse, his greeting yips and yaps were music to my ears. I picked up his wiggling, wriggling little form and buried my face in his sweetly scented, silky black and white fur. He withstood my affection for at least ten seconds before reminding me he hadn't been outside yet with a polite little woof. I kissed his little button nose and set him down so he could scamper outside to do his business.

While King Foo was occupied and didn't require my immediate attention, I unloaded my design bag, stashing it in my office, and slipped out of my shoes, tossing them vaguely in the direction of my closet. Wiggling my toes and scrunching them into the thick pile of my bedroom Flokati, I closed my eyes and took in a cleansing breath, glad to be home.

Sally Edgerton's guest room had been the first of a handful of projects that I had to keep on top of today, and while I loved the fact that business was booming, I also relished coming back to my wonderfully quiet space. I rolled my head from side to side, wincing at the ensuing crackles and pops, and tried to gauge whether or not I'd have enough time to change before Foo finished his business. A polite clicking of claws on the glass slider told me I didn't, so I headed for the kitchen to let my little man in.

As usual, he literally ran circles around me, begging for fresh water and more kibble in his bowl and, of course, the post toilette treat. He was clearly feeling particularly saucy, because he actually sat up on his haunches and waved his paws at me for his treat. He didn't get half this time; he got a whole one. It's almost shameful how easily manipulated I am by anything with big brown eyes and fluffy paws.

After dutifully refilling Foo's bowls, I perused the contents of the fridge, hoping it had been magically filled with things that seemed appealing. Sighing, I saw that the refrigerator fairies had failed me yet again. The only things mocking me from the chilly confines of the fridge were a crusty, half-filled container of fried rice and a packet of sliced turkey that was looking decidedly shady.

"Looks like it's takeout again tonight, little buddy," I murmured, closing the fridge.

Foo, intent on emptying his bowl, didn't even spare me a snort as I tapped on my phone, bringing up the list of my favorite delivery places.

"Ooooh, Slim Chickens," I murmured with delight. Slim Chickens was a bit of a misnomer, at least for what I typically ordered, but they make lightly breaded chicken strips that melt in your mouth and a potato salad that isn't typically seen this side of the Mason-Dixon line. Champaign, Illinois, has its pluses, but an abundance of places serving the kind of creamy, dreamy potato salad that I'd had before when visiting the South isn't one of them.

I placed my order and headed back to the bedroom to change, after clicking on the TV. I tried to tell myself that after I ate, I would just watch a movie with a glass of wine before bed, but I knew better. I'd turn on the TV and let it play in the background while I worked on Sally's guest bedroom design. Her explanation about why she'd hired me didn't surprise me in the least. I often function as the bridge of harmony between "design opposite" couples. This wasn't my first rodeo, and I knew I could create a room that would give Sally her pink without nauseating her beloved.

It felt glorious to take off my work clothes and slip into well-worn yoga pants and a light sweatshirt from my college days. I let my hair down and just fluffed it with my fingers rather than taking the time to brush it, the dark waves falling between my shoulder blades. Knowing I'd be eating soon, I secured it loosely at the back of my neck with a scrunchie. There are few things worse than a hunk of hair falling forward onto a pile of potato salad…although a bowl of soup ranks right up there.

Burrowing my toes into fuzzy electric blue slippers, I scuffed back down the hall to the living room, my heart leaping to my throat when I saw what was on the television. It was a live feed of the house across the street from Sally Edgerton. There were now more police cars present than when I left, and the word "HOMICIDE" was displayed in big letters across the bottom of the screen, along with the address.

I grabbed the remote and turned up the volume, transfixed. Foo pawed at my shin, and I picked him up, cradling him against my chest, my chin resting on his head, as I stared at the television. Moving as though in a dream, I eased down onto the couch and focused on the news report. The lady of the house, Rosalie Bennett, had apparently been murdered. A picture of her in a gown at a formal event appeared on the screen, making my heart thrum even harder. She looked so sweet—a classy, elderly woman who probably served at soup kitchens on holidays just because she wanted to.

"That's horrifying," I whispered into Foo's fur.

The news anchor, with his perfectly coiffed hair and expensively capped teeth, looked gravely into the camera and directed anyone with information about the crime to come forward and contact the police. My heart skipped a beat as I realized with a jolt that I might just fit into that category. I was there when all of the emergency vehicles showed up, and right before they did, I saw a technician come out from between the victim's house and the house next door. Could I have been glancing at a cold-blooded murderer? The thought made me shiver, and my stomach did a queasy little flip.

"Oh, crudmuffins, Foo, I don't want to talk to the police."

Foo responded with a few licks to the underside of my chin before settling into my lap for a nap. The number for the police department hotline scrolled across the bottom of the screen, taunting me.

It was probably nothing, I rationalized, trying desperately to dissuade myself from making the call.

I'm not a busybody. I lay low and am thankful that my interactions with law enforcement have been nearly non-existent. This stems largely from the fact that I have an absolutely unwarranted guilty conscience. If I see flashing lights in my rearview mirror, I'm convinced that the encounter is going to result in my long-term incarceration, even when I have no idea what I could possibly have done wrong. I've never even had a traffic ticket, but when I'm instructed to roll down my window by someone in a uniform, I suddenly become sweaty and tongue-tied. I would not do well in prison. There are no lattes in jail.

On-screen, the police phone number still scrolled by, over and over. I decided to mind my own business and keep my mouth shut. I didn't want to get some poor, hardworking electrician in trouble after all. He was just doing his job...right? I felt utterly secure in my decision right up until I saw the gurney with a black body bag on it wheeled into the coroner's van. Poor lady. Even if I was wrong, I had to report what I'd seen.

It was my civic duty.

The doorbell rang, nearly making me jump out of my skin. Slim Chickens. In my horror over what had happened across the street from Sally Edgerton's, I had completely forgotten about food, and that takes a bit. Foo exploded into a cacophony of yapping that drowned out the television and, I'm sure, drove the poor Slim Chickens driver to dash away as quickly as possible. I brought the food inside and set it on the kitchen counter, unable to even consider eating at the moment.

My stomach churned with dread as I held my phone, staring at it as if it might come to life and bite me.

"I can do this," I muttered, trying to work up the nerve. "I must do this."

Taking a deep breath, I punched in the number that had been scrolling across the bottom of the TV screen and picked up the remote to mute it, pacing while the phone rang on the other end. I briefly considered hanging up but didn't have time to employ that cowardice before a bored-sounding policewoman answered my call. I stuttered and stumbled but managed to get part of my story about seeing the electrician out before she cut me off abruptly.

"Stay on the line, please. I'll transfer you."

Confounded that now I'd have to tell my story a second time, I was startled when a rough voice barked into the phone, "Detective Griff."

"Oh, uh, hi," I stammered. "I think I may have been accidentally transferred to you. I was calling about…" I began to explain, only to be rudely interrupted by the detective.

I may have issues with expressing myself in front of law enforcement, but these folks needed to work on their manners.

"I know *why* you're calling," Detective Griff cut me off. "Name and address, please."

"Oh, well, I don't know her name, but the address is on Carrington Street…" I tried again, only to be interrupted. Again.

"Not the victim's name, ma'am, your name," the detective clarified, rather brusquely, I thought.

Glad that he couldn't see me blushing from my neck to the roots of my hair, I supplied him with my info, though I couldn't for the life of me understand why he needed it.

"Got it. I'm going to need you to come down to the station to make a statement," he declared, sending my heart into palpitations.

"I've never been to a police station," I murmured to myself, or so I thought.

"It's downtown. Just go to the reception desk, and they'll direct you to my office."

"Oh. Well, ummm…" I stalled, panicking. I could hear the tremor in my voice, and despite my best intentions, I doubted that I could get control of it anytime soon. My knees shook, and I had a sudden urge for wine.

There's a huge difference between making a phone call to report something I saw and actually going to the police station to talk to a real live detective. I hadn't geared up emotionally for that reality. Thus far, I'd only seen detectives when I watched my true crime shows.

"I haven't had dinner yet, and…" I faltered, blushing again because I sounded so guilty.

"I could come to you for the statement, if that's easier." There was a warning in his tone.

The thought of a detective in my house, being suspiciously sniffed by Foo, definitely nudged me in the right direction.

"I'll head out now," I promised, hanging up before he could say any other

13

scary things.

I did the speed limit all the way to the police station, as if they were going to be on the lookout for me now, and pulled into the parking lot, my heart in my throat. When I stepped into the reception area, I was more than relieved to see that the police station here in central Illinois bore little to no resemblance to the street-grimed, chaotic interiors filled with criminals in my favorite police shows.

The interior was a light green color that functioned well beneath the glare of the overhead fluorescent lighting, and the tile underfoot was a checkerboard of well-buffed, earth-toned linoleum, with two rows of molded plastic chairs in a sage green facing each other, against the walls. Very governmental, but in a sort of oddly Zen way. Maybe the décor was some sort of psychological experiment designed to put people at ease so that they'd be more likely to confess.

A stout, uniformed woman was behind the reception desk, and once she spoke, I deduced that she had been the one who answered the phone when I called. In the same bored voice, she asked me my name and why I was there, then told me to take a seat. I was acutely aware of the ticking of the simple black and white clock on the wall that was much too high for anyone to reach, and as more seconds ticked away, the more fidgety I got. I wanted to leave, but more than that, I wanted to avoid anything that might prompt the fireplug-shaped woman to chase me down and tackle me. I envisioned her pulling my arms behind my back and throwing me in the slammer.

I stayed put.

"Ms. Samson?" a now-familiar male voice drawled.

I glanced up and saw a tall, muscular, hatchet-faced man, with a seemingly perpetual frown, gazing down at me. I shot to my feet, startled.

"Umm...yep." I nodded far more vehemently than was necessary.

"I'm Detective Marcus Griff. Come with me, please," he ordered, then turned on his heel and stalked away.

Oh no. This is it.

I took a quick glance at the outside world through the glass entry doors, in case it was the last glimpse that I had for a while, and hurried after the detective. He was so tall and broad in his dark brown suit that I felt like I was following a giant sequoia, and he took such gargantuan strides that I had to jog to keep up with him. Which meant my chubby little self was going to be glowing by the time we reached our destination. Would the indignity never end? This was what I got for trying to be a good citizen.

I was more than a bit relieved when the detective led me to a messy, but otherwise non-threatening office rather than a cell or interrogation room.

"Have a seat." He nodded at the worn Naugahyde chairs on the visitor side of the desk.

The poor man had no sense of décor. The walls were off-white, the desk was nondescript grey metal, and his desk chair was old, creaky, and tattered. At least it was leather.

I sat, hands folded in my lap, trying my absolute best to appear respectable and trustworthy. The detective stared at me for a few seconds before grabbing a pen and a yellow legal pad and scribbling my name and the date on it. I swallowed hard. I really would have felt much better doing this anonymously.

"Tell me what you saw this morning." The detective seemed to be examining me closely.

I tried my best not to squirm under his scrutiny and relayed the story of seeing the electrician coming out between the two houses.

Griff's brows rose. "Why didn't you come forward while you were still at the scene?"

I swallowed hard.

"I just figured that maybe someone was sick or something. Sally told me that the neighborhood was filled with older people. And besides, it's not like I knew that someone had been murdered. I didn't find that out until I saw it on the news after I went home. When I went to my car while everything was happening, a policeman actually told me to clear the area because the cul de sac was going to be closed." I now felt guilty that I had just slunk away initially, and I loathed how defensive I'd just sounded.

"Did you know the victim, or anyone in her family?"

"No." I shook my head.

"Have you ever been in that neighborhood before?"

"Not that I recall." I frowned, trying to remember.

"The scene is pretty close to where you live." Griff's tone seemed too casual, his eyes glittering like those of a snake about to strike.

"Less than a mile." I nodded again.

"Where did you go when you left Ms. Edgerton's home?"

"I just went home. It was the end of my workday."

"What did the electrician look like?" The question came out of left field.

"Umm…he had on a bright yellow vest, like for safety."

"Hair color?"

"I'm not sure…I think he may have been wearing a hard hat." I twisted my hands together.

"I'm thinking that would be a detail that would stick in your memory," Griff replied dryly.

"I…I didn't stare at him or anything. He was just a movement that caught my eye when I was measuring a window." I blushed scarlet.

"How tall?"

"I don't know, exactly. It's kind of hard to tell from the angle that I…"

"Tall? Short?"

"Uh, medium?" I bit my lip.

"Thin? Fat?"

He was on a roll with the single-word questions, fired in rapid succession.

"Average…I guess," I winced.

The detective compressed his lips and stared at me. I felt like a bug under a microscope and laced my fingers together so I wouldn't fidget.

"What did his vehicle look like?" Griff tried again.

"It was a white van with writing on the side." I was so glad to have been able to answer at least one question decently. My elation was short-lived.

"What did the writing say?"

I gulped.

"Not sure," I mumbled.

"Did you get a license plate number?" Griff's brows rose.

"No."

"Are you even certain that it was an electrician's van?" He pursed his lips.

"Not exactly. No."

"Ms. Samson, are you trying to lead me on a wild goose chase? Because if so, I have to wonder why." His tone was vaguely menacing as he leaned forward, and rather than causing me to cower, his tactic offended me. I'd seen too many crime dramas on television to not know what he was up to.

"What are you trying to imply, Detective?" I bristled, straightening in my chair.

"The easiest way to deflect blame is to throw someone else under the bus," Griff pointed out.

My mouth dropped open, and when I turned red this time, it wasn't because of embarrassment.

"Are you *serious* right now? I called in, trying to help. I volunteered information. I went without dinner to come down here and talk to you, and now you have *the nerve* to imply that I might be involved in the very crime that I came to report?"

"I think it's rather convenient that you can't seem to quite remember anything concrete about the alleged electrician." Griff's voice dropped a notch, as he stared me down.

"Convenient? Trust me, Detective, this little visit has been anything but convenient. Why did I even bother?" I huffed, standing so quickly that the metal legs of the chair screamed across the linoleum. "Since I obviously have no information that you can use, I'll just be on my way, Detective."

I strode beet-faced to the door and had my hand on the knob when Griff spoke.

"I wouldn't leave town if I were you," he suggested, his tone neutral.

That one stopped me in my tracks. I turned slowly to face him, eyes narrowed.

"You know, I always wondered, when I saw detectives say that in cop shows, whether it was really a thing. Turns out, it is." I grimaced. "Goodnight, Detective Griff." I took my parting shot and hurried out, glad that it was over and that I had survived and was still a free woman. The tremble had even left my voice momentarily.

"Ms. Samson..." I heard from behind me when I had almost made it to the end of the hall.

I whirled, terrified, only to see Detective Griff standing in his doorway, my purse dangling from his fingertips.

"Forgot something?" he drawled.

My color rose yet again, and I stomped down the hall, practically snatching it from him.

"Thank you," I muttered, utterly humiliated.

This time, I made it outside, having never been more glad to climb into the safety and comfort of my little blue car.

Chapter Three

After a rather restless night's sleep following my harrowing trip to the police station the night before, I needed a dose of girl time. I arrived at Sun Singer, a cute little wine bistro that's literally walking distance from my house, and ordered a Pinot Noir, knowing that my friend Charla, who was meeting me for lunch, would be late. How she can function that way is a mystery to me. She is always late. Always. I can give her a time that's an hour ahead of our reservation, and she'll still be fifteen minutes late. Fortunately, she has enough breezy charm to get past any frustrations that I, or anyone else, might have with her chronic tardiness.

For best buddies, we are as opposite as can be. She's as thin as I am…fluffy. Blond hair vs. jet black. Blue vs. green. Bold as brass vs. closet introvert. Carefree vs. neurotic. And somehow…we work. We met at a celebrity bartending event for a local charity, that I only agreed to be a part of because of the business growth opportunities, and have been besties ever since.

So, there I sat, sipping my Pinot and enjoying the lovely early spring day, with no expectation that Charla would arrive anytime soon. She surprised me by being only half an hour late. I hadn't even finished my wine; it must've been some kind of record.

"That stuff is loaded with carbs, you know," she announced, kissing me on the top of my head and enveloping me in a cloud of some lovely vanilla-based perfume as she slid lithely into her seat and reached for the menu, bangles jangling.

"Don't begrudge me one of life's simple pleasures." I rolled my eyes and took another sip.

To say that Charla is a health nut is the understatement of the year. She starts every day with more than an hour at the gym, she barely eats enough to keep a squirrel alive, and she doesn't drink coffee or alcohol. How is life even worth living? But, then again, she's my age, early thirty-something-ish, and still looks like she could be in college. When we go out, the college guys hit on her, and yes, she loves it.

"You need to get high on life, girlfriend," Charla mused, scanning the menu as though we hadn't been here a thousand times before.

I chuckled, raising my glass. "I'm working on it."

We ordered lunch—or I should say, *I* ordered lunch. Charla ordered what looked like a plate of grass, with a hint of lemon juice on it, and a water. I made a face and went with a cranberry and goat cheese spring mix salad, pretending not to hear Charla's warnings about the digestive issues associated with dairy. It was a big step for me to get a salad, rather than a burger bursting with sauteed mushrooms and capped in ooey-gooey cheese, so I wasn't going to let her fanaticism bring me down.

She flirted shamelessly with the server, as is her custom. She swears that she gets better service that way, and I have to admit that she's often correct. And then she proceeded to grill me about the murder and my meeting with a real live detective. She enjoys *Law and Order* almost as much as I do, so, of course, she found my dilemma enthralling. We've had post-breakup marathon sessions of watching *L&O* nonstop in our jammies. I eat cartons of ice cream while she munches happily on baby carrots. Each to their own, I guess, but I can't imagine finding comfort in baby carrots.

"Was he hot? Please tell me he was hot," she breathed, forking her way through the pasture on her plate.

"No, he wasn't hot." I made a face, thinking of Detective Griff. "He was all cheekbones and eyebrows and jawline." I shook my head.

"He totally sounds hot." Charla waggled her eyebrows. "You're just salty because he was an aggressive conversationalist."

"No, hon. *You're* an aggressive conversationalist," I corrected. "This guy is a human bulldozer."

"Mmm...sounds right up my alley." Charla gave me a wicked grin.

"Ew." I grimaced and changed the subject. "So, what do you know about Rosalie Bennett?" I poked around in my salad, shoving aside various botanicals in search of more luscious nuggets of chevre.

Charla Beguile, real estate agent extraordinaire, knew everyone in town, having been born and raised here, and she also knew all of their secrets somehow. My thought was that she plied everyone with wine, and being the only sober one, she mined them for info. She had the hot girl advantage and employed it willy-nilly.

"Hmm…let's see," she mused, sipping at her lime and cucumber sparkling water. "She and the hubby are pillars of the community. Part of the university art crowd, big donors to charity. He's owned all the dry-cleaning shops in town since back in the fifties, and they're Champaign Country Club, rather than Urbana Country Club, if you know what I mean." She gave me a knowing look.

I vaguely knew what she meant. The two towns, right next to each other, are very different. Champaign has a more traditional Midwest-values thing going on, and parts of Urbana might make you think that you'd suddenly been transported to southern California, complete with Birkenstocks and granola.

"So, the Bennetts are nice people?"

"From everything I hear, yes," Charla confirmed. "Lots of money."

"It's just so sad. Why would someone kill a nice old lady?" I lamented, my ersatz sympathy evaporating into delight when I found a candied pecan in my salad.

"Duh. She was loaded." Charla looked at me like I was a dolt.

"Yeah, I suppose. But that makes you wonder who stood to benefit from that." I sighed, putting the last forkful of sadly, mainly lettuce into my mouth.

"You don't have to clean your plate, you know," Charla said, judging me a little bit over the rim of her water glass. "That's a harmful childhood myth."

"Do you honestly mean to tell me that you're not going to finish your bale of hay?" I challenged, looking pointedly at her plate.

"Nope, I'm not. Their portion size is off." She regarded her plate disdainfully and pushed it away. "Don't even think about it," she warned when she saw me eyeing the greens thoughtfully. "You don't even like microgreens that much."

"Sure, I do. I just like something with flavor in it more."

"And sugar and fat."

"Mmmm...yeah. Keep talking like that, and I'll order dessert," I threatened, only halfway kidding.

Just her mention of sugar and fat brought to mind glorious visions of ice cream, cake, cookies, and brownies. I was probably gaining weight just thinking of them.

"So, where are you off to today?" Charla broke into my food-fueled reverie.

I glanced at my watch and gasped when I saw the time.

"Yikes! I'm supposed to be meeting Tang at Flooring Fiesta in twenty minutes."

Charla casually waved a hand. "Plenty of time." It's not like she cared whether or not I was on time to meet my other bestie, Tang. The two of them were like oil and water—no, scratch that,—they were like oil and gasoline. Unpredictable, a bit unstable, and potentially explosive when mixed together.

"I still have to walk home to get my car." I grabbed my purse and extracted my credit card, scanning the patio for our server.

"Settle down, Miss Worry Pants. I'll drop you off at your house after we pay the bill." She waved coyly to the server, who gave her a piece of cake, to go, when he brought the bill.

"What are you going to do with that?" I eyed the innocuous little bag, after the server disappeared with our credit cards.

"I'll probably give it to Marge when I get back to the office. Why?"

"I'm a better friend than Marge. Why are you giving it to her and not me?"

"Because I care about you, and Marge ticked me off this morning." Charla coolly examined her ruby talons.

"So, you're giving her cake...why?" I frowned.

"Because she's trying to lose weight for her daughter's wedding in June." Charla grinned at me, looking very much like the Grinch...before his heart grew.

"You're evil," I whispered, impressed.

Charla shrugged.

"Geez, girl, I'm glad I'm on your good side."

"As far as you know." She winked at me as the server approached.

"Here you go, ladies. And just to say Happy Spring, I took care of your drinks for you." He looked hopefully at Charla.

"Oh, aren't you just too sweet!" She let her fingers linger just for a moment on his when she took the credit card folder from him.

"You ladies have a great day, and come back and see us."

Charla had to move three real estate signs and two contracts out of the passenger seat of her Escalade so that I could sit down, and she drove me home in her usual bat-on-the-wing style.

"Say hello to your little friend for me," Charla drawled sarcastically when I got out of the car.

"I'm sure Tang will send you his best." I batted my eyes at her.

The two of them weren't exactly fond of each other. Tang was the first person I'd met when I moved to the Midwest, and we hit it off immediately, becoming besties in a heartbeat. He and Charla knew each other professionally but would never have dreamed of seeing each other socially. Each was too much of a diva for the other, I think.

"I'm sure." Charla smirked and waved as she backed out of the driveway.

I felt more than guilty slipping into the garage like a thief and leaving quietly so that I didn't wake Foo from his nap. If I woke him up, he'd want snuggles and to be let out, and I just didn't have the time for that. Which also made me feel irrationally guilty.

I pulled up at Flooring Fiesta and went inside, glancing at my watch to make sure that I was on time. Not only had I made it on time, I was actually a bit early, so I was able to enter with the swagger of unreasonable pride that comes with being more than prompt. Tang wasn't due to arrive for another five minutes, and he was always right on the dot, so I wanted to get a head start on checking out the area rugs for Sally's guest room—one of my favorite parts of the design process. I've literally built entire rooms around museum-quality area rugs.

My dear Tang was literally the best architect in town, and he loved taking his breaks to shop décor with me. He really loved it when we had to go to Flooring Fiesta, and it wasn't all about the rugs.

"Hey, Brad." I smiled at the co-owner of the flooring store.

Brad Gentry is the human equivalent of a golden retriever. He's helpful, sweet, and loves everyone. He gives me discounts for my clients, and his installers are the best in the business, so I always try to find what I need at his store rather than other retailers.

"Hey, Sari! How's business?"

"Interesting, as usual," I said with a laugh. "You are not going to believe what I need today."

His manner changed like the flip of a switch, and he instantly became Flooring Man. I swear, one of these days, I'm going to buy him a t-shirt with a giant F in a gold shield on the front.

"Bring it," he challenged, his ever-present notebook in hand.

"I need an area rug that will coordinate with pink."

Brad didn't bat an eyelash.

"Okay, so we're looking for pink blends or cool-toned neutrals, unless you're working with a warm pink?" He paused in his notetaking to glance at me for confirmation.

"No, strictly pink. No warmth, no hint of coral. She would drench the room in Pepto Bismol if she could, but we're not going to let her do that. I'm counting on you, Brad. I wanted it muted and light. And if we can find something with neutrals thrown in, I'll be all about it."

"I just got a pallet of new styles and colors of area rugs in last night." His eyes lit up. "I haven't had a chance to hang them up yet, but you can come to the back room and dig through them if you'd like."

I had to stifle a laugh. Seeing Brad, a man's man from the word go, excitedly discussing the nuances of his collection of pink-friendly area rugs would truly be a treat.

"Trying to lure my girl into the back room again, Bradley?" Tang's voice made the two of us turn around.

"Right on time, as usual." I grinned, drinking in the smell of Tang's cologne when he hugged me.

"Of course. Hug it out, Bradley?" he offered, opening his arms wide.

"Nah, I'm good, thanks," Brad replied, looking as though he'd like to find the nearest rock and crawl under it.

Tang was perfect in every way. His ultra-white shirt was crisply pressed, with the cuffs turned up just far enough to make him look hardworking, but casual, showing off his tanned forearms. His trousers had knife-like pleats, his teeth were straight and white, and not one hair was out of place. Ever. Even his shoes were fashionable. He was a genius architect, spoke several different languages, and played every sport with athletic grace. Why on earth he hangs out with me is one of the mysteries of the universe, but I love him dearly.

"Are you sure? It's 'Be Nice to Asians Week,'" he teased.

"It is?" Brad frowned, wondering what to do with that.

"Stop it, you!" I elbowed Tang, letting poor Brad off the hook. "Let's go look at pink area rugs."

"Wait. Pink?" Tang's brows rose.

"Yes, pink. I told you this one was going to be fun." I grinned and followed Brad to the back of the store, through the EMPLOYEES ONLY door, and into the warehouse.

"Who on earth wants a pink area rug?" Tang made a face.

"Sally Edgerton. It's for her guest room."

The three of us spent the next hour or so flipping through rugs, the stray fibers sticking in my hair and going up my nose, but we eventually narrowed it down to four contenders. While we looked, I told Tang and Brad what had happened with the detective.

"Murder?" Tang's eyebrows went so far up his forehead that I wondered if they were going to become one with his glossy mane of perfect hair. "Okay, honey, I'm sorry, but you need to stay as far away from that case as possible," he advised.

Brad nodded. "I agree."

Tang looked at him and smiled. Brad averted his eyes, pretending to brush lint from one of the rugs.

"Seriously, girl," Tang continued. "You don't need that kind of drama in your life."

"I know." I sighed. "The detective even made it sound like he thought that what I did was suspicious."

Tang's brows rose again, and his mouth fell open slightly. "What did you do?" he asked, resting his hands on his slim, designer-clad hips.

"Nothing wrong. I just didn't say anything about what I'd seen while I was still at the crime scene, because I didn't know it was a crime scene. When I got home and found out on the news that there had been a murder, I called the hotline."

"And the detective found you suspicious because of that?" Brad asked.

"Apparently." I made a face.

"And how did you handle the fact that he was suspicious?" Tang asked. The man knows me so well. I don't get mad often, but when I do…

"I yelled at him and stormed out," I admitted sheepishly.

"Good for you," Brad chimed in.

Tang signaled his approval with a high five.

"But now, it's like…I have to find out what happened," I said. "I can't stop thinking about it. I just feel so bad for that poor old lady."

"That's fine. Just feel bad from a distance, young lady. Sweet little old ladies die every day, and you don't have to be involved with them." Tang shook his finger at me.

"I suppose you're right." I let it drop.

"I'm always right. Now, make a decision on your rug, and I'll tell you if it's the correct one or not." Tang waved a hand at the line of pallets that were stacked high with rugs.

"Okay, Brad, do you have a favorite picked out?" I asked.

The three of us did this every time, until we reached a consensus on the right choice. They'd make their selection, but not announce it, then I'd announce mine and see if we all chose the same one.

"Yes, ma'am." He nodded, folding his arms over his chest.

"Okay, I like the Coco Loco Blush, what say you?" I looked from one to the other.

"Yep," Brad agreed.

"Nailed it," Tang approved.

"Well, that was easy. Thanks, you two." I smiled at the two very different men.

"See, Bradley, we make a good team." Tang winked.

"Uh…yeah. So, Sari, you want me to deliver this?" Brad changed the subject, turning a shade of pink that was brighter than Sally Edgerton's new rug.

"Yep, I'll text you the address when I get home, but hang onto it until the painting and closet installation is done, please."

"No worries, just let me know."

Tang took my arm, and we skipped, arm in arm, from the store to my car, with Brad staring after us and shaking his head.

"So, we need to do ice cream soon. I haven't fed that habit in a bit," Tang informed me.

"Oh, heck yes! I had a salad for lunch today." I made a pouty face.

"Awww…I'm so proud of you." Tang reached out and squeezed my face, so I made hilarious fish lips at him. "I had a lusciously nasty cheeseburger with spiral onion rings."

"You're just cruel. How on earth do you keep those abs with the way you eat?" I poked his six-pack.

"It's all in the gym time, baby." He proudly slapped his rock-hard abs.

"Then I'm doomed." I chuckled, kissing him on the cheek and getting into the car.

He shut the door behind me, calling out, "Now go make good choices!"

While I knew that Tang and Brad were absolutely right and that I should just stay out of all that murder mess, my curiosity was killing me. And both of them should know that the quickest way to get me to do something is to tell me that I can't…or shouldn't. For now, I'd go back to being an ordinary, law-abiding citizen, but I couldn't promise what tomorrow might bring.

Chapter Four

Sally Edgerton practically dragged me inside when I rang her doorbell. Her caftan was a shocking shade of purple, and she was wearing eyeliner to match. I was carrying so many samples in my design bag that I felt like a pack mule and was relieved when Sally's boyfriend, Matt, took it off my hands, toting it to the dining room table. The man was absolutely stunning—he had movie star good looks—and I had to remind myself not to stare.

"He wasn't supposed to be here today," Sally whispered, fretting. "The sole on one of his favorite hiking boots split, so he took it as a sign, and now he wants to be involved in the design process with us." Her eyes darted toward the dining room.

"No worries," I whispered. "I've got this. He's really handsome, by the way." I grinned.

"I know, right?" Sally lit up. "He's younger than me, too, rawr!" She made a clawing motion with her hand, cracking me up.

"You go, girl." I laughed.

"What are you two giggling about out here?" Matt appeared in the kitchen, where we'd stopped for bottles of water before heading to the dining room.

"Sari was just telling me how devastatingly handsome she thinks you are, and I was agreeing," Sally replied lightly, as I gasped in horror.

"Oh, how I love the way you lie to me, my dearest." He grinned at Sally and swooped in for a kiss.

Why can't I have that? He clearly adores her. The only men I meet are either unavailable, or there's something tragically wrong with them. Tang doesn't count in that regard. He's entirely awesome, but he wants to hang his hat in Brad's closet, not mine, so there's that.

"You silly boy." Sally playfully pushed Matt away, her eyes warm. "Sari and I are going to go over her plans for the guest room."

"Shall I stay and cause trouble?" He slung an arm over her shoulders.

"Of course. You don't mind, do you, Sari?" Sally asked.

I looked for hidden messages in her eyes, and, seeing none, I shrugged.

"Nope. I think it's great that both of you are here," I answered truthfully.

There were few things worse than successfully completing an installation and having one of the partners hate it. It didn't happen often, but when it did, it was a nightmare for everyone involved. If there were going to be objections from an interested third party, it was better to get them out of the way early.

"Perfect!" Sally beamed, leading the way to the dining room.

"Now, I'm going to do a little magic here, so please don't make any judgments until I pull up the design on my laptop and set all of the samples out together," I advised.

They both agreed. Sally was practically bouncing in her seat with excitement, and Matt stood behind her chair, arms folded. His posture could mean anything from skepticism to an open mind, and I was quite obviously hoping for the latter. I opened my laptop, pulled up the design, then unloaded the samples that I had in my bag. Sally's eyes grew bigger with each item that I pulled out.

"Okay, you two, gather round." I eased into a white tulip dining room chair that had probably belonged to Elton John at some point. Or Austin Powers. It was funky and mod and wonderful, and I hoped against hope that it would support my weight.

Sally scooted her chair so close to mine that she was practically in my lap, and Matt moved with her, his hands on her shoulders, absently massaging while he looked at the screen. He was the first to speak.

"Wow," he murmured.

"Good wow, or bad wow?" I braced myself for the reply.

I was confident in my design, but you never know what a client is thinking until they say it. And this was, after all, a study in the subtle art of pink.

"Great, wow." He nodded, impressed.

"So much wow!" Sally's eyes roved over the screen, her hands clasped under her chin.

"Awesome—let me walk you through the design." Now that they were on board, I could get into the nitty-gritty with confidence. "We're going to keep your existing wood flooring, since it's consistent throughout the rest of the house, but we're going to use this area rug…" I clicked over to a photo of the rug and handed Sally the 4x4-inch sample that Brad had given me.

"Oh my, it has that lovely pale pink with some beige and cream…it's beautiful!" She held it out to Matt, who took it, ran his fingers through the long, soft fibers, and nodded his approval.

"It really is," I agreed, hitting my stride early. "This is the fabric for the accent chair. You'll notice that the pink background and cream polka dots are the same colors that are in the rug, and the driftwood legs will coordinate with your wood flooring. The comforter is a beige and cream raw silk…" I handed her another sample, and she and Matt oohed and ahhed over it. "…and we'll use the same pink and cream polka-dotted fabric for the throw pillows, along with some solid cream ones. The curtains are in the polka dot, and the sheers are cream. What do you think so far?" I already knew the answer.

"I think you're magical." Sally squeezed my arm.

"Magical? That's a new one, and I'll take it, thanks." I chuckled. "But that's not all. Wait until you see your new bed and breakfast coffee and storage center."

I clicked over to another screen that had a 3-D rendering of the storage center, built into the existing closet, made out of pickled oak that looked like driftwood. There were drawers and shelves, along with hidden storage and easy access to an outlet for making coffee. I'd even put an adorable mini pink lamp in the unit for a pop of color.

"Oh honey, you have outdone yourself." Sally clapped her hands together. "Don't you think so, babe?" She turned to Matt.

"I love this room." He agreed, visibly impressed. "I would never have thought that I'd like a room with so much pink in it, but this is the epitome of understated and elegant. Well done, Sari."

"Thank you." I grinned. "I loved this project because I got to use my favorite color."

"I may have to call you about redoing and organizing my garage. But please, no pink out there; it'll just get dirty," Matt teased.

"I'll wait for your call," I said, gathering up my samples.

"Oh, that reminds me, Sari, dear. I have a referral for you." Sally patted the table.

"Oh?"

"Yes, her name is Agnes Hackles, and she lives right down the street."

"Agnes Hackles?" I tried not to giggle maniacally.

"It suits her," Matt commented dryly.

"Oh, hush you." Sally shushed him. "She's a bit…"

"Much," Matt supplied.

"Eccentric," Sally finished, shooting him a look. "But she's in need of a decorator, and since her husband passed a couple of years ago, she has the means to do her dining room properly. And trust me when I tell you, Sari…she really, really needs your help."

"No problem. Do you have her contact info?" I asked, finished with loading my bag.

"Yes, I do, and if you can stop by for a quick chat with her, I'll give her a call now. Just so you two can meet and see if you want to work together," Sally offered, picking up her phone.

"Oh. Uh…yeah, sure. I can meet with her now, I suppose."

I gave a quick internal cheer. Locking in another client when I've just completed the design for the previous one is my ideal scenario. I'd be able to move seamlessly from one to the next, with no dip in income or productivity. That would definitely help keep me on the ball. The fact that it was in the same neighborhood, conveniently located close to mine, was a bonus.

Sally went into the kitchen to have a quick phone conversation with Agnes, who apparently wholeheartedly agreed to have me come over and take a look at her dining room. I thanked Sally and Matt and told them I'd email their installation schedule once I had everything all set up. Bag in the car, quick glance in the mirror to straighten my hair, and on to Agnes Hackles' stately home…right next door to the murder house, on the far side.

I tried not to stare at poor Rosalie Bennett's house as I drove by. Death, in theory, is fascinating, but death, in reality, freaks me out just a bit, forensic curiosity aside. I don't have a ton of experience with it, and I must admit that I'm curious about the circumstances surrounding it, but I still get the willies when I know that I'm in, or even near, a place where someone has died.

Most people crane their necks and stare at traffic accidents. As long as help has arrived and I'm not needed, I tend to avert my eyes. I don't want to impose on something as intimate as someone else's suffering…or demise. Now, when it's a crime drama on television, that's a different story. I can solve murders alongside the best of them, as long as they're fictional.

I went to the end of the street to turn around in the cul-de-sac so that I could park in front of Agnes' house and still be heading in the proper direction. Agnes opened the front door as soon as I got out, waving frantically.

"Yoohooo! Over here," she trilled, beaming.

If Sally's fashion idol was Endora, Agnes's was clearly Rosanne. She wore baggy blue jeans with an elastic waist and a sweatshirt with pictures of birds on it that added a bit of bulk to her already round midsection. Her feet were clad in navy blue Sperry boat shoes, ankles puffing out over the sides, and her only pieces of jewelry were pearl earrings that hung from long slits in her wrinkled earlobes. She radiated a Midwest grandma vibe.

Grabbing my initial consultation bag, which was much smaller than my presentation bag, I raised a hand in greeting and trotted toward her.

"You're Sari," she announced as I mounted the steps to the porch.

Her lips were assaulted by a slick of lipstick in a color that went out in the seventies.

"Yes, I am. And you must be Agnes. It's a pleasure to meet you."

We shook hands, and she led me into an interior that made me feel as though I had just stepped into a museum gone wrong. The furniture pieces would have been beautiful, don't get me wrong, but with all of the scary, oddly colored fabrics, I had to wonder what she'd been thinking when she selected them. The carpet was of the highest quality, but appeared to be originally from the sixties, and the area rugs clashed with the furniture. It was an expensive nightmare. This was going to be interesting.

"So that's some kind of foreign thing, right?" Agnes asked as I scanned the foyer and living room, looking for design direction.

"Excuse me?" I turned, giving her a puzzled look.

"Your name. Sari. That's foreign, right? Where are you from?" Agnes smiled, and I saw a smudge of Curiously Coral on her teeth.

"California." I smiled sweetly. "Which way is the dining room?"

I had no intention of telling Agnes that the reason I'm named Sari is because my parents are trippy hippies who love other cultures. We once had a ferret named Chakra when I was growing up. Somehow, I didn't feel that Agnes would relate.

"Right this way," she gestured, her smile dimming a bit. "I'm sure you've noticed; my home is quite different from Sally's. Why she chose to go all Austin Powers on that beautiful home is beyond me. She's created her own flashback pad, and that works for her, but I have much more…classic taste."

Classic? That's one way to put it. Yep, good call on not revealing where my name came from.

"I see that." I nodded. "So, what are you looking to do in here?" We had just entered a dining room that would've made Louis XV on psychedelic drugs proud.

"I want to be a bit daring in here." Agnes' eyes brightened, and she clasped her hands under her chin with delight.

"Oh?" I replied neutrally, finding it hard to envision what she might find daring.

Agnes gripped my arm excitedly and made a sweeping gesture with her other hand.

"I want to incorporate…blue!"

"Blue?" I repeated, surprised that she hadn't mentioned circus tents or carnival rides. "What sort of blue were you thinking?"

Agnes released my arm and blinked at me.

"Well, isn't that your job to figure out?" She wrinkled her nose, hands on hips.

Oh, this was going to be fun.

"Yes, of course, I just figured that since you did such a lovely job on the rest of the house you might have a vision for this room," I explained patiently, refusing to get my hackles up. Ha-ha.

"I just told you my vision. I want blue. Now, how are you going to make that happen?" Her brows rose.

There was no need to go to Agnes's closet. Based on the rest of her home and what she was wearing, I had enough information. Her bold aesthetic was very much in keeping with her brash personality. At least, that's what I would tell anyone who asked.

"Are you going to want to retain any of the furnishings or art in here, or does everything go?" I hoped against hope that I didn't have to work with any of the existing pieces.

"Out with the old, in with the new." Agnes jerked her thumb toward the front door.

"Got it. Okay, now there's the matter of my fee. This initial consultation is free, but before I start working on the design for this project, I'll need to draw up an estimate for the cost of my services, plus the materials that will need to be purchased. Did you have a particular budget in mind?"

It was a standard question that I asked most of my clients when they called on the phone to book their initial appointment. I could already tell that Agnes was going to be a high-maintenance client, and I would take that into consideration when calculating my final bid. Yes, there is absolutely such a thing as a diva tax.

"Young lady, are you questioning whether or not I can afford this project?"

Oh boy.

"Not at all. I just need to know what you're willing to spend on the project," I assured her, holding up my hands as if in surrender.

"Well, whatever it costs. What a silly question." She frowned at me.

"So, you're okay with me spending forty thousand on a gravy boat?" I intentionally tossed out a ridiculous number to prove my point.

"No, I'd fire you." Agnes crossed her arms over her ample bosom.

"Exactly. So, what I need to know from you is what range you'd like me to stay in for this project, so that you don't feel as though you've spent too much."

"Well, let's do it this way…" Agnes' lips pursed as she thought. "Since it's not *my* job to put a proposal together, why don't you come up with three different levels of cost, so I can see what I'd get for each, and then I'll pick one that appeals to me."

"That's three times the work when we only need one design," I countered. "I think I can determine, based on the pieces that are here now, where your price points will be. I'll come up with a proposed budget, and you can decide whether it works for you or not. How about that?"

Agnes raised an eyebrow and tapped her foot.

"Well then, let's just hope you nail it the first time."

"Indeed." I pasted on a smile. It hurt my face. "I'd like to take a look at some of the furniture labels and take some photos and measurements while I'm here, if you don't mind." I tried to get her attention by raising my voice a bit.

She was staring at something outside of the picture window, the corners of her lips turned downward.

"Yeah, fine, whatever," she murmured, still looking toward the house next door. "It's such a shame what happened to poor Rosalie."

"Were you friends?" I didn't know what else to say.

Agnes flicked her eyes briefly toward me.

"We didn't run in the same social circles, if that's what you mean."

No kidding.

"My Wally made a good living, but he had used car dealerships, so we're not high-society enough for most of the neighbors around here." Agnes shrugged. "I'll be comfortable for the rest of my life; I don't need a country club membership. You're not a member, are you?"

There seemed to be more resignation than bitterness in her tone when she assessed her circumstances. Agnes Hackles, for all of her bravado, apparently knew her place in the world and was at least somewhat content with it.

"Uh, no." I shook my head.

"Course not. You wouldn't be, being a foreigner and all," she mused.

My eyebrows rose, and I blinked. Yep, she had just said that. She hadn't moved away from the window, so I bit back the retort that was dying to fly from my lips, took out my tape measure, and got to work. Agnes stood, rooted to the spot for a bit, staring, without seeing, out the window, then seemed to shake off her reverie.

"You want coffee or something?" She headed for the kitchen.

"No, thank you. I'll just get some measurements and photos, and I'll be out of your hair in a jiffy."

No sense in trying to build a relationship over coffee. Chances were good that when Agnes received my estimate, she'd no longer be interested in my services.

"You need anything else from me?" Agnes seemed tired.

"Nope, I'll be fine, thanks," I assured her, writing down a measurement.

"Go ahead and let yourself out when you finish then. I have things to do." She waved a hand absently and left the room. I stared, open-mouthed, after her.

"Well, alrighty then," I muttered, getting back to work.

At least I'd get done faster without having to make conversation. So much for my referral. I finished up as quickly as I could, then called out, "Bye Agnes, nice to meet you!" on my way to the door. I'd draw up a proposal and present it, with a grim certainty that she'd likely send me packing. I'm perfectly okay with that. Some clients aren't worth the headache. Although, I must admit, I was curious about what made her tick. I like figuring out the difficult ones, and I view the skeptics as a challenge that my design skills can overcome. If I wanted to, I was confident that I could even win over Agnes. I just wasn't sure yet that I wanted to.

On the way to my car, I noticed a middle-aged man with thinning mousy hair, swept over the top of his head in a manner designed to disguise a glistening pate, watering the bed of flowers that separated his yard from Agnes'. I smiled and said hello, never dreaming he'd actually reply. I always try to be polite when dealing with people, but I've also learned to drop any notion that they'll respond in kind. If I don't expect acknowledgment, I'm never disappointed.

"Are you friends with Agnes?" He sounded surprised.

"Not exactly. I'm a decorator."

"Totally makes sense. You have your work cut out for you." One corner of his mouth lifted slightly in a sad smile.

"Yes, I do." I tried to laugh, but it came out sounding flat.

I felt so awkward. This man was obviously a relative of the deceased, and I had no idea what to say to him. I've never been a touchy-feely sort of person, despite my zen upbringing. I think maybe I was always so embarrassed by my parents' effusiveness that I may have gone too far in the other direction. Tang had attacked my impenetrable fortress of standoffishness with a fiendish glee, determined to break me out of 'toxic patterns.' It was starting to work...a bit.

"She's a nice lady, even if she seems a bit off-putting at first," he offered up with a shrug.

"Yeah, she seemed nice. Well, have a good day." I moved toward the car, cursing my insensitivity the moment that the words left my mouth. *Have a good day?*

"You too." He raised a hand in farewell, looking forlorn.

The reality of death, staring me in the face like that, makes me truly appreciate the normal, boring life that I have. Somehow, though, despite my yearning for a simple, laid-back existence, I tend to get myself caught up in things that are bigger and scarier than I could've imagined. It wouldn't surprise me if the same curiosity that led to the demise of the feline might just do the same for the decorator, but that possibility didn't dissuade me from my insatiable need to know things.

The man in the yard looked as though he was staring after me as I made my way to the car, but the vacant look in his eyes spoke volumes. He wasn't looking at me. In fact, I was quite sure that whatever he was thinking about consumed him so entirely that he'd probably forgotten my very existence. Not that I could blame him. Under the same circumstances, I would be a quivering mass of jelly, shivering in the corner in my most comfy pair of sweatpants.

Chapter Five

The sad and weary look in the eyes of the thin man who was watering Rosalie Bennett's flowers haunted me for the rest of that day, and I thought about it again when my head hit the pillow at night. Such a sad situation. Judging by the age of him, he must have been her son. I can't even begin to imagine the basket-case that I'd be if something like that happened to one of my parents. They hadn't said what precisely had happened to Rosalie, but it really wouldn't matter, would it? Murder was murder, and I'd be furious and grief-stricken no matter what the means or motive.

The murder was still on my mind a few days later, when I drove to Tish's Ceramic Shop to pick up the gift that I'd commissioned for Sally Edgerton's design. I had given Tish samples of the colors that I'd used in Sally's guest room, and she'd incorporated them into a planter that resembled a crinkled paper bag. Around the mouth of the planter, she'd made a ridge that Buster's collar, which I'd borrowed from Sally, fit into perfectly, his heart-shaped name tag hanging down right in the front. Sally could take the collar off when she needed to clean the planter, and it would be a lovely tribute to place on the built-in desk in her guest room. My next stop was at a floral shop just down the street from Tish's, so that Kyle, an absolute artist with flowers and plants, could fill the new planter with hardy succulents.

Seeing Buster's collar around the planter that was now filled with life made a lump rise in my throat. I swallowed hard and blinked rapidly for a moment.

"Yeah, it hit me like that, too." Kyle gave me a shaky, understanding smile.

"How's BooBoo?" I hoped that Kyle's ancient cat hadn't passed since I last spoke with him.

"She's hanging tough. But when something does happen..." Unable to continue, he lifted Buster's planter and nodded, his eyes moist.

I nodded too and accepted the beautiful arrangement when he gingerly handed it over, spontaneously giving him a hug.

"Take care and hug that sweet furry kitty for me." I needed to dash out before I broke down. I couldn't even bring myself to think of what life would be like if Foo...

"I will, and likewise to Foo," Kyle replied.

Back in the car, I put the arrangement in an oversized gift bag to transport to Sally's. I couldn't wait for her reaction when she opened it, and I hoped that it brought her more joy than pain. She was at the door waiting for me when I pulled up. That could either be a good sign or a bad one.

"Oh, Sari, can I just say again, you are a genius!" she hollered as I came up the walk with my gift bag in hand.

"Anytime." I chuckled. "How's the makeover going?" I actually knew every detail of what had happened thus far.

"The area rug is down, the new bedding is on the bed, the walls have been painted, the art is installed, and everything looks amazing," Sally gushed.

"And right on schedule. So, all that's left is the installation of the coffee station in the closet." I handed Sally the bag. "Perfect. Let's go take a look."

"Yes, let's! I can't wait to show you. What's this?" She held up the bag.

"It's my gift to you and Matt for being such delightful clients."

"Oh, how thoughtful of you." Sally moved in for a hug, then led me into the house. "Matt is already in the guest room. He wanted to be there when you saw it, so I'll open this once we're all up there together."

"That'll be great." I agreed, assuming that she'd probably need his support when she saw the tribute to Buster.

The installation was spectacular. The barely-there pink paint that I had selected had a pearl-like finish that made the room seem to glow, and it looked as cozy and warm as I had envisioned it.

"Fantastic job, Sari." Matt smiled at me when I came in.

The man had dimples. Dimples. Sally was one lucky lady.

"And after all this amazing work, Sari got us a present. Can you believe it?" Sally held up the bag.

"I love presents." Matt grinned. "Can we open it?"

"Please." I nodded, the anticipation killing me.

Matt held the bag by the bottom while Sally peeled back the tissue.

"Oh, it's a gorgeous succulent arrangement!" She reached in to pull it out. "Oh, and look, the planter matches the—" She stopped suddenly, unable to continue.

She had seen the collar, and she pointed it out to Matt, as tears welled in her eyes. Without a word, he took her into his arms, kissing the top of her head while she cradled the planter.

"I hope that was okay…" My heart leapt to my throat, and I unconsciously crossed my fingers, hoping that I hadn't offended them or crushed them with painful memories.

"Oh, you dear, dear woman." Sally reached for my hand and pulled me into a hug. "This is the most precious thing you could've done," she whispered as tears spilled down her cheeks.

Tears were not something that I could typically deal with, but since they were happy tears, I just hugged her back and didn't worry about trying to say the right thing.

"*And* it matches the décor." Matt was transparent in his attempt to lighten the moment while blinking rapidly himself.

"Baby, go get Sari's present from my dresser," Sally directed, extricating herself and wiping her eyes.

"You didn't have to—" I began.

"Oh honey, after what you just did for us, don't even try to refuse. I was out shopping, and I saw something for you that just spoke to me. I could not leave it on the shelf. It needs to go home with you."

"Good thing I love presents too, then, huh?" I replied.

I could feel myself blushing, my typical reaction to emotional displays and/or compliments. As an introverted chubby girl, I didn't usually have to deal with compliments, so I had zero practice in how to accept them gracefully.

"Here we go." Matt returned, bearing a small box.

"What is it?" I asked.

"One way to find out." He held the box out to me.

Sally set the planter on the built-in desk, and I opened the box. It was a chakra necklace, and it was stunning.

"Oh wow! This is amazing. Thank you." My mouth dropped open.

"It's a chakra necklace," Sally explained.

"Oh, I know." I held up a hand to interrupt. "My parents are into crystals and energy and vibrations and all that stuff. We had a pet ferret named Chakra when I was in middle school. This is truly beautiful. Thank you so much."

"You're more than welcome, sweetie." Sally hugged me again.

I had to do some tall talking to convince her that I did not need to take home half a pound of Belgian chocolate when I left, though I was sorely tempted. I did, however, accept a sample of it, rationalizing that it would put me in such a good mood that even Agnes Hackles couldn't dampen it. I was heading to her house next to present my plan. I was secretly hoping that Tang might be available for a cocktail later. After a visit with Agnes, I might just need one. Or three.

I rang the doorbell, armed with my laptop and presentation samples. I didn't have much hope for actually securing the contract—and I was kind of okay with that—but I had brought one with me just in case.

Agnes opened the door, chewing. "You're three minutes early."

"Oh, I'm sorry. I finished up earlier than I had expected at Sally's. I can sit in my car for a few minutes if you need some time."

We were off to a great start.

"Nah, you're here, might as well come on in." She turned, retreating into the house. It wasn't the warmest welcome that I'd ever received.

I hurried into the house behind her and closed the door once I got inside. She was taking a plate of half-eaten food from the dining table to the kitchen.

"Feel free to finish your lunch while I talk, if you'd like." I was suddenly stricken with guilt for interrupting the older woman's meal.

"I'm fine. Shouldn't be eating as much as I have been lately, anyway. Seems like I just look at food these days and gain weight," Agnes grumbled.

"I know the feeling." I glanced down at the soft mound of my stomach, cleverly concealed beneath a blazer that I'd have to unbutton before I sat. Don't even get me started on my thighs.

"So, are you ready for my proposal?" I asked brightly, trying to elevate the mood a bit before I began.

"Let 'er rip." Agnes eased into a chair.

"Are you familiar with Monet?" I asked, having seen some nice reproduction art in her...unique home.

"Like the faucet?" She frowned.

"No, that's Moen. Monet was a French Impressionist..." I began.

Agnes waved off my explanation.

"Yeah, sure, I've seen his stuff."

"Okay, so I based my design off of his painting, *Nympheas en Fleur*." I pulled a small reproduction of the famous painting out of my bag.

"Oh. I like that." Agnes nodded, brows raised in approval.

Well, color me gobsmacked.

"Good, because your kitchen is predominantly green, and your living room is purple. This painting incorporates more muted shades of both of those colors, as well as bringing in a whole spectrum of blues." I handed her the print.

"Well, I'll be darned, it sure does. Can we get a bigger one?" She held the painting up against the backdrops of the kitchen and living room and squinted.

"I can order a large version of it for the focal wall over here." I pointed to the wall, where, at present, a large and very baroque hutch loomed over the room. My rule of thumb has always been *If it's baroque...fix it.*

"But the hutch is there." Agnes frowned.

"Yes, but it won't be in the final design. Would you like to see the plan?"

"That's why you're here, isn't it?" She cackled, seeming pleased.

This was not at all how I thought this appointment was going to go. I didn't know whether to be excited or terrified at the idea of having Agnes as a client.

"It sure is. Let me bring up the design for you." I opened my laptop and took a seat.

She loved it. Every furniture piece, paint color, and accent, from top to bottom. Go figure. Now, I'd be in a working relationship with Agnes Hackles for at least a few weeks. To be fair, she had become much more pleasant over the course of our design chat and hadn't balked at the considerable price of the design at all. Score.

"You know who I think did it?" she blurted as we were enjoying diet orange soda over ice after my presentation.

"Did what?" I tried my best to conceal the belch that was bubbling up in the back of my throat.

"Killed poor Rosalie," she whispered, leaning forward, as though the killer himself was standing just behind the drapes, waiting to pounce.

"Oh!" I was startled by the casual reference to a rather sensitive matter. "Uh…who?"

"It's gotta be that Buck Lumpkin." Agnes sat back in her chair and folded her hands over her stomach, nodding as though the matter was settled.

"Who is Buck Lumpkin?" I was instantly drawn in, wondering if he might be the electrician that I had seen.

I was still more than a bit salty that Detective Griff had sort of accused me of potentially being involved, so if Agnes Hackles had the dirt on what had gone down next door, I wanted to know.

"Buck Lumpkin is the neighbor on the other side of the Bennetts. I was the oddest duck in the neighborhood, until they moved in. At least my Wally had been a business owner, like everyone else around here."

Her tone had more than a degree of contempt, and she leaned forward again, her eyes darting toward the door and the window.

"Buck Lumpkin actually works for a living," she whispered, as though she was revealing a crime.

Before I could think of something suitably pithy to say, she continued.

"And that's not all. I don't know if you've noticed, but he and his wife, Vikki is her name—not Victoria, just Vikki—they have this huge RV that they leave parked in their driveway. I don't know how many times the Homeowner's Association board has warned them about it. Not only that, but because the RV is taking up their driveway, they park their shiny new oversized pickup truck *on the street,* for crying out loud," she groused. "Who does that?"

Not knowing what to say, I just stared at her. She barely paused to draw breath.

"They come and go at all hours, and the pickup truck has a loud motor that wakes us all up." Agnes shook her head in dismay. "And can you believe this? He mows his own lawn!"

Her eyes went wide, as though she expected me to recoil in horror at the news.

"Well, that might make him a bit of an oddity in this neighborhood, but I wouldn't say that makes him a homicidal maniac, exactly…" I took another swallow of soda, trying to keep my smirk to myself. Apparently, I *can* be pithy sometimes.

"Well, you say that now, but I've overheard him having rather loud disagreements with Cliff over him not keeping the dandelions at bay in his yard and some other things too. The rest of us work so hard to not have dandelions and Buck Lumpkin just lets them run rampant," Agnes pursed her lips and folded her arms.

"So, you pull your own dandelions?" I arched an eyebrow at her.

"Don't be ridiculous. My lawn guy takes care of that." She rolled her eyes.

"Do you know what their other disagreements were about, besides the dandelions, I mean." I was intrigued.

Even if Agnes had a skewed perspective, it didn't erase the fact that Buck and his family were an anomaly in the neighborhood. That fact alone made him worth checking into.

"Of course not. Their arguments were none of my business," she declared primly.

I had to work hard to contain my reaction to the screaming irony.

"Have you personally ever had any run-ins with Buck Lumpkin?" My curiosity was clearly getting the best of me, but I couldn't help myself. I was sitting with a bona fide gossip, and I was going to make the most of it, by golly. The detectives on Law and Order learned a great deal by casually asking questions, so maybe I could, too.

"I sure as the dickens told him how I felt about that hulking RV sitting in the driveway when I was out for my walk, and he and the wife were doing yard work. She wore a tank top, for goodness sake." Agnes sighed and shook her head.

I bit my lip to suppress a giggle fit.

"And was he mean to you?"

"He told me to mind my own business. The sheer nerve of the man! And when I started to give him a piece of my mind, he turned up that vile country music station that he was listening to, so that it drowned me out. Rude!"

I was now dying to meet Buck and Vikki-not-Victoria Lumpkin. They might either know who committed the heinous crime…or they might be suspects themselves. If neither of those things were true, I had to believe that, since Agnes found them insufferable, I might just enjoy them. As Agnes droned on about the transgressions of Buck Lumpkin, I formulated a plan. It was bold, it was foolhardy, and with any luck, it might just work. If not, I might not live to tell the tale, so at least I wouldn't have to endure the shame of failure.

Chapter Six

When I finally extricated myself from Agnes, with a signed contract in hand—clearly miracles never cease—I drove two doors down and parked in front of Buck and Vikki Lumpkin's house. Taking the car seemed prudent in case I might need a quick getaway. Grabbing my initial consultation bag, I marched right up their front walk and rang the doorbell before I could chicken out. Buck Lumpkin answered the door and immediately frowned at me. He wore an ancient t-shirt that looked like it had once been a greenish-blue and jeans that drooped over his frame, making me thankful he'd worn a belt.

"Hi, I'm Sari." I smiled and held out my hand.

He ignored it and looked confused.

"What're you sorry for?"

"Oh, ha-ha." I manufactured a laugh that came out sounding rather off-balance. "Sari is my name," I explained. "And you are?"

"Wondering what you're doing on my porch." Buck folded his arms, eyes narrowed.

"Oh, right, sorry." I giggled nervously again, hoping that I sounded more competent than I felt at the moment. "I'm an interior decorator, and I'm looking to build my client list in this neighborhood, so I've selected a couple of homes to offer a free room makeover, and yours is one of them," I announced, trying to make it sound like he'd just won the lottery. "Surprise," I added, complete with jazz hands, when he didn't immediately respond.

"I don't know if I'd be interested in that." He frowned again and sucked his teeth. "You trying to sell something?"

"Nope, not at all. I'll just redesign one room in your house, and if you like the design plan, you can tell all of your friends and neighbors." I made up the ruse on the fly. "It's a form of advertising for me. Word of mouth is a powerful thing." I tried my best to squelch the image of Agnes Hackles' pursed lips that flitted through my mind.

"Well, I don't deal with all that kind of stuff. You're gonna have to get with my wife on that and see if she wants to set something up. You got a card or something?" He gazed at me as though I might leap past him at any moment and ransack his house.

"Absolutely."

I dug into my purse and produced a card. Buck took it and studied it as though he would be tested on the information it contained.

"Alright," he said finally. "I'll have her give you a call if she's interested."

He closed the door before I could open my mouth to reply.

"Gee, thanks for considering my free offer," I muttered, making a face at the door before I turned to go to my car. Hopefully, they didn't have a doorbell camera.

I glanced at my watch. Old fashioned though it may be, yes, I still wear a watch. I refuse to pull out my cell phone just to check the time. It can stay in my bag where it belongs, and all I have to do is take a quick look at my wrist. The good news? I'd be right on time for my date at the nail salon with Charla, which meant that I'd get to soak my feet in the pedicure basin for at least fifteen minutes before she showed up. Some things you can just count on.

* * *

"Hey Kenny, how was your trip to Vegas?" I asked my favorite nail tech when I entered the salon.

Kenny was a hot, hilarious, way-too-young-for-me Vietnamese man who was a wizard with nail art.

"Ate too much, drank too much, gambled too much." He grinned.

"Oh, so it was awesome." I chuckled, easing down into the pedicure chair

48

and slipping off my shoes. "Oh, man, that feels good." I groaned when my feet were submerged in the warm sweetly-scented water that bubbled up over my ankles.

"Exactly." Kenny nodded. "Charla coming today?" He looked at the clock.

"Yep, but she won't be here for a bit, I'm sure."

I rolled my eyes. Her lack of ability to keep a schedule was legendary.

"I'll have Lindsay start running her water so she can sit in the chair next to you when she comes in."

"Not Lindsay!" I hissed.

He frowned. "Why not? She does good nails."

"She's mean, and every time she does Charla's nails, all Charla does is complain that she's too slow," I whispered, my eyes darting to the front of the shop, where the tiny dragon lady, Lindsay, was busy ringing up her most recent customer.

"I could have her do *your* nails, and I'll do Charla's," he teased.

I gave him a withering look. "I'm just going to pretend that you didn't say that. What about Phil? I think I saw him when I came in."

Kenny shook his head. "Phil just went on his break."

"I'll double your tip if you can get him to do Charla's nails instead of Lindsay," I offered in a low voice.

"Deal." Kenny grinned.

"Why do I feel like I've been set up?" I wondered aloud.

I tapped at the buttons on the remote control for the massage function on my chair and was soon being happily pummeled while sipping at the Coke Zero Kenny provided. Charla breezed in, a vision in turquoise, with so many bangles on her wrist that she jangled when she moved.

"Hey, girlfriend." I raised my soda in greeting, and Kenny sat down to work on my toes.

Charla slid into the chair next to me, her perfume announcing her presence.

"Oh my gosh, you would not believe the clients that I've had to deal with today," she muttered, taking off her shoes and rolling up the legs of her linen pants.

How she manages to wear linen and not end up looking like a crumpled tissue, I'll never know, but she has that knack.

"I mean seriously..." She paused briefly to send a flirtatious smile to both Kenny and Phil. "They wanted me to require the seller to leave their grandma's antique armoire behind. I'm sorry, but in what universe is an armoire considered a fixture?" She shook her head and accepted a bottle of sparkling water. "Oh, thank goodness I got Phil today." She let out a breath and leaned back in her chair.

"You're welcome. If I hadn't bribed Kenny, you'd have gotten Lindsay," I informed her.

"You're a saint." She shot a scathing glance at Lindsay's back. "So, what's happening in your world, girl?" She took a sip of her water and hit the massage function on her remote.

"I need info, since you asked." I kept my voice low, leaning toward her.

Phil glanced at Kenny and said something in Vietnamese. I didn't want to know.

"Oh, do tell." Charla's big blue eyes sparkled.

She loved being the font of all knowledge about the local society set.

"What do you know about Buck Lumpkin?"

She pursed her cherry-glossed lips. "The name rings a bell, but I can't place him."

"He lives right next door to Rosalie Bennett's house. The house on the corner with the huge pool." I leaned back and closed my eyes, enjoying the sugar scrub Kenny was massaging into my calves.

"Oh, *that* guy! Right!" Charla nodded, remembering. "He's an interesting story. I don't know much, but what I do know is, well, weird."

"Really?" I opened my eyes. "Weird, how?"

"He apparently came into a lump sum of money somehow...I think it was, like, the lottery, or some sort of casino thing. He and his wife ran through most of it in a hurry—trips to the Caribbean, big cars, expensive clothes, the normal stuff that people waste their money on—and they spent the last bit of it on that house, from what I understand." Charla raised her eyebrows in her patented "I'm-not-judging-I'm-just-judging" look.

"Well, if they spent all their money, how can they afford to live in that house?" I glanced about to ensure that no one besides Kenny and Phil could hear me.

"Oh, you're going to love this," Charla said, turning around to look me in the eye. "Scuba diving."

"Excuse me...what?" I frowned at her, utterly confused.

"He uses their massive pool to teach scuba diving, so he's able to write off all of his pool expenses and keep it open for most of the year. I'm assuming that it helps pay the other household bills, too." She chuckled and took another sip of her water.

"Stop it." My mouth dropped open.

"Nope, it's true. He really does give scuba lessons in his backyard." She nodded.

"Hmm. I guess I never realized that there would be enough of a market in the Midwest to support a scuba lesson business."

"People from here vacation in warm places. They take lessons before they go so they don't have to waste the time when they get there. He certifies them and everything."

"Well, color me surprised."

"Why do you need info on Buck Lumpkin, of all people, anyway?" Charla frowned. "He's married and totally not your type." She wrinkled her delicate, tip-tilted nose.

"Ew...no. I'm not interested in him personally. He just happens to live next door to a murder victim, and I'd love to solve the case before that surly detective does."

Kenny burst into a low-voiced, rapid-fire conversation with Phil, and the two of them cast surreptitious glances at Charla and me while we chatted.

"Seriously? You need to mind your own beeswax, missy," Charla warned. "You don't know the first thing about investigating a murder, other than what we watch on TV."

"I'm not going to let that detective think that I had something to do with this," I vowed, clamping my teeth together at the mere thought of him.

"Wow. He really got under your skin, didn't he?" Charla poked at me playfully. "Really, though. Leave it alone and let the man do his job. You're innocent, so there's nothing to worry about. I wouldn't mess with Buck Lumpkin either; he's too much of a wild card."

"I already offered to do a free room makeover at his house," I confessed, wincing in anticipation of her response.

"What? Why?"

"Because I had to think of an excuse to talk to him, and that's all I could come up with on the spot." I bit my lip, giving her a sheepish look.

"You talked to him? You are out of your ever-loving mind, woman." She shook her head.

"He didn't make an appointment, but I gave him a card to give to his wife…" I trailed off at her look of disbelief.

"Well, when she calls, you need to tell her that the offer expired or something. I'm serious. You stay out of this thing. If Buck Lumpkin is a murderer, you don't need to be anywhere around him," Charla warned as Kenny began another Vietnamese monologue.

"Yeah, I suppose you're right." I made a face. "She probably won't even call."

"If she does, you back away from your offer. I mean it. She might even be the one who did the deed, for all you know." She shook her finger at me.

"Fine!" I laughed at her expression. "Okay, Mom, I get it."

"You behave, young lady." She attempted to maintain the stern look, then grinned. "Kinda exciting though, huh?"

"You better believe it."

Heading home with pink, sparkly nails and toenails, I was almost to the turn that led to my street when I saw something that made my heart skip a beat. An electrician's white van with a light bulb logo on the side. It looked very much like the van that I had seen from Sally Edgerton's guest room window. Heart thumping, I grabbed my phone and took a picture of it before it drove away when the light changed. I didn't know what I was going to do with the info yet, but it seemed important to record it. I wasn't at the right angle to see either the driver or the license plate, but at least I had something to go on. Rattled, I drove home, where Foo and food awaited me.

* * *

You gotta love dogs. Whether I'm gone for ten minutes or an entire day, Foo loses his mind when I come home. This happy little creature, who is so adorable that he gets away with almost everything, is just filled with complete love and excitement when he hears my car pull into the garage. That kind of adoration is good for the soul. And it's mutual. Foo Dog has been the keeper of all of my secrets, and his fur has absorbed so many stress tears that I swear he should have a salt problem, so I feel like I can cut him some slack when the occasional sock gets chewed. I can always buy more socks, but there'll never be another Foo.

I opened the door from the garage to the house, and he assaulted my ankles until I picked him up and planted a kiss on the top of his head. Once the formal greeting process concluded, he wanted to be let out, immediately, and expressed it by dancing and hopping in front of the back sliding doors, every now and again letting out a little chuff to prod me along faster.

I let Foo out, then slipped out of my shoes and trotted to my room to change after admiring Kenny's artistry on my toes. I had just pulled on my jogging pants, which were definitely not used for jogging, and a shapeless grey t-shirt when I heard my phone, which I'd left on the kitchen counter, ringing.

"Crudmuffins." I tossed my hair up into a messy bun, securing it with a scrunchy as I hurried toward the sound. "Impeccable Interiors," I sang out, managing to sound only slightly out of breath.

Foo rained down blows on the slider, demanding to be let in, so I rushed to the door, opening it before he made little doggie nose prints all over the glass.

"Hi, this is Vikki Lumpkin. My husband said you stopped by today for some free makeover or something."

Dangit. A vision of Charla's forehead creased with faint lines as she gave me her stern look flashed through my mind.

"Hi, Vikki. Thanks for calling. How are you?" I cradled the phone to my ear with my shoulder while I grabbed a treat from the jar for Foo.

"Curious. Why don't you tell me what this is really all about?"

Great, she sounded just as pleasant as Buck. Lucky me. I considered following Charla's perfectly rational advice to tell Vikki that the offer had expired or something, I really did, but when it came right down to it, abject curiosity won out, and I caved.

While performing various contortions to get Foo's food and water, with my neck cramping because of the odd position of my shoulder, I explained the free makeover to Vikki in the same manner that I had described it to Buck.

"What's the catch?" she snapped.

I had to wonder for a moment what on earth was happening in these people's daily lives that made them so unpleasant to total strangers. I mean, knowing that they'd murdered the neighbor would probably do it.

"No catch. It's just a way to get word out about my services," I assured her, sinking down into the sofa.

"And it's totally free?" she asked. Again.

"One hundred percent." I fought hard to keep a smile in my voice.

"It better be, because I'm not paying a dime. I didn't ask for this, and the second you even mention money, I'm tossing you out," Vikki growled.

What fun. Did they not teach manners or people skills when Buck and Vikki were in school? Those two took abrasiveness to a whole new level.

"Not a problem." The brightness in my voice was more contrived than a locally produced television commercial.

We set a time to get together the next day, and I hung up the phone feeling troubled. So, I did what I always do when I'm feeling troubled. I called Tang. He was less than pleased to hear that I was going over to the Lumpkins', particularly when I told him who they were and why I had contacted them in the first place. I was hoping he'd volunteer to go with me, and when he didn't, I asked him to, but unfortunately, he wasn't available. Whatever I encountered behind the out-of-style double doors of the Lumpkin house, I'd encounter alone. Gulp.

I gave myself a pep talk. What were the odds that I'd actually be inside the home of a killer? I mean, that never happened, right?

I spent the rest of the evening cuddled up with Foo, watching Netflix, and when I woke in the morning, my stomach was a fluttering ball of anxiety. Which did nothing to diminish my appetite, of course. It would take more than potentially facing a cold-blooded killer to do that. I could eat in the midst of any crisis, and when it was emotional, my consumption was astonishing. Lucky me.

Soon, I'd be in the private spaces of someone who may or may not be a killer and who had already been hostile to me once. Yes, I wondered if I had lost my mind like Charla had declared, and no, that wasn't going to stop me. In for a penny, in for a pound, it was too late to back out now, consequences be darned.

Chapter Seven

I rang the Lumpkins' doorbell, and my eardrums were nearly shredded by a high-pitched cacophony inside. It sounded as though a pack of hyenas had taken possession of the home, and I had to wonder if there were any survivors. Foo's bark could pack a punch, but his singular series of well-intended woofs paled by comparison. I sighed inwardly. There were few things as frustrating as trying to conduct an appointment in the company of nonstop barkers. I could only hope that their barks were worse than their bites.

An overly tanned, harried-looking, middle-aged bleach-blonde answered the door. She held off the screaming horde with her foot, opening the door just wide enough to peek out and regard me with nearly palpable suspicion.

"Hi! I'm Sari Samson," I hollered with a smile, trying to be heard over the din. "We made an appointment yesterday."

The woman frowned and yelled, "Tater, shut up!" into the house.

Tater? All that noise was coming from one dog? Her directive did absolutely no good, and Tater kept up the chorus.

"I'm Vikki. How does this work?" She kicked backward with her foot but didn't make contact with any living creature, as far as I could tell.

The door was only open maybe six inches, and her body was wedged into it, blocking the dog, or dogs…or demons…whatever was in there. Apparently, I was going to have to continue to shout at her from the porch. Great. I had told her over the phone what the appointment would entail, but clearly, she required a recap.

"You choose a room that you want to work on, then we go in and get to work. I brought samples of paint, flooring, wallpaper, and fabric, so we can put together a complete design. I also have a program on my computer to do a 3-D image of what the room will look like," I yelled, wishing that I had brought some of Foo's Zen treats with me. I was going to have a sore throat if I had to do much more of this.

Vikki sighed. Or at least I think she did. There was no way on earth that I could hear something as subtle as a sigh at this point. She pursed her lips, apparently considering whether or not she was going to let me in, so I decided to push her a bit.

"May I come in?" I yelled.

"Hang on," she barked, abruptly closing the door.

Not knowing what else to do, I hung on, as directed. Waiting on the porch for her to open the door, I strongly considered hightailing it back to my car, but as soon as I moved toward the steps, the noise stopped, and Vikki opened the door, cradling a tiny, snarling chihuahua, who was wearing a Cubs jersey, in her arms. That little thing had been the source of that explosion of sound?

"Awww…" I smiled at the dog.

I've found that people like it when you think their dog is adorable, or at least pretend to. Dogs were typically easier for me to relate to than people, but I had my doubts about this one. At least he wasn't wearing a Cardinals jersey.

"This is Tater." Vikki stepped back so I could enter the house, which smelled oddly of chlorine and cigarette smoke.

"He's so cuuuute," I cooed, knowing better than to attempt to pet the grumbling, rumbling little tyrant.

"He's a pain in the tuckus." Vikki rubbed the top of the dog's head.

He snapped at her hand, and she snatched it away before he could draw blood.

"See?" She made a face and shook her head.

I merely blinked and smiled uncertainly.

"So…which room were you thinking about for your makeover?" I asked.

The sooner we got down to business, the sooner I could get her talking, get my info, and get out. The living room, which I could see clearly from the foyer, was strangely empty. There was a black leather reclining sofa and a flat-screen television perched on a glass coffee table. That's it. No art, no area rug covering the oak flooring, and no other furniture. The walls were done in a light greenish-blue DIY attempt at Venetian plaster, and the foyer ceiling fixture looked like it hadn't been updated since the seventies. Surely, she'd pick this room.

"I saw on your website that you do custom closet designs, so I want you to give me more room in my master closet," Vikki replied, setting Tater down.

He immediately lunged at my ankles, and I started hopping from one foot to the other in an attempt to avoid his snapping teeth, cursing my decision to wear a skirt and hose.

"He won't hurt ya." Vikki waved a hand in Tater's general direction. "He just makes a fuss at first. He'll settle down."

"He must smell my dog." I gave the standard dog owner response and tried my best to smile past my irritation. "Let's take a look at that closet."

I followed Vikki down a dark hall, thinking that Tater would eventually tire of snapping at my ankles. I was wrong. The little booger kept it up, every step of the way, along with the snarling and barking. So pleasant. There are some times that I deserve hazard pay.

The master bedroom was nearly as sparsely furnished as the living room, but messier, so I thought that the closet would be a piece of cake. I couldn't have been more wrong. I think every possession that Buck and Vikki owned was in the small walk-in closet, including a full-length wetsuit hanging on the door that scared the bejeebers out of me when Vikki snapped on the light.

"I saw that you do that organizing thing too. I want it organized."

"Life is much easier with a little organization," I murmured automatically, trying not to gape at the odd assortment of items in front of me.

The closet was teeming with clothes, sporting equipment, linens, boxes of files, and a sizable collection of miscellaneous stuff, some of which I couldn't identify. I'd run into some pretty strange things in clients' closets before, and I was not looking forward to what I might find in this one.

"So...what were you wanting to do in here?" I glanced around at the chaotic clutter, thinking that they needed a magician or an intervention, not a decorator.

"I don't know. Some shelves, and more hanging space, and maybe some cabinets or something."

"Gotcha." I nodded, thinking.

Tater disappeared into the closet, much to my relief, burrowing under a stack of what I hoped was clean laundry. Now I could get down to business, without worrying about his little claws and teeth assailing my pantyhose.

I like to draw closet organization clients into the process by having them help me measure the space. In a clean closet, it's much quicker to do it myself, but in a messy one, I sometimes need help, and it's a tried-and-true way to build rapport with the client. I needed to get this lady talking, so I could accomplish what I'd set out to do.

"First things first, will you help me measure the space?" I rested my bag in one of the few clear spots on the floor and grabbed my tape measure, a notebook, and a pencil.

Vikki gave me a strange look but stepped into the closet to help. I handed her the end of the tape measure, and we got to work, with me carefully stepping over various piles of things to record the measurements. I moved a stack of shoe boxes aside and had to stifle a gasp when I saw a stash of rifles, handguns, and ammunition boxes.

"Oh yeah." Vikki nodded, noticing what I'd just seen. "We'll need a gun cabinet in here too."

I swallowed hard, managing a shaky smile and making a note. Even more highly motivated to take care of business and get outta Dodge now, I hurriedly finished up the rest of the measurements and tasked Vikki with counting clothing, shoes, and "stuff" while I took photos of the closet and put the measurements into my computer program. When she gave me her figures, I made some adjustments, and we moved to the living room so that I could start designing.

A couple of kids rode by the house on their bikes, and Tater came charging out of the closet, screaming his head off and lunging at the living room's picture window. Vikki shushed him several times, but he didn't quit until they were completely out of sight, and even then, he kept emitting low growls.

I had a brilliant inspiration, if I do say so myself, and it was one that could open up a dialogue relating to the murder.

"Wow, that poor little guy must've been losing his mind when all those lights and sirens were at the house next door the other day." I made a sympathetic face at Tater, who merely gave me the stink-eye, his upper lip twitching.

"How'd you hear about that?" Vikki whirled to face me, drilling me with a glare.

"I was across the street, redoing Sally Edgerton's guest room, when it happened," I replied with a nonchalant shrug. Or at least, what I hoped would pass for a nonchalant shrug. I've never been a good fibber.

Vikki's eyes narrowed.

"If you're already doing a house in this neighborhood, why do you need to offer a free makeover to grow your business?" Her low, accusatory voice made Tater advance, growling.

Oops. This was the problem with making up things on the fly. Tater emitted a single, shrill bark that shattered my eardrums and made me jump and crept closer, his tiny body trembling with barely contained malice.

I'm an animal lover since birth, but I grabbed my paint fan deck, fully prepared to swat at the menacing little beast if he lunged at my ankles again.

"Well, while one testimonial from someone in the neighborhood is good, some people require more than one reference before they'll commit to a project," I hedged, surprised at my newly-acquired ability to create flash fiction.

"And you wanted to use me as a reference?" Vikki put her hands on her hips and stared me down, clearly skeptical.

"Look, you're a tough lady, and if my work pleases you, that could carry a lot of weight." I winced inwardly at perpetuating my ever-spiraling tale.

Before Vikki could reply, the doorbell rang, thank goodness. Saved by the bell. Tater lost his mind, and Vikki chased after him, trying to grab the incensed, wriggling creature before opening the door. She managed to corner him and avoid his snapping teeth long enough to pick him up and tuck him under her arm so that she could answer the door. I was both dismayed and relieved to see that it was Detective Griff on Vikki's porch.

"Mrs. Lumpkin, I need to follow up with you on some questions that I had after the last time that we spoke," I heard him say.

I closed my laptop and started packing up my consultation bag.

"Oh, what now?" Vikki sighed and let the detective in while Tater snarled and snorted in her arms. Then she saw me packing up, which apparently infuriated her. "And just where do you think you're going?" she demanded as Detective Griff walked in, raising an eyebrow when he spotted me on her sofa.

"Well, I have all I need in order to draw up your design, so I'll do that at home and mail it to you," I declared as I rose from the couch and edged toward the door.

"And when is my free closet getting installed?" Vikki just wouldn't leave it alone and apparently didn't care at all that Griff stood, arms folded, watching our exchange with great interest.

"Oh, Vikki, the closet isn't free," I explained quickly. "The design is. If you like the design, we have to draw up a contract, and you pay for the closet."

"That there's a bait and switch. That's illegal. I knew you weren't on the up and up, offering me something for free and then tricking me. You hear that, Detective?" She turned to Griff. "She just committed a crime. You should leave me alone, once and for all, and arrest her."

I uttered an involuntary gasp.

"That is absolutely not bait and switch. My designs are valuable and are the product of years of training and experience. The value that I'm offering you is huge."

If she wanted to get aggressive with me, I was more than capable of squaring off with her. Even if my 'free' plan had actually only been a ruse to get inside and talk to her, she had no right to make accusations.

"Free means free, and you lied to me."

I knew from experience that my face had flushed a brilliant scarlet, because it felt like I'd been set on fire, but it wasn't embarrassment that had amped-up my thermostat.

It was fury.

No one called me a liar. I may have fudged a bit, or had ulterior motives, but I hadn't lied. I fully intended to give her my design ideas, right down to the paint colors and wood tones. I think Griff saw my reaction and decided to intervene before he had to break up a catfight.

He stepped between us, holding up his hands. "Ladies, while this is all very fascinating, I have official police business to conduct. If you'll excuse me, Ms. Samson…" He looked pointedly at me and then at the door.

"My pleasure," I snipped, moving to the door and shooting Vikki a scathing glance.

Griff handed me his card before I left. "Please contact me this afternoon."

Just as I approached the door, I heard Vikki light into the detective.

"How do you know her?" she demanded shrilly. "There's something fishy going on here, and you better tell me what it is. Is she working for you?"

I shut the door behind me, glad to have escaped intact, and could only hear the muffled sounds of Vikki haranguing the detective. His timing had been perfect. Even if I looked shady to Vikki, I had been given the chance to make my exit before anything potentially dangerous happened.

Based upon the sheer number of firearms and ammo boxes in the closet, plus Vikki Lumpkin's testy and suspicious manner, I was convinced that I was on the right track in my quest to ferret out a murderer. It was just super-duper inconvenient that the detective had discovered me at a potential suspect's house, and I wracked my brain as I drove home to come up with a plausible explanation for it.

I pulled into the garage and groaned when I heard Foo's adorable little yips and yaps.

Foo does not share.

I'm not talking about food or toys. He's very good-natured about those things, because he knows that there are plenty more where those came from.

Foo does not share me, his human.

So, when I came home smelling of Tater, with dog spittle undoubtedly slathered about my ankles, Foo decided to make me pay for it.

He greeted me at the garage door, like he always does, but instead of happily smiling at me and waiting to be picked up, he immediately started sniffing me from the knees down, not even pausing to give me a dirty look. When I picked him up to give him his customary forehead kiss before letting him outside, he turned his head away, refusing to look at me.

"Oh, come on, little buddy, not you, too." I sighed, taking him to the slider, where he shot me a decidedly frosty glance before trotting outside to do his business.

There were multiple snags in my pantyhose, *thanks, Tater,* so I peeled them off and threw them into my bathroom trash can. I soaped up a washcloth and cleaned my ankles, thankful that at least the skin didn't seem to be broken, then headed straight for my sweatpants. Slipping quickly into the most shapeless, colorless, comfy clothes that I could find, I went to the back door to let Foo back in, and my phone rang. I recognized Detective Griff's number on the screen and made a face. Couldn't I even have a moment's peace? I contemplated ignoring the call, but then figured that if I did, Griff just might come to the door for a most unwelcome visit.

"Impeccable Interiors." I pretended not to know who was calling. Petty, yes, but it gave me a measure of satisfaction.

"This is Detective Griff. I'm going to need you to meet me at the station this afternoon. I have a few questions for you."

Crudmuffins.

"Can't you just ask me the questions over the phone?" I glanced down at my less-than-presentable attire. The last thing I wanted to do was get dressed in normal clothing and leave the house.

"I can, but I'm not going to. I'll be back in the office in one hour, and I'll see you then." He hung up before I could protest.

"Are you this rude to every law-abiding citizen?" I complained to the dead line.

Foo barked to be let in, and I went through the routine of food, water, and affection in a very preoccupied state. I'm always nervous around law enforcement, and this time, I actually had reason to be. It was going to be tough not to act guilty when I had engaged in behavior that could be *technically* construed as interfering in an investigation. Dangit. My palms were going to sweat, that much was certain. I could only hope that my upper lip didn't bead up with telltale sweat as well. I'd wear light clothing just in case my underarms decided to join in on the fun.

Why, oh why, hadn't I just ignored my initial impulse to call the police? Life would be so much easier if I had. I'd just be working on interiors and living my life like a normal person. But no, I'd tried to do the right thing. It was maddening.

* * *

I sat across from Marcus Griff again, and so far, my lip wasn't sweating, so I had that going for me.

"What were you doing at the Lumpkins'?" He was watching me like a hawk.

"Their master closet," I replied, sitting on my hands so I wouldn't fidget.

"Vikki doesn't exactly strike me as someone who would call an interior decorator."

"And yet, she did," I replied truthfully.

"But only after you approached her husband with a free design offer." Griff quirked an eyebrow at me.

Yikes. The gloves were off. Time to turn on the charm and hope for the best. Why couldn't I just channel Charla's easygoing, flirtatious manner at times like these?

"Well, yes. Judging by their front door, I thought that they could probably use my help. You saw the inside of their house." I gave him a pointed look. "They needed me. Badly."

"Mrs. Lumpkin said that you acted nervous and questioned her about the murder." The detective leaned forward, making me feel like a bug under a microscope.

"I *was* nervous! She was mean, and her dog was meaner. As far as questioning her about the murder, I did no such thing. I merely remarked that the sirens must've hurt her dog's ears."

It was true, but I still felt a rush of guilt.

"She was very suspicious about your motives for being in her house." Griff gave me a look.

"She strikes me as someone who is defensive about everyone she meets," I shot back.

As self-serving as that sounded, it was true.

The detective crossed his arms and stared at me. "I find it more than a bit odd that you were in the area when a murder victim was found, and now you've cooked up a scheme to worm your way into the neighbor's house."

"I didn't *worm my way in*. I employed an advertising technique that I use when I want to spread the word about my business in a certain neighborhood." I cringed at how lame the excuse sounded.

"Then I want a list of every homeowner that you've approached with this type of offer, so that I can verify your technique."

He called my bluff. Now what?

Panic, then bluster.

"Did you know that they have guns? Well, they do, lots of them. I even have pictures on my phone. I can show you," I blurted, reaching for my phone.

"Not necessary, thanks." Griff held up a hand.

"These people live next to a crime scene, they have a closet full of guns and ammo, and you think *I'm* a suspicious person?" I snorted in disbelief.

"I just find it highly unusual that I keep running into you in connection with this case. If curiosity is what motivates you, I'll remind you that curiosity killed the cat. If it's something else that motivates you, you need to tell me," Griff replied.

"Is that a threat, Detective?" My stomach clenched.

"That, Ms. Samson, is reality."

I left Detective Griff's office with a sick feeling in the pit of my stomach. Was I going to let him deter me from trying to find out more? Heck no. If anything, I was even more determined. He's going to believe Vikki Lumpkin and look at *me* suspiciously? That is so not okay. I'm going to get to the bottom of this murder if it kills me. But I mean…I'm hoping it won't.

Chapter Eight

Agnes Hackles called again. She calls me at least twice a day to either complain or ask a question that I've usually already answered. This time, she was utterly convinced that the painters had brought the wrong color of paint, and she was refusing to let them continue until I came over and verified the color.

While I was en route, Dave, the owner of the painting company, called.

"You know, Sari, this lady...I'm about to pack up and leave, and if I do, I'm gonna charge her for my time and my guys' time, and the product that we've used. I got no problem leaving, you know what I'm saying?"

"I hear you," I said, trying not to hyperventilate.

Dave has the best painting crew around, by a long shot. His time slots go fast, and he does quite a bit of work in Chicago, so I was lucky to even be able to snag him for Agnes's project. He's a south-side Polish Chicagoan who has no problem speaking his mind, which totally works for me, but the thought of Agnes squaring off on him gave me palpitations, so I tried to defuse the situation.

"I know that she can be...a lot," I began, trying to tread lightly. "But I'm on my way over there to smooth down her feathers, so if you could just stay there until I try to work some magic on her, I'd really appreciate it."

There was a moment of silence on the other end that made me believe Dave might have already left, but when I heard his deep sigh, I let out a relieved breath.

"You know, days like this, Sari, they sometimes make me wish I was a drinking man."

"I know, believe me, I know. I'll handle it, I promise," I said, hoping that I could.

"My guys are still on the clock you know," Dave warned.

"I completely understand. How's Christina?" I asked, changing the course of the conversation to his favorite subject—his wife—who's as sweet as she is gorgeous, and one of the best cooks ever. It was a sure-fire way to put him in a better mood.

"My angel is amazing as always," he replied. "And I don't have any problem getting out of here and going home for a good meal if that's what I need to do."

"I think I'd want to do that even if I didn't have a difficult client," I replied, relieved when I heard him chuckle.

"I'll bring you some of her Pho after this job is over," he promised. "The end of this one will definitely be a reason to celebrate with food."

"Oh, that's amazing—her Pho is the best. I'll do my best to see that we both live through this, Dave."

"Fine then. See ya."

He hung up before I could say goodbye, but I felt pretty confident that he'd still be there when I arrived.

As I turned the corner and pulled into Agnes's neighborhood, my heart leapt into my throat. Once again, I passed a white van that looked just like the one I had seen across the street from Sally's house, leaving the neighborhood. I wrestled with the idea of whipping a U-turn and following it, but Agnes was expecting me, and the painters were surely eager to get the job over with, so I continued on my way, wondering if it had been just a coincidence. I kept glancing in my rearview mirror, irrationally expecting to see the van following me, but I managed to make it to Agnes' house unscathed and without a van on my tail.

Agnes rushed out onto the porch, her hair sticking out in all directions and a splotch of paint on the elbow of her sweatshirt.

"Well, it's about time you got here. I've been losing my mind with this whole renovation thing, and wondering if it's all a big mistake," she fretted, as she did several times a week.

Fortunately, I deal with nervous homeowners on a regular basis, and Agnes was no more neurotic than most.

"Everything will be fine, Agnes. Even if it *is* the wrong color, that's an easy fix."

I hurried into the house after her and came face-to-face with the painting crew, who stood staring at us, arms folded. Dave stood near a ladder, texting.

Please let it be Christina.

"Hey Dave, how are things?" I called out, waving.

He looked up, raised a hand briefly in greeting, then went back to his texting without a word. When he finished, he came over to where Agnes was pointing at the wall and holding up a color chip.

"See," she insisted. "It's not the same. It's way too bright. I can't live with this."

Dave and I exchanged a glance, and I gave him my don't-worry-I've-got-this look. We'd been in this situation before and I think that by now, he trusted me to take care of it.

"Okay, I see what's happening here," I declared, after assessing the situation. "First of all, Agnes, come stand right here by me." I pointed to a spot.

"Why?" She blinked at me, puzzled.

"Because you need to be at least three feet away to see true color." My explanation drew a suspicious glance from her, but she stood next to me and folded her arms.

"Okay, I'm three feet away, and it's still too bright." Agnes shook her head, her mouth set in a stubborn line.

"A couple of things are making it seem that way," I explained patiently. "First, you have a cool-toned blue being painted over the top of a light coral. Coral and blue are complementary colors, which means, when they're next to each other, they're going to look more vibrant. Also, paint darkens when it dries, so what you're seeing here is extra brightness because the paint is still wet, even though it may not feel wet to the touch. It has to cure for hours before you'll get true color."

Agnes took it all in, but raised an eyebrow, clearly still skeptical.

"Let me show you something." I took her arm and led her over to Dave's ladder.

I picked up the plastic cover from Dave's five-gallon container, which, thankfully, had dried paint on it.

"See? See how dark this paint is?"

I walked back to the patch that had been painted on the wall and held the cover up to it.

"See how the paint on the cover is darker? That's because it's dry, and the paint on the wall isn't."

Agnes pursed her lips and stared, then relented.

"Well, I'll be darned."

I glanced triumphantly over at Dave, who rolled his eyes, shook his head, and put his phone in his pocket.

"So, Dave's going to get his guys back to work, and you'll have a beautiful blue room in a couple of days, when the paint has cured, and I assure you it will be the exact color that you selected." I smiled.

Dave took the paint lid and got back to work, mouthing a quick 'thank you' on his way. Crisis averted, and now I might even get some of Christina's homemade Pho once the project was done. Agnes walked me to the door.

"I saw that you were over at the Lumpkins the other day," she remarked, clearly jonesing for some good gossip.

"Oh, uh...yes," I stammered, surprised. "I was redoing their master closet."

"I hope you got the money up front; I wouldn't trust those people further than I could throw 'em." Agnes made a face.

Before I could summon a response, she spoke again.

"You need to be more careful about the company you keep." She glanced in the direction of the Lumpkins' house. And since you do master closets, I need to have mine done, too. Next time you come out, you can take a look." She waved me out the door.

"Perfect," I replied, with a wan smile.

Shaking my head, I was headed to my car when I heard raised voices coming from the Bennett house. I stopped in my tracks, trying to listen, and an elderly man came storming out of the house. He was pale and staggered a bit when he rushed to his car, looking uncomfortably out of breath. Dropping my bag, I ran over to check on him, thankful that I'd worn flats.

"Oh my goodness! Are you okay?" I asked as the old man sagged against the car.

You could tell that he'd been strikingly handsome once, and his face sported a golf-course tan, despite his pallor. He was a bit thin and tall, and I hoped he didn't faint because I didn't think I could catch someone that size.

"He's fine," a voice that was vaguely familiar called out. I turned to see the man whom I'd met while he was watering the garden, come trotting out of the house. Looking tired and out of sorts, he helped the older man into the driver's seat. "He's just stubborn, that's all."

"I'm stubborn? Heh!" The older man waved a hand.

As soon as the car door was shut, he put on his seat belt, started the car, and drove away.

"Should he be driving?" I asked. "He didn't look so good."

"He's fine. His allergies are just acting up, that's all. Listen, I'm sorry you had to witness that. It's been a trying time around here for us, and tempers are a little on edge." The man patted down his comb-over as an errant breeze tried to flip it.

"No worries. I hope he feels better soon."

I turned to go, and the man stopped me.

"Hey, you're the decorator, right?"

"Yep, Sari," I replied, holding out my hand.

"Oh, don't be sorry, it's okay." He smiled. "I'm Byron Bennett. And you are…?"

"Nice to meet you, Byron." I laughed. "I'm actually Sari. That's my name. Sari Samson."

"Interesting." He nodded, seeming a little confused. "We're going to be selling the house, so I wondered if you might be able to come over and tell us what things we need to do to get it ready for sale."

"Sure, I'd be happy to." I dug in my purse and handed him a business card. "Just give me a call, and we'll set up an appointment."

"Sounds good, thanks." He stuck the card in his pocket, and I went back to

Agnes's porch to collect my bag, then headed home, inexplicably exhausted.

* * *

Foo and I had just settled in on the couch with a bowl of popcorn, fully prepared to watch a movie and chill for a bit before I got back to my design work when my phone rang.

"Hey, Mom," I answered the phone with a delighted grin, pausing the movie. "What's up?"

"Are you stressed, honey? You sound stressed," my mom observed accurately, without even bothering to greet me first. The woman was truly eerie at times. I wondered whether there might actually be something to their crystals and energies and connecting to the universe.

"Always." I laughed. "What are you up to?"

"Your father and I decided that it's high time that we come out for a visit now that the weather is getting nicer," she announced.

Oh geez. Not now. Why did they have to want to come visit now? I love my parents dearly, but I think it's fair to say that I had quite a lot on my plate at present.

"It's umm…it's still pretty chilly here, actually, Mom."

For two people who have spent the entirety of their lives in southern California—Temecula, to be exact—it *was* chilly. Anything under sixty degrees would be chilly to them.

"I checked the forecast and it's going to be in the seventies next week," Mom assured me.

"Next week? Wow, isn't it expensive to buy plane tickets at the last minute?" I gulped, my mind racing as I desperately tried to think of a reason to dissuade them…beyond the obvious.

"Sarisara Samson, you tell me right now what's going on."

I swear she can read me like a book, even over a phone line, from a few thousand miles away. I told her a bit about what had happened to Rosalie Bennett, without going into much detail, or mentioning that I was poking my nose where it very much didn't belong.

"Oh, sweetie, that's such bad juju. You need to make sure that you stay far away from that place and the whole situation. Do you have any sage?" Her tone was hushed. *"I really feel like you need to smudge your house as soon as possible."*

"Yep, I still have the bundle that you sent me for Christmas." I rolled my eyes, having no intention of lighting a bunch of herbs and walking through the house, making it smell like a Thanksgiving dinner gone wrong.

"You need some fresh ones. Their potency diminishes if you let them just sit around and get dusty. So go buy those today, do you hear me?"

"Got it."

"I'll bring some things with me, and we can do a full cleanse of the house and your aura when I get there. Let me write that down..." Her voice trailed off, and I heard some fumbling sounds on the other end. *"I really feel like the universe prompted me to come visit you next week, sweetie. You just be super careful until we get there, okay?"*

"I am, Mom." I smiled at her concern. I'd always be her baby, and while that could be annoying at times, it was also very sweet and comforting.

After a few more minutes of chitchat, we hung up. I'd have to go shopping for organic food before they got here. Thank goodness Charla knows all the best places for that type of thing. Now that I was totally distracted, I turned the movie off and headed for my room to change into a swimsuit. A nice long soak in the hot tub would soothe the stiff muscles in my neck, and it'd be easier to relax and get to sleep later.

Once suited up, I headed for the condo hot tub, across the parking lot from my unit.

I was elated to see that I would be the only one in the humid confines of the hot tub room. I tossed my towel and robe onto a lounger, piled my hair on top of my head, securing it with a scrunchy, and hit the button to turn on the jets for fifteen minutes. I'd love to stay longer than that, but truthfully, I was afraid that I might fall asleep if I did.

I slowly made my way down the steps into the water, giving my body time to acclimate to the shocking heat, as the water burbled around me, swallowing me up. It was glorious. I found a spot where one of the jets hit me squarely in the lower back, humming and thrumming and soothing my soul. Closing my eyes, I leaned my head back, feeling the tension of the day beginning to ebb.

The door to the hot tub room opened with a jarring *screeeee...* and in walked the last person that I wanted to see at the moment. My least favorite neighbor, Gabe Lennon, whom I always referred to in my mind as Nick Offerman's unattractive twin, because of his wild sideburns and bushy mustache, had been trying to get me to go out with him since I moved into the complex. He was at least a decade older than me and had a bulbous stomach, which was now hanging out over the top of swim trunks emblazoned with superheroes. How do they even make those for men? They'd be appropriate for a four-year-old. And don't even get me started on the monstrous feet that scuffed along in rubber flip-flops... Sasquatch came to mind.

"Sari, Sari...sweet, sassy Sari." Gabe greeted me, practically licking his lips.

"Hey, Gabe." I manufactured a polite smile.

I didn't have the strength to actually pretend to be nice. Polite would have to suffice.

"Got room in there for me?" He whipped off his t-shirt and waggled his eyebrows.

"Nope."

"You're such a jokester." He brayed out a laugh and headed down the steps into the water. "What have you been up to? I haven't seen you around much." He sat a few feet from me, thankfully out of reach—I swear I'd die on the spot if his leg brushed against mine—and talked loudly to be heard above the jets.

So much for my glorious solitude.

"Just busy working." I closed my eyes again and leaned my head back, hoping he'd take the hint and be quiet.

Clearly, Gabe is not one to take a hint.

"Yeah? Business is booming, huh?"

Sigh.

"Yep," I replied, not opening my eyes.

"You're too young to work so hard. You need to get out and have fun. I have a pair of tickets to the basketball game this weekend if you want to go."

Everyone who knows me, even a little bit, knows that I love basketball. It's one of those quirky things that makes no sense. I'm not athletic; I don't like to sweat, but give me snacks and put me in front of a group of guys trying to throw a ball into a hoop and I'm a happy camper. It's probably because basketball is the only sport that I actually understand, and there were a few occasions when I was a kid that my dad would take me on a special trip to see a Lakers game.

My love of the game is not quite so profound as to make the sacrifice of being in Gabe's company for an entire evening, however. Besides, Charla has season tickets, with really good seats, and I was almost certain that she was going to ask me to go with her to the game. I'm always her basketball date when she's between guys, so I hoped that she hadn't met anyone recently.

"I have plans already." I yawned, still keeping my eyes closed. "Thanks, though."

"Yeah, no worries." Gabe sounded hurt, but I knew, based on past experience, that he'd, unfortunately, bounce back quickly, and his disappointment wouldn't dissuade him from offering another invitation. "We could maybe go to dinner this weekend, if you want."

And there it was. He'd nursed a bruised ego for less than twenty seconds before trying again.

"My parents are coming to town next week, so I'm going to be busy all weekend."

"I wanna know when you and I are gonna get together. You're young and hot, and I'm a successful guy with a lot to offer. I think we'd hit it off."

"I'm focusing on my career right now," I gave him the standard brush-off, resenting him mightily for intruding on my brief moments of zen.

"That's the problem with girls your age. Obsessed with careers." He made a disgusted sound.

"Well, if you can't deal with that, maybe you shouldn't try to date us." I opened my eyes and froze him with a look.

He started to protest as I moved across the tub toward the steps to exit.

"Aww…c'mon now. You don't have to be like that," he wheedled.

I cannot stand wheedling. I was poised and ready to slug him if he tried to grab for my hand, or anything else, as I left the hot tub, but he must've seen the look on my face, because he sank back down into the water and looked away.

"Have a good evening," he called after me. "I'm just across the parking lot if you get bored, and I make a mean clam linguine."

How enticing. I waved a hand in his direction without turning around. I hurried to throw on my robe so that the fleshy parts of me that weren't contained by my nearly full-coverage swimsuit wouldn't gross him out or, worse yet, make him even more determined. Yep, even in front of Gabe, my insecurities rose up like the Ghost of French Fries Past. Getting hit on was one thing, suffering through pity from *that* source was entirely another.

Part of me felt sorry for hurting his feelings; the other part wanted to give him a quick lesson in feminism and appropriate behavior. He was harmless, if repulsive, but I had bigger fish to fry. Every minute lately had seemed to produce a fresh new level of stress that I previously hadn't imagined, and somehow, I felt like all that I had endured thus far…was only the beginning.

Chapter Nine

"Be glad you're a dog," I told Foo as I towel-dried my hair after a post-hot-tub shower. "People can be gross sometimes."

Visions of Gabe in his superhero swim trunks flashed through my mind. At least it hadn't been a speedo. I shuddered.

I hung up the towel, put on some jammie pants and a tank top, and headed to the kitchen for wine and a snack. I was much too tired and relaxed to bother fixing an actual dinner. Fortunately, there was a tray of boiled shrimp, with a container of cocktail sauce in the middle, in the fridge, so I grabbed it and a sleeve of crackers, along with half a bottle of pinot grigio, and headed for the couch.

I flipped through the channels long enough to find a good crime drama, and Foo and I watched it while I munched shrimp and sipped at my wine. I'd start working on designs after I ate, but for the moment, my entire focus was on food and entertainment. The drama was a good one—the leading guy was tall, dark, and handsome, as well as clever, and the woman was sassy and sharp. It was a murder mystery, of course, and I turned it up when the detectives were talking about the clues.

The murderer ended up being the pool guy, which made me really want to find the electrician that I'd seen leaving the scene right before all of the emergency vehicles showed up. And then I wondered...did the Bennetts have a pool? I'd be on the lookout for one when I met with Byron, the victim's son, whom I'd encountered outside.

After the show, I plugged in my laptop and powered it up. I was still waiting for my design program to load, when suddenly my entire condo went dark and quiet. The TV turned off, and so did all of the lights. The refrigerator ceased its endless light humming. Even the faint glow from my laptop screen seemed to be swallowed up in the darkness.

"The electrician!" I hit the flashlight button on my phone and swept the beam randomly around the living room while Foo, picking up on my panic, growled low in his throat from his perch on the sofa next to me. "He must've seen me taking a picture of his van," I whispered, snatching up Foo and running for the one place in the house with a locking door...the bathroom.

My heart beating ninety miles an hour, I hit speed dial. It took Tang forever to answer his phone, and when he did, I whispered at him so low and fast that he couldn't understand a word I said. Frustrated, I got as far away from the locked door as I could, so that the sound of my voice wouldn't carry into the house, then I realized that put me right in front of the window, where I'd be easy to see under the glow of my phone.

"Crudmuffins!" I hissed, carefully stepping into the tub, Foo tucked under my arm.

The shower curtain rings made a metallic scrape against the rod that sounded as loud as a gunshot to me, but, wincing, I slowly pulled it closed anyway. Why? No idea. It wasn't as if a killer would be deterred because I happened to be hiding behind a shower curtain. I quickly and quietly explained the situation to Tang, who told me to call the police. When I refused, asking him to come over instead, he didn't hesitate.

"I'll be right there. Just stay on the phone with me and don't say anything unless you're in danger, got it?"

"Got it, hurry," I pleaded.

Foo started to whine, and I stroked that special spot between his eyes to get him to be quiet. With the phone to my ear, I heard Tang's car door slam shut, and the engine start up. Help was on the way. But...what if the killer found me before Tang arrived? Terrified, I huddled in the shower, rhythmically petting Foo, while straining to hear any unusual sounds. Nothing.

The white noise coming through the phone cut off after a series of thumps, leaving dead air.

"Tang?" I whispered into the phone, wondering what on earth had happened.

No response. I was about to say his name again when I heard something that made me go quiet, freezing in place. A creak. A loud creak. Someone had just opened my front door. Heart in my throat, I clutched Foo to my chest, willing him to be quiet. Listening.

Footsteps, slow at first, then faster. They came closer and closer, then stopped at the bathroom door. Foo barked, and I almost wet my pants.

"Sari?" Tang called out. He'd obviously used the key that I had given him for emergencies, and he must've been nearby, which was more than fortunate.

"Oh my gosh!" I came bursting out of the bathroom and flung an arm around him, with Foo between us. "I thought something had happened to you." My heart still pounded as adrenaline coursed through my veins.

"Why?"

"Because the phone went dead."

Tang chuckled and patted my back to soothe my hysterics before gently disengaging himself from my iron grip.

"I hung up when I got here, Sari. I checked the entire condo, and there's no one here. Where's your fuse box?"

"In the laundry room. Be careful." I was feeling a bit sheepish, but still wary.

He disappeared, and moments later, the lights came blazing to life, as did the TV, which was now playing a thriller, so of course, the first sound that I heard as the lights came on was a bloodcurdling scream. I jumped, and Tang came down the hall toward me with an amused grin on his face.

"Tripped a breaker."

I sagged with relief.

"Sorry that I made you come all the way over here."

"Yep, you're gonna pay for that, and you'd better have at least a half-gallon of my favorite strawberry cheesecake ice cream in the freezer."

"There's a whole gallon. I knew I'd need more for when Mom and Dad got here."

"Your parents are coming? Cool. But I thought they were vegan?"

"They are. The ice cream is for me, so I don't die of stress." I let out a shaky breath, heading for the kitchen.

"Good plan. Now, I'm assuming that there's a reason why you suddenly freaked completely out at a tripped breaker." Tang gave me a pointed look as I set Foo down and got the ice cream out of the freezer.

I told him that I had thought it might be the electrician from the Bennett investigation, and he stared hard at me.

"Honey, you need to stop this," he insisted, hands on hips, brows raised. "I mean, I get why you don't want to just leave it alone, but you are not a cop, and you have no idea what you're doing. I worry about you, and worrying gives me wrinkles, and that's unacceptable."

"You sound like Charla." I emitted a weak chuckle.

"Ew. Don't ever say that again." He shuddered.

They aren't exactly BFFs.

"It's true." I pointed the ice cream scoop at him for emphasis.

"Why are you doing this, Sari?" Tang asked quietly, sitting at the breakfast bar and resting his chin on his hands.

"You didn't see the way that detective looked at me." My cheeks burned with shame at the memory.

"Well, you know you have a habit of blushing and stammering when you're speaking to authority figures." He accepted a heaping bowl of ice cream and dug in.

"I know." I sighed, putting the lid back on the carton and licking my sticky fingers before returning it to the freezer.

"Why are you even like that?" Tang wondered, his mouth full. "I mean, your mom and dad are like the sweetest people in the world. It's not like you had autocratic tyrants bringing you up."

"That's probably why." I savored my first creamy, dreamy bite of ice cream and felt my heart rate finally begin to slow.

"Huh?" was all Tang could muster through a gigantic bite.

"I was never around authority figures much. Teachers loved me, and my parents' friends were like kids themselves, so I never had to deal with serious people who had rules and laws and stuff." I shrugged. It made perfect sense to me.

Tang nodded. "Which is why that detective really got under your skin. Is he cute?"

"Oh, stop it. You're as bad as Charla when it comes to men." I pointed at him with my licked-clean spoon. "His face looks like it's carved out of granite, and I don't think he's even capable of smiling." I made a face and shuddered.

"So he *is* cute." Tang waggled his eyebrows with a mischievous grin.

"If you're into tall, dark, and grim, maybe." I rolled my eyes and scraped the sides of my bowl for the melted joy that clung there. "How's Leo?" I desperately needed a subject change, and a question about Tang's cockatoo would certainly do the trick.

"Still swearing like a sailor."

I laughed. "That bird is incorrigible. And you encourage him. Although I'd probably swear a ton, too, if I lived with you."

"I can't help it. It's hilarious when this amazingly beautiful cockatoo busts out a sentence that would make a New York cabbie blush." He chuckled. "Nice change of subject, by the way." He gave me a sly glance.

"Be quiet and eat your ice cream," I said, busted.

"Look, that detective hasn't even called you for follow-up questioning, so clearly, he doesn't actually think you had anything to do with the murder. Just let it go." Tang tipped up his bowl to drink the last few drops of melted goodness.

"If your fancy friends could see you now," I teased.

"This is why I don't go to their houses and have ice cream. I can only be free-to-be-me over here." He winked.

"Lucky me." I rolled my eyes.

"Yes, lucky you." He headed to the dishwasher with his bowl. "I hate to eat and run, my love, but some of us work for a living." Tang glanced pointedly at his watch and moved in for a hug, enveloping me in some expensively amazing cologne. "Gotta run." He disengaged and headed for the door. "Next time something odd happens, don't assume it's a killer on your trail."

He closed the door before I could summon a good retort. That's Tang for you, always a parting shot.

Was I being an idiot? Maybe. Did I have any idea whatsoever as to what I was doing? Definitely not. Was I going to let that stop me? Heck no. I would figure out who the murderer was, just to spite the detective. Who is *not* cute. At all.

Chapter Ten

The parking lot at McDonough Electric, which was the only electrical company that had a lightbulb logo, only had two cars in it—one a battered compact, the other a fairly nice sedan—next to two white vans that were nearly identical to the one that I'd seen leaving Rosalie Bennett's neighborhood the other day. My car's tires crunched over the gravel lot, and I couldn't help but wonder whether or not my strappy heels would survive the trek into the building. Fortunately, there was a sidewalk out front, so if I could make it to the sidewalk, I'd be home-free.

My heart pounded, and I had the beginnings of a headache. Stress. I wasn't cut out for being a private investigator, that much was certain, but I was consumed by morbid curiosity, a strong sense of self-preservation, and a diehard determination not to let that detective get the best of me.

I walked like Bambi on ice, wiggling and squiggling on my heels, over to the safety of the sidewalk, then made my way to the nondescript brown cement-block building. There were bells over the door that clanged like someone had dropped a drawer of silverware when I came in, and the plump young woman who sat behind the desk looked up and gave me a surprised once-over. I was pretty sure that she didn't often see customers coming in wearing designer sunglasses and strappy shoes. Why shoes and sunglasses? Because they always fit, even after a too large bowl of ice cream. I felt like a complete imposter. Maybe because I was.

"Help you?" She uttered the simple question like it was an accusation.

"Hi! Yes!" I said in that horrid, overly-bright tone that comes out when I'm trying to do something that I shouldn't. "I'm looking for an electrician, and I want to use the one that a friend of mine had, because he's highly recommended." My fib tumbled out much more successfully than I thought possible.

"What's his name?" the young woman asked, looking as though she was holding back a sigh.

"Well, now, that's a great question. I don't know his name." Doggone it, here comes the blush, starting at my jawline and creeping over my face in a Pepto-pink glow. I could feel it.

Understandably, the clerk gave me a baleful stare.

"But," I continued, in a hurry, "I know that he was at my friend's house two weeks ago, on a Tuesday. I can give you their name and address, if that helps."

She gave me a withering glance and tapped at her computer. I gave her the Bennetts' name and address.

"Tuesday, two weeks ago?" she asked, frowning at her computer screen.

"Yep." I nodded vigorously. I probably looked like a possessed puppet.

"We didn't send anyone out to that address on that date."

"What about the house next door?" I chewed on my lower lip, sure that I had seen their van there.

"Nope. None of our techs were in that neighborhood at all on that date." The clerk shook her head.

"That's odd."

"Yeah. Maybe you should just ask your friend for the name of the person that they used." She cocked an eyebrow, adorned with a metal stud, at me.

"Right, of course." I barked out an extremely fake laugh. "Gotta run. Thanks for your help." I pasted on a smile and practically bolted for the door.

Now I was stumped. If I hadn't seen an electrician's van...what had I seen? Scenes from the crime show that I'd been watching flashed into my mind. The pool guy! I had to find out if the Bennetts had a pool, and if so, had it been serviced two weeks ago? Fortunately, I was heading over to my initial consultation with Byron Bennett next. I could simply find a way to ask him about a pool and a pool guy. I was off on a new quest, imagining the look of surprise on Detective Marcus Griff's face when I revealed the killer. I just had to find him first. Or her. I try to be politically correct, even when hunting a murderer.

* * *

It felt very strange, pulling up to a house where I knew that a woman had recently been murdered. I'd been in some strange homes before, but never one, at least that I knew of, where a homicide had been committed. The nervousness I felt when I entered the electrician's office was nothing compared to the jittery heebie-jeebies I experienced when I parked at the Bennetts'.

"Focus on the house, focus on the house, focus on the house..." I took several deep breaths before opening my car door and grabbing my consultation bag. I was such a chicken—the idea of me investigating a murder was beyond laughable, despite the vast amount of knowledge I'd gleaned from Law and Order and the Discovery Channel.

I was glad that I at least had no idea about the circumstances surrounding the murder, so I wouldn't have a clue as to where Rosalie's body had been, or in what condition, other than dead, it had been in. I could do this...even if my stomach wanted to contest that assertion.

Byron, Rosalie's son, opened the door before I had a chance to ring the bell.

"Hi, Sari, thanks for coming over," he greeted me with a sad smile, poor guy.

"My pleasure." I followed him into the house, which looked like it had been grand in the eighties, but which clearly needed some serious updating before it could be sold.

"So, you can see that it needs to be updated," Byron echoed my thoughts.

"It seems so," I replied, nodding, taking notes, and trying to take my mind away from the murder.

"I don't know why they never redid the house." Byron gazed about, hands in his pockets. "It's not like money is an issue, and this place has needed a facelift since I was in college. So, now you've seen the living room and foyer. Over here is the dining room."

He walked me to the dining room, and I took more notes.

"Through this door is the butler's pantry, and past that is the kitchen." He pointed.

"Okay, great. We'll go there next."

Brass light fixtures, plastic switchplate covers, Wedgewood blue everything...

"Okay." I made some notes about the dining room furniture. "Let's see the kitchen. That's one of the most important rooms when selling a home, so we may have to put a good chunk of the budget there, depending on how much updating it needs." I braced myself, waiting for pushback.

Most homeowners never want to admit that their home is outdated, and many of them balk at the mention of spending money, but I had to get that out there early. If they wanted to go cheap and quick on this project, I needed to know that before I started designing.

"It's a hot mess, and budget won't be a problem. Houses in this neighborhood are in demand, so we'll get our money back out of it."

Wow. That was easy.

"The kitchen is this way." He led me through the hall, past the butler's pantry, which could be really cute with a bit of a makeover, and into the kitchen. The dusty rose, Formica-covered kitchen.

"Oh!" I exclaimed before I could stop myself.

"Yeah, told you. My mom didn't cook much, so the kitchen was barely used, but it still has to go."

"These vintage appliances are in perfect condition," I marveled.

They were ugly, to be sure, but it was miraculous to see how pristine they still were. They looked like they had just come out of the box...sometime in the seventies.

"Perfectly heinous." Byron chuckled.

"But retro is in right now, so we can sell them and put the money toward the design." I used a tried-and-true trick to make the financials easier to stomach.

Byron shrugged. "If you think you can sell them, go right ahead. I don't have time to do something like that."

"Sure, I'll take care of it."

I glanced out the back window, and my heart practically stopped. A pool!

"Oh, you have a pool." I tried mightily to reign in my excitement.

"Yep, and it has a new pump and new liner as of last year."

Inspiration struck.

"Wow, it really looks great. Who do you use for pool maintenance? My condo complex isn't happy with the service we've been getting for our pool, so we're on the lookout for someone who is really good."

I felt beyond awful for fibbing, but I crossed my fingers behind my back and went for it, because it was a means to an end. My heart stopped for a moment when Byron gave me a funny look.

"Great Waves Pool and Spa," he replied, his eyes locked on mine.

"Oh yeah." I nodded. "I've heard of them. So, does someone come out like once a week?"

"Yeah, our guy comes out on Tuesdays."

Tuesdays! Rosalie had been murdered on a Tuesday. I somehow managed to keep my expression neutral, though my stomach did an excited little flip. Maybe I wasn't so bad at this whole murder-solving thing after all.

"Gotcha. Is it the same guy all the time?" I winced inwardly when Byron frowned.

"You're awfully interested in the pool."

"No, I'm selfish." I laughed nervously. "I'm actually interested in *my* pool, and obviously, whoever works on yours does a good job, so I want to recommend him to the condo board."

Byron nodded, then smiled sheepishly.

"Sorry, things have been more than a little weird around here lately. It's like I don't even know how to talk to regular people anymore." He looked contrite. "The pool guy's name is Ralph, or Rich, or something like that. I don't know his last name."

"Regular people?" I grinned, arching an eyebrow at him.

"Non-law enforcement people," he clarified. "I'll be so glad when the investigation is done and whatever maniac that did this is behind bars, so my dad can start rebuilding his life." He sighed, running a hand through his thinning combover.

"I bet." My heart broke for him. "So, let's check out the rest of the house," I suggested, with an upbeat tone, hoping to take his mind off the family tragedy, at least for a little while.

"Do you have a realtor yet?" I asked as we made our way down the hall toward the bedroom suites.

Charla and I gave each other referrals all the time.

"No, we haven't gotten that far. Dad knows that he needs to move, but he's dragging his feet." Byron shook his head. "He can be...stubborn at times."

"It must be tough for him. Losing his wife, particularly...under the circumstances,"

"It is, but of course, the only emotion that he feels comfortable sharing is anger. Right now, he's mad at the world, beyond furious at the killer, and embroiled in an entirely unnecessary conflict with my brother, Broderick, because he doesn't know if he can make it to the funeral. He walks around the house ranting about it." Byron grimaced.

"Grief can do awful things to people sometimes," I agreed, remembering the twenty pounds that I put on after breaking up with my last boyfriend, three years ago. Unlike the boyfriend, the pounds had stuck around, tormenting me on a regular basis.

"I'm sorry, I shouldn't be venting to you like this." Byron cleared his throat.

"No worries at all. You vent as much as you need to; I'm a good listener." I gave him an encouraging smile.

"Thanks. You asked about a realtor." Byron changed the subject, looking uncomfortable. "Do you know someone?"

"I know the best one in town, and I'll give you her card before I leave."

"Thank you, I appreciate that." Byron smiled faintly, seeming relieved. "That's just one less thing that I have to worry about."

"This has been hard on you." I'd have hugged him if he weren't a total stranger.

"I'll get through it," he said dismissively, looking as though he was trying hard not to cry. "Anyway, take your time going through the house. I'll check back with you in a bit."

He left me alone to assess the rest of the house, and I hoped that I hadn't offended him with my comment. I do tend to stick my foot in my mouth on occasion. I quickly finished up, taking photos and measurements and jotting down ideas of what I wanted to do. Most of the furniture needed to be replaced, so, since they'd be moving anyway, I would recommend that they rent furniture from a staging company that I like to use.

The entire interior needed to be painted, so I'd need to try to convince Dave to work me into his schedule, the flooring needed to be replaced, and I'd go through Brad for that, and even the fixtures and art pieces, while high-quality, needed to be updated as well. I'd be taking a boatload of authentic home decor treasures to Furniture Lounge, my favorite retro shop downtown.

I left the Bennett house with plans to google Broderick Bennett—estranged family members were often the culprits—and Joe, the pool guy. It had been a productive day, in more ways than one. I was truly going to enjoy the design work for this project, and I'd gleaned what could be some very valuable information about potential suspects.

Pleased with myself, I headed for Strawberry Fields, the health food store, to stock up for my parents' visit. Fortunately, a clerk who remembered my parents from previous visits was working, and she hooked me up with all sorts of things that I couldn't pronounce, assuring me that they'd love them. I had just returned home with a boatload of organic, fiber-filled, antioxidant, non-GMO food after signing a credit card slip that made my eyes bug out when my phone rang. Hurriedly setting the bags down in the kitchen, I pulled the phone out of my purse and saw that it was Charla.

"Hey, what's up?" I was out of breath from toting in the groceries all at once.

I let a dancing Foo out and refilled his bowls while we chatted.

"We're going out tonight," Charla informed me.

"No." My reaction was immediate and consistent.

Foo darted back inside, making a beeline for his food. I'm thinking that's learned behavior from hanging out with me.

"You always say no, but you're going. You need this. You're not a nun, and you're too young to be a spinster. Put on a hot skirt and a tight top, and I'll pick you up at eight."

I sighed, knowing that she was not going to take no for an answer. I glanced at my watch. I still had plenty of time to shower, get dressed, and actually play with a bit of makeup before she arrived on my doorstep to drag me out into the world.

I closed my eyes and shook my head. "Fine, but I'm not staying out late."

"Okay, Cinderella. I'll see you at eight." She hung up before I could change my mind, filling my introverted heart with dread. If she was driving, that meant that I was stuck wherever she took me until she decided that it was time to leave. The unfortunate reality was that, despite the fact that Charla was always late, she also had a fierce desire to be the "last woman standing" when it came to nights out on the town. She saw posted bar closing times as mere suggestions and had been the last patron to exit on multiple occasions. I'm an early-in-early-out kind of gal on the rare occasions when I actually acquiesce to participating in human interaction scenarios.

With a sigh of resignation, I headed toward my closet to find an outfit. Charla would undoubtedly disapprove of whatever I chose to wear, but I needed my social interaction armor. Nights out with her could prove to be…interesting.

Chapter Eleven

I checked my look in the mirror at eight o'clock sharp, not at all surprised that Charla hadn't arrived yet. I looked okay, I supposed. I was wearing a cute pair of slightly baggy distressed jeans and a faux-vintage t-shirt, with a scarf knotted around my neck. Dangly earrings and short black boots completed the look, and I had done fairly spectacular smoky eyes with my Barely Brown shadow. A spritz of perfume and I was ready to hit the town. Or at least sip my drink quietly and listen to the band play while Charla hit the town.

Charla was bold when it came to men and always on the prowl. I had given men up for Lent and never went back. Sure, it was lonely sometimes. Okay, *much* of the time. But I had Foo, and after my last breakup, I wasn't quite ready to trust anyone just yet, no matter how hard Charla tried to "hook me up."

The doorbell rang and I jumped. Charla was only seven minutes late; it was a miracle. Wouldn't you just know it—the one time that I hoped she'd be ridiculously late, she shows up almost on time. I opened the front door and she looked spectacular, decked out in a hot pink, sequined tank top, a denim skirt, and stilettos that made her just over six feet tall. I was immediately enveloped by a cloud of perfume and noticed that her lipstick had sparkles in it.

"Wow." I blinked.

"I know, right?" She grinned, then gave me a once-over. "When are you going to get ready, girl? We're running late." She showed me the clock on her phone. Oh, the irony.

"I *am* ready," I protested, glancing down at my outfit, which now seemed just this side of dowdy. "I even wore makeup, geez."

"Oh honey, no." Charla pursed her lips, shook her head, and brushed past me, heading to my closet.

"What? I like this outfit." I trailed after her.

"You've got the curves, sugar. You gotta flaunt them," she replied, flipping through my skirt collection.

"Here we go." She pulled out the shortest, most clingy black skirt that I own. I bought it because it was on sale, and I had been a few pounds lighter then. "The t-shirt and scarf are fine, but those jeans have to go, and I think your boots will work with this skirt. Put it on." She thrust the hanger at me.

"It's too short. It'll ride up, and I'll be tugging at the hem all evening." I put my hands up and backed away.

"Stop acting like you're ninety." Charla placed the hanger in my hands. "You're still young and beautiful, and you deserve some fun in your life. You're going to rock this skirt, and if it creeps up a bit, you just be proud of that luscious thigh."

"Ew…no." I shook my head, staring at the skirt in my hands like it was a rotten banana peel.

"Yes. And hurry up about it." Charla took me by the shoulders and turned me toward the bathroom. "I will not let you leave the house like that." She shoved me into the bathroom and closed the door behind me. "Just put it on, and if it looks awful or trashy, I'll tell you."

"How do I get myself into these situations?" I muttered, staring at the bathroom door and knowing that Charla wouldn't give up. "Here goes nothing." I sighed, resigned to my fate.

I slipped out of my comfy jeans and wiggled into the skirt, holding my breath while tugging up the zipper. It wasn't as tight as I thought it was going to be, and I didn't feel as though it was going to split at the seams the moment that I sat down. I opened the bathroom door to show Charla, and she spritzed me with perfume.

"Hey!" I laughed, coughing after inhaling a bit of the fragrance. "Are you trying to tell me something?"

"Yes, you need to smell as amazing as you look." She capped the perfume and put it back in her purse. "And you do look amazing. Your makeup is on point, and that skirt is pure Betty Boop." She gave me a once-over.

"Is Betty Boop a good thing?" I smoothed down non-existent wrinkles in the skirt and headed for the full-length mirror on the back of my closet door.

Charla nodded sagely. "Boop is best. Now let's scoot, girl!"

She wasn't kidding, I actually did look pretty good in the skirt. I had qualms about how it might shimmy up my thighs when I sat down, but I guess I'd just have to deal with that. I could throw on a jean jacket before we left and use it to cover my legs whenever I sat. I kissed Foo goodbye, and we left.

In the car, I turned down the volume on the radio so that I could hear myself think. "So where are we going?"

"Rose Bowl." Charla flashed me a wicked grin.

My mouth dropped open. "Are you kidding me right now? Why on earth would we do that?"

"Because Billy Galt is playing tonight, and I love me some Billy Galt," Charla replied, drumming her hands on the steering wheel in time with the song on the radio.

"Have you…?" I gave her a look.

"With Billy Galt? No." She cracked up. "I don't even know him. I just love his music. I think Jeff Kerr will be there too, on guitar."

"Do they have snacks?" I asked. At least the music would be good. I could sip on a couple of cocktails and munch on snacks while I listened.

"Have you forgotten what going out means? You're going to be out on the dance floor, shaking your thang. You might even meet someone cute." Charla laughed, doing a little dance in her seat.

"You should really keep at least one hand on the wheel. And no, I have no intention of dancing. Shaking my thang is more shaking than I'm prepared to do. I need to lose a few pounds before I subject the public to my savage dance moves."

"You need to stop finding excuses for not living your life, my friend."

Charla gave me that look that made my soul squirm…because I know, deep down, that she's right.

"I'm just not ready to meet someone yet." I shrugged, knowing what she was really getting at.

"And if you wait until you feel like you're ready, you'll never meet anybody," she shot back. "Don't worry about dating, or meeting a guy, or whatever, just go out there and feel the music rippling through you, and let go, be free. Just have fun. Is that really so hard?"

"Apparently."

"Then we'll just have to get you drunk."

"Oh boy." I shook my head.

"Now, I know you're delicate," Charla began, before we got out of the car, "so I'll sit with you for a bit and let you get warmed up with a drink before I drag you onto the dance floor."

"Better make that three drinks."

"One drink, then we dance. Got it?" Charla raised her eyebrows in a manner that clued me in to the sheer futility of mounting a defense.

"Whatever." I opened the door and exited the car before she could badger me anymore.

She wasn't winning this one. I love to dance. At home. With no one but Foo to see me, as I bop around the house doing my weekly cleaning with my classic rock playing at a volume that competes with the vacuum, washer, and dryer.

Going out at all was a stretch for me. If I agree to go out, it's going to be on my terms, even if I was browbeaten into wearing this rockin' skirt…that I'll be tugging at all evening.

"Woohoo!" Charla hooted with joy when a wave of sound engulfed us upon opening the door to the venue. Throwing her hands into the air, she danced toward a table at the edge of the dance floor, drawing several looks of admiration from dancers and drinkers alike. Yeah, she's shy and subtle like that.

The Rose Bowl hadn't changed since the last time I'd been there. It probably hadn't changed since it opened, decades ago. Wood floors, a tiny stage spanning the width of one side of the room, an ancient bar with cheap beer on tap, and lights that look like they came out of the Brady Bunch's basement. No wonder they kept the lights down low. I'm a fan of low lighting. It makes me look younger…and hopefully thinner.

I plunked down into a chair that faced the band, and Charla went to go get us the first round of drinks, making sure to make eye contact and flirt along her way. It was a fifty/fifty gamble as to whether she'd make it back to the table with my drink before hitting the dance floor. She surprised me. Merely five minutes later, she came back to the table, sipping from her drink, and trying not to slosh mine while she shimmied and swayed, before taking her seat.

"Isn't this great?" she yelled while leaning over to hand me my drink.

"It is!" I smiled and nodded.

It was. The band was killing it, and they were playing seventies tunes, which I absolutely love. It reminded me of the music that I grew up with, when Mom and Dad would dance in the living room, making goo-goo eyes at each other. The place was packed, and the energy was high.

I held up my drink. "What did you get me?"

Charla clinked her tumbler of club soda with lemon against my glass.

"Vodka tonic, extra lime," she yelled. "I got you, girl!"

My favorite drink. Maybe I'd actually make it through tonight relatively unscathed. I only hoped that I'd get home at a decent hour. My parents were coming in the next day, and if my mother thought that I looked even remotely tired, she'd be trying to pump me full of herbs, teas, and supplements that smelled like freshly mowed grass.

"Check that guy out!" Charla leaned in and directed.

I followed her gaze to the bar, where a tall guy stood, ordering a drink.

"All you can see is the back of his head."

"Yeah, but he has broad shoulders, great hair, and a cute tushy." She waggled her eyebrows and rose. I grabbed her by the wrist.

"Please tell me you're not ditching me already."

"Gotta strike while the iron is hot, sweetie." She grinned, pulling her hand away. "Or the guy, in this case. I'll be back. Just enjoy your drink." She waved a hand at me and was gone, beelining for the guy at the bar.

I had to laugh. Charla lived her life with great enthusiasm and wasn't afraid of anything. Why she chose to be friends with someone like me, I had no idea. Balance maybe? Chances were good that she and the guy would hit it off. It always worked out in the beginning, but none of her conquests seemed to have much staying power. She didn't seem to mind, flitting from one man to the next, like a bee gathering pollen, but I often wondered why nothing ever seemed to work out long-term for her. She's an amazing human being…but also a princess, which may be part of the issue. She knows what she wants and won't settle for less. I like that about her.

The bar was far enough away that even when the guy turned toward her to speak, I still couldn't tell what he looked like, though he seemed familiar somehow. I watched Charla work her wiles on him for a while—the hair flip, the touch on the arm, the head tilt—then turned away, sipping my drink and watching the band when she dragged him toward the dance floor.

The lights were low, I could feel the bass beat in my midsection, and the vodka was making me relax, whether I planned to or not. It was lovely.

"You wanna dance?" I was shaken from my place of public solitude by a man with a mustache and a kind face. He was dressed in jeans, much like the ones that Charla had made me take off, and a plaid shirt.

"Oh, no, thank you. I'm waiting for my friend." I replied with a smile, hoping to soften my response.

It was true, I was waiting for Charla.

"Well, if you change your mind, I'll be around." He nodded politely.

"Thank you." I grinned, relieved that I hadn't hurt his feelings.

He turned to go, and I took a sip of my drink. When I looked up, I saw Charla coming toward me with an elated grin, and my stomach did a queasy flip-flop. There was a reason that the guy at the bar had looked familiar. It was none other than Marcus Griff. *Detective* Marcus Griff. I paled, and my hands went clammy when we made eye contact, and he frowned.

"You've got to be kidding me," I muttered under my breath, shooting Charla an accusing glance.

"Sari, this is Marc. Marc, this is Sari, my bestest buddy in the whole wide world."

Neither of us spoke. We merely stared at each other. Charla looked from me to him and back again, puzzled. The band stopped playing.

"Do you two know each other or something?" Charla smiled uncertainly.

"No!" I rose from the table, beating a hasty retreat.

"Sari, where are you going?" I heard Charla call out as I scurried away, cursing myself for further underscoring the detective's impression that I had something to hide.

Of all people that she had to pick up, did it really have to be Detective Griff? Seriously?

I hailed a cab outside the bar just as the band started playing again, and I managed to slip into the backseat and close the door before Charla came outside, wide-eyed. I waved to her and gave her the universal sign that I'd call her, just before the cab turned the corner and disappeared from her view. I leaned my head back against the seat and decided that the chance encounter had been the universe's way of telling me that I shouldn't have gone out in the first place.

Chapter Twelve

Everything was freshly scrubbed with environmentally friendly cleansers because my mom could sniff out hazardous chemicals like no other. The guest room was freshly made up, and the fridge was stocked with all of the strange things that my oddball parents like to eat. They were picking up a rental car at the airport, and based on my mom's last lengthy text, where she described everything they'd encountered on their trip from California, they'd be here any minute.

Foo could tell that today was not an ordinary day, and he moved from room to room with me as I made my last inspection, sticking to me like doggie Velcro. When I heard the rental car pull up in the driveway, I ran outside to greet my parents, whom I hadn't seen since last Christmas.

Mom got out of the car and met me halfway, kissing my cheeks and wrapping me in a bear hug.

"Sarisara, my beautiful baby!" She hugged me with more strength than I knew she had.

She and Dad were determined to live as long as possible, keeping their rail-thin bodies fit and inflammation-free.

"Hi, Mom, it's so good to see you, finally." I buried my face in her long, curly, salt-and-pepper hair. She smelled so comfortably familiar, like home... mixed with patchouli.

"I see how it is. Leave the old man to take care of the luggage while you two catch up." My dad came over to join the hug.

The two of them, not caring a bit about looking strange to the neighbors or the general public, kept me wrapped in a warm family embrace for nearly a full minute. I didn't care either, at that point. All I felt was loved, and I needed that.

Eventually, they let go, and Mom studied me as we walked to the car to unload their baggage.

"Are you eating properly, dearest?" A rare frown creased her smooth brow. "Your color is a little off. How's your colon? Are you regular?" she demanded, taking my arm.

"Geez, Mom! My colon is awesome, thanks." I laughed, shaking my head.

Dad was taking the suitcases out of the car, and it looked like they were going to be moving in permanently, but I knew them well enough to know that there was probably at least one suitcase dedicated to herbal supplements, cleanse formulas, energy enhancers, and other types of all-natural wizardry. I took a small bag from Mom, and the contents inside shifted. I nearly dropped it when a strange growling noise came from within it.

"What the...?" I gasped, holding the bag away from my body.

"Oh, don't be afraid, peaches, that's just Safira," Mom smiled fondly. It was a smile that I recognized, that was reserved for cute animals.

"What is Safira?" I quirked an eyebrow at her.

If Safira happened to be a python or some other reptilian creature, I was dropping the bag and running for the hills. Last I knew, though, snakes didn't growl, so I'd probably be okay.

"Safira is the newest addition to our family. We've had her for about six months, and she's just delightful." Mom clasped her hands together and beamed.

"But what is she?" I asked again as the bag shifted.

"She's a hairless cat, and she's just an adorable beauty," Mom said proudly. "We were at a flea market in Murrieta, and there was a breeder there. Safira is a retired breeder cat. The breeder had sold all of her kittens, but he couldn't sell her because her tail was broken, poor thing. So, we got this divine creature for an amazing price." Mom clapped her hands together with glee.

"Your mother drives a hard bargain." Dad beamed with pride.

"You bought a hairless cat at a flea market." I blinked at my mother. "How much did it cost?"

"I was able to talk the breeder down to just fifteen hundred dollars."

My mouth fell open.

"Oh, Mom…" I shook my head.

"Now you just hush." Mom put up a finger to shush me. "That was a steal for this breed, and I would have paid double. I can't wait for you to meet her; she's the sweetest thing. A little cranky after her plane ride, though."

"Foo is going to be a little cranky that she's in his house. They let you on a plane with a cat?" I wondered aloud.

"Well, I mean…technically she was carry-on…" Mom faltered, looking at Dad for support.

I gasped.

"Wait, you smuggled a cat onto a plane?"

"She was perfectly content to rest in the bottom of my bag during the flight, and then I took her to the restroom during our layover. She was fine." Mom waved a hand.

"What do you mean you took her to the restroom?" I frowned.

"Your mother has taught our girl to use the commode." Dad cast a loving gaze at Mom, who seemed rather pleased with herself.

"Nothing should surprise me anymore." I shook my head and handed the cat bag back to Mom, then picked up two small suitcases that weighed a ton. Each. "Let's get inside and get you settled." I led the way.

There were cries of delight when Mom saw Foo, who circled her ankles, begging to be picked up. My mom has this thing with animals. They all love her, and she loves them. She's cuddled everything from Madagascar hissing cockroaches to tarantulas and several species of fish. She's the best snorkeling buddy in the world because even aquatic creatures are drawn to her. So, needless to say, Foo was beside himself when he saw his Grammy arrive.

"You used Earth-friendly laundry soap on the linens." She inhaled and smiled with satisfaction, looking around the guest room. "That's my girl."

She set the bag with Safira in it on the bed and beckoned to the cat to come out.

"Come on, Saffie, sweetie." She patted the bed.

Foo cocked his head to the side, staring up at the bed. The bag rustled, and he let out a nervous bark, looking at my mom for an explanation.

"It's okay, Foo." Mom addressed him like she would a human child. "This is Safira, and there's no reason for you to be afraid of her."

The bag rustled again, and something pink and wrinkled that vaguely resembled a paw poked out of it.

"Ew," I spoke before I thought.

"All living creatures are beautiful, young lady," Mom reminded me. "Come on out, sweetie."

She tapped the bed again, and a creature as wrinkled as its paw emerged from the bag, head low, looking ready to pounce. Foo lost his ever-loving mind, erupting into an apoplectic fit of barking that I was worried would give him an aneurysm. The cat, if we can call it that, looked down at him and hissed. He bounced up and down on his hind legs, his front paws scrabbling at the comforter, trying to get to the intruder in front of him, yapping and snarling.

"Foo, hush!" I snapped, irritated by the racket he was making.

"There's no need for negativity, dear." Mom brushed her forefinger under my chin. "Now, Foo…" She turned to the dog, whose eyes were round as saucers. He wasn't scared; he was furious that there was another animal in his house. "There's no need for this." She got down on his level and stroked his head while she looked into his eyes.

It was like turning off a radio. I have no idea how she does this, and it amazes me every time.

"There's a good boy." She rubbed the sides of his face with her thumbs. "Now, we're going to meet Safira, and we're going to be sweet to our new friend." Her tone was serious, and I swear Foo understood every word.

Dad and I exchanged a glance, looking like we both wanted to place bets on the outcome of this interaction. Mom picked up Foo and set him on the bed a few feet from Safira, who growled low in her throat.

"That's not okay," Mom reminded the cat in the same voice that she'd used to hypnotize Foo.

Safira settled down, folding her front paws under her body, her eyes on

Foo. Foo slowly approached the strange creature, his button nose wiggling a mile a minute. He sniffed her nose, her face, her head, and moved slowly around her to sniff her body. He found a spot on her side that he seemed to fixate on, sniffing and sniffing. Suddenly, without warning, he turned, lifted his leg, and peed all over Safira's side. The cat rose up and took a swipe at him.

I gasped in horror. Dad cracked up, and Mom nodded sagely.

"He marked her." She dug in a bag for cleansing wipes. "They'll be fine from here on out. The hierarchy has been established, and she has accepted it." Mom wiped the dripping creature down, while Safira gave Foo the stinkeye. "Foo, we see your point, and we'll respect it."

I looked at my dad, who was still trying, unsuccessfully, to suppress his mirth, while stripping the bed.

"Want some carrot juice?" I felt as though I'd stepped into another dimension.

"Love some." He grinned, following me to the kitchen, dropping his armful of bedding into the washing machine on the way.

I was sitting with Dad at the breakfast bar when Mom came out of the guest room with Foo under one arm and Safira under the other.

"Their auras are serene," she declared, setting down both animals and taking a seat at the bar.

"Well, that's a relief," I snickered.

Mom merely raised an eyebrow at me. She was a dear, gentle soul, but you didn't want to mess with her.

"Carrot juice?"

"Do you have grapefruit?"

"Coming right up." I was of the firm opinion that drinking grapefruit juice was akin to drinking straight-up battery acid, but Mom loved it, so I'd purchased a couple of bottles of the caustic stuff.

"Sari, dear, whatever happened with that murder case? Has it been solved yet?"

I could feel Mom's eyes boring into the back of my skull as I poured the battery acid.

"Not that I know of." I hedged, setting the juice down in front of her.

"How awful." Mom shook her head. "You're not still trying to become involved in that, are you?"

My phone rang. Saved by the bell. And thank the lucky stars above, it was Tang.

"Hey, girlfriend. Do you need me to manufacture a crisis so that you can get away from the parental units for a bit?"

"No, they just got here." I chuckled as I headed down the hall for privacy.

"Everything going okay?"

I told him about the Foo incident, and he laughed so hard that he couldn't speak. When he recovered a bit, he gasped, *"Oh, I would've paid big money to see the look on your face."*

We chatted for a few seconds, and then I hung up, heading back to the breakfast bar. I had barely settled into my seat when there was a knock on the door. Without bothering to wait for me to answer it, Charla breezed in.

"Mr. and Mrs. Samson, how are you?" She greeted them like old friends.

"Charla, darling, it's been too long." Mom gave her a kiss and a hug, and Dad did the same.

"Good to see you, young lady. You eat healthy. It shows on your face," he observed.

"You're not so bad yourself, Steve." Charla winked at him.

Good gravy, my best friend was flirting with my dad. Lucky for her, both I, and my mom, knew that it was just a reflex and didn't mean anything.

"Why, thank you, young lady. The check's in the mail." He winked right back. Dad was no dummy either, though I'm sure that Charla's harmless flirtation stoked his ego just a tad anyway.

"So, what brings you over on the busiest day of your week?" I asked. I knew that my bestie wouldn't have dropped by on a Saturday without a specific reason, and I hoped it wasn't that she wanted to chew me out for ditching her at the Rose Bowl last night.

"I just wanted to say hi to your mom and dad." She gave me a secret look that spoke volumes. "Wanna walk me to my car?"

"Are you leaving already?" Mom protested.

"Yep, I'm afraid so. I couldn't wait to see you guys, but I have appointments stacked back-to-back all day long." Charla favored them both with her killer, white-toothed smile and hugged Mom one more time.

As soon as we shut the front door behind us, Charla turned to me.

"What the heck happened to you last night? I was worried sick when you just ran away and then didn't answer your phone."

"I texted you when I got home," I said, evading her question.

"Why did you even leave? We were having fun."

"That guy you met at the bar was a detective…" I began.

"I know, isn't that sexy?" Charla grinned.

I grimaced. "He's not just *a* detective, he's *the* detective. The one I told you about, who thinks that I might be involved in Rosalie Bennett's murder."

Charla's mouth dropped open.

"You've got to be kidding me." She shook her head. "Figure the odds. I meet a hot guy at a bar, and he's the one who wants to put my bestie behind bars. Oh well, it doesn't much matter. By the time I got back into the bar after trying to chase you down, he was gone. He didn't even get my number before he left."

"He probably didn't want your number after he discovered that you were my friend," I pointed out.

"Oh honey," she vamped, fluffing her hair and pursing her lips, "it'd take more than that to make him forget about this."

We both cracked up. I wish I had just an ounce or two of Charla's self-confidence. If she could bottle that stuff and sell it, she'd be a wealthy woman.

"Be good or be sneaky." She waved, getting in the car.

"You too, young lady." I giggled.

I'm firmly convinced that everyone needs a Charla in their life. I went back in to rejoin Mom and Dad.

"You know, that Charla is a special young woman," Mom commented when I returned.

"I agree." I nodded, wondering what she was up to.

"I'm surprised that she doesn't have a man in her life." Mom's tone was too casual. She was looking for information.

"She has several." I chuckled.

"Well, at least she's out there trying." Mom arched an eyebrow at me. "You'll never find your soulmate if you keep hanging out eating ice cream with Tang."

"What if Tang and ice cream are my soulmates?"

"I may be old, but I'm not so out of touch that I don't realize that that handsome young man bats for the other team, sweetie." Mom booped my nose with a fingertip.

"Mom!" I gasped.

"What? There's nothing wrong with that. It just means that he's out of reach for you, so you need to find yourself someone who's actually available."

"Or just be content with my own company."

"Uh-huh." She gave me a look and went back to sipping her juice.

Chapter Thirteen

Mom, Dad, and I had been enjoying a lovely afternoon on my patio, just chatting and catching up, with Foo and Safira curled up, side by side, under Mom's lounger when my phone rang.

"Oh geez, I have to take this." I apologized, holding up my phone.

"No worries, honey." Mom waved a hand and took a sip of her coconut water.

"Hi, Agnes," I answered the phone, wandering inside so that I could talk.

She spoke so quickly that I couldn't really tell what the issue was, but the bottom line was that she needed me to come over, right away. Again. I hit the End button on my phone and rushed back out to the patio to let Mom and Dad know what was going on.

"Hey guys, I'm really sorry to break up our chill day, but I have a super needy client who just gave me a distress call. I need to go talk her down from her décor drama ledge and I'll be back."

"No worries, sweetie. We're going to do some yoga and meditation and then maybe hit the hot tub, so you go take care of business and we'll see you when you get back," Dad replied languidly, sprawled on a lounger.

Dad owns a yoga studio, and both he and Mom lead classes there. I felt much less guilty after hearing that they'd already made plans that I didn't need to be around to participate in, so I headed back into the house and hurried to my room to change into something a bit more professional than basketball shorts and a t-shirt. Once properly clothed, I sped toward Agnes' house, thankfully hitting almost every light green.

"Agnes, what is it?" I asked, without preamble, when she opened the door.

105

"I can't even explain it, Sari, you just have to come see." Her tone seemed odd, and my stomach did a little flip-flop.

She stepped back, and I followed her inside. The dining room was done, and it looked absolutely spectacular. I made a mental note to take 'after' pics before I left. Unless of course, Agnes decided to throw me out because she hated it.

"This looks amazing. Everything is just exactly how I envisioned it. Is something wrong with the custom closet installation?" I was baffled.

The installers had confirmed that the closet was done and had assured me that everything had gone as planned with no issues.

Agnes looked at me, her hands clasped under her chin, and tears filled her eyes.

Oh, heavenly days! What had gone so wrong that it was making her cry??

"Sari, I just want to let you know that I'm so happy about the job that you've done in this house. You took my eclectic choices and made them work, and I'm so grateful. I never dreamed that my house could be this beautiful." She beamed, wiping her eyes. "Stay here for just a second." She hurried off toward the kitchen and came back moments later, carrying a pink cardboard box.

"I baked you a cake." She set the box on the dining room table and opened it.

The cake was stunning. It was frosted in light pink and covered with roses, sweeping ribbons of frosting, and pink pearl candies.

"Wow, Agnes, that's so amazing. You didn't have to do that." I swear I felt my thighs grow just thinking about that gorgeous cake.

"I know I didn't." She patted my arm, smiling through her tears. "I wanted to. You've done a very special thing for me, and every time I look at your precious gift, it makes me smile." She glanced toward the window.

The special gift I'd given her was a pair of curtain tie-backs fashioned from her late husband's silk neckties. They were perfect accents for the window treatments and were clearly of tremendous sentimental value to Agnes.

"I'm so glad." I smiled, relieved. "So then there actually wasn't anything wrong?" I clarified. With Agnes, it behooved me to always clarify.

"Not a thing." She beamed. "Thank you so much," she blurted, surprising me with a hug.

I took solace in the fact that it was as odd a gesture for her as it was for me and we both held up admirably.

"You're more than welcome." I hugged her back, then moved to the table to pick up my cake.

"It's lemon cake with strawberry mousse filling and strawberry frosting," she explained, walking me to the door.

"Lemon cake is my absolute favorite. I'm really going to enjoy this," I assured her, stepping outside.

A commotion to my right caught our attention. Agnes and I looked over, and our eyes went wide when we saw Detective Griff leading Buck Lumpkin out of his house. Buck spotted me, and his eyes turned to slits of rage.

"Why don't you arrest her? She was in my house, so whatever evidence you think you found, she probably put it there. She set us up, man."

I stood there with my mouth hanging open in shock, and Agnes turned to me, stunned.

"You were in his house. I forgot about that," she whispered.

"They wanted a closet consultation." I avoided her eyes.

Detective Griff drilled me with a glare, and as soon as he was done putting Buck Lumpkin in the back of a patrol car that had pulled up behind his nondescript police sedan, he made a beeline for Agnes's porch.

"Thanks for the cake. I've gotta go."

I hurried to my car and put the cake on the passenger seat, propping the front edge of the box up with the strap of my purse so it wouldn't tilt and make the cake stick to the inside. When I stood up and shut the door, Marcus Griff was leaning against my car, his gaze icy.

"Why is it that I can't seem to come to this neighborhood without encountering you?" he wondered aloud, staring hard at me.

I shrugged, done with his rudeness. I had done nothing wrong, and I was more than a bit tired of being badgered when I was just trying to help.

"Coincidence? I can't even enjoy live music without encountering you, apparently."

"You ran out of there awfully fast. Almost like you had something to hide."

"Maybe I was just disappointed in my friend's choice of a dance partner." I found it incredibly satisfying to taunt the overbearing detective.

"I've got my eye on you, Ms. Samson."

"Aww...that's too bad. Charla will be so disappointed. Now, if you'll excuse me, I have things to attend to, and judging by the look on Buck Lumpkin's face, you have a fun afternoon ahead of you as well. Goodbye, Detective Griff."

I waved and got into my car, leaving him standing there, speechless. It felt good. I'd have to work on this empowered woman thing that came so easily to Charla. If she could do it, I could, too. Watch out, world, here comes Sarisara!

I drove home riding the wave of adrenaline and empowerment that my encounter with Griff had inspired, and when I got out of the car in my garage, I could smell the incense before I even opened the door. Mom was clearly in the process of bringing my environment into a more zen state. I had to smile. At this point, it certainly couldn't hurt to be more zen.

That thought faltered for a moment, however, when I went into the house and saw batiked cloths covering my lampshades, handwoven throws tossed on my couches, and floor pillows scattered about. It looked like a commune had taken over my condo, and the air was a bit hazy with the fog of incense. Candles burned on every available surface, and Mom was in the kitchen, making a mess. Foo and Safira were curled up together in front of the dishwasher.

"Hello, love, how was your appointment?" Mom called out, raising her voice to be heard above the hum of the food processor, which currently contained something bright green.

"Umm...fine, I guess." I frowned, surveying the kitchen.

My counters were filled with every conceivable kind of fruit, vegetable, nut, and grain known to mankind, along with some items that I didn't recognize.

"What's going on?" I asked when the grinding and whirring of the food processor stopped.

"I knew you were working, so I figured that I would help you out by making dinner tonight." Mom poured the goop into a glass bowl.

I blinked for a moment.

"You do realize that it's only three o'clock in the afternoon, right?"

"Of course, I know what time it is, Sari." Mom chuckled. "But by the time I'm done cooking, it'll be time to eat. Oh, and your father and I ran into a nice young man down at the hot tub, and I invited him to dinner." She was clearly pleased with herself.

"Wait, what?" My eyebrows went skyward. "Who did you invite, and why?"

You don't just spring offhand dinner invitations on an extreme introvert. Mom knows this. If I'm going to be forced to socialize, I need time to prepare mentally for the event. And to have a stranger in *my* space? My thoughts were whirling into a full-on panic spiral when my mom dealt the final blow...with a sledgehammer.

"Oh, don't worry, honey, he's the sweetest man. I think you'll really like him, and you should definitely try to get to know your neighbors if you insist upon living alone out here in the Midwest." She pointed a slotted spoon at me.

"Who is it?" I repeated, my stomach doing a flip-flop at the thought of chatting with a stranger over dinner.

"His name is Gabe Lennon, and he's in insurance," Mom announced, as though she was expecting me to swoon.

"You can't be serious." I closed my eyes and grimaced, my mind racing to find or invent excuses so that dinner would have to be canceled. I wondered if I could pull off saying that my client had been exposed to Ebola and was just letting me know as a precaution.

"Totally serious. He'll be here for pre-dinner cocktails at six." She apparently chose to overlook my utter dismay.

"Cocktails? Mom, you and Dad don't even drink." I knew full well that I sounded like a petulant teenager, and I didn't care in the least. My heart rate accelerated, and suddenly, my cozy little condo seemed to close in on me.

"No, but *you* do, and you're going to show Gabe Lennon some hospitality. It's a settled matter. Human interaction is vital to your well-being, so you need to embrace this, love."

She went back to slicing and dicing something that looked vaguely like it might be a turnip. My mother is sweet and loving and kind, but you do not mess with her once her mind is made up. I knew that arguing would be futile, so even though I found the idea of eating vegan food while entertaining Gabe Lennon to be about as appealing as oral surgery, I gave up. Truthfully, I'd rather have oral surgery. Without anesthesia. I looked over at my dad to see if he'd rise to the occasion and be my ally in the battle, but he merely gave me an apologetic smile. Even he knew better than to cross my misguided matchmaking mother.

"Tang!" I hissed into the phone, hiding in my bathroom so that Mom wouldn't hear me. "You have to come to dinner tonight and pretend that you love me so much that you decided to switch to women."

"Sorry, honeybun. I do love you tons, but that ain't gonna happen," Tang said. "What's going on?"

I told him about my mother and Gabe Lennon, and he seemed to derive an unconscionable amount of amusement from the situation.

"He's icky," I whispered. "You have to save me. Do you have a guy friend or something who'd be willing to pose as my boyfriend?"

"I'll see what I can do." He chuckled. "This is going to be fun."

"No ice cream for you," I growled. "Be here before six. That's when Gabe is supposed to show up."

Tang promised to do his best to scour his friend network for a hot guy who could be bribed with cocktails and a vegan dinner. I told him that I'd cut off his ice cream supply for a year if he didn't show up with someone good.

First, I yet again encountered Detective Griff, and now, this. Could the day possibly get any worse? I'd soon come to realize that the universe seemed to take that morose thought as a challenge.

Chapter Fourteen

Ordinarily, if I had a guest coming over for dinner, I'd go all out. I'd curl my hair, put on makeup and perfume, and find the cutest outfit and shoes in my closet. I might even wear heels, because I'd be sitting most of the time anyway, so my feet wouldn't hurt. This occasion was something entirely different. When my mom shooed me away to go get ready, I took a glass of wine and went to my room with a knowing smirk. Foo, the little traitor, finally managed to pry himself away from my mother and hopped up onto the bed, curling up next to me while I scrolled through social media on my phone.

My plan was to waste time until it was nearly six, when I'd don my oldest jeans, along with the most shapeless, ill-fitting top that I could find, scrub my face clean of any trace of makeup, take off my earrings, and do anything else that I could think of to make myself positively unattractive. I wouldn't come out of my room until I heard the doorbell ring, so my mother wouldn't be able to send me back to change.

Was it childish? Yes.

Was I the least bit repentant? Absolutely not.

I hoped Gabe Lennon would find me so unappealing, maybe even repugnant—I was pretty sure I could pull off a repugnant look—that it would make him finally give up. Tang would be horrified, but he'd seen me in worse shape, particularly when I was going through my breakup, and he'd been wonderful. I wondered absently how many of Tang's shirts had been ruined by my tears and smeared mascara.

Foo and I had some quality quiet time while Mom bustled in the kitchen—

even if I had offered to help, she would have shooed me away—and Dad snored in my easy chair in the living room. It was actually nice to be able to just hang out for a while. That was a rare occurrence in my world. I had design work waiting, but I intentionally left my laptop closed and just enjoyed the wonderful nothingness of the moment.

"Sarisara, are you almost ready?" Mom called out, just before six.

"Almost." I closed the article that I had just finished reading on my phone and rose languidly from the bed to wash my face and change into my sloppy clothes.

I showered, dressed in a lime green polo that had seen better days and the required sloppy jeans, and slipped my feet, unpolished toenails and all, into pink rubber flip-flops. My mom would be horrified. When I caught a glimpse of myself in the mirror, I was grinning like a Cheshire cat. An ill-dressed Cheshire cat.

At two minutes before six, the doorbell rang, and I heard Tang, as well as someone with another voice that sounded familiar, talking to my dad. I dashed out to the living room and saw that Tang had brought Brad, from the flooring store, with him. Tang guffawed as soon as he saw me, and Brad's eyes went wide. Unlike Tang, he'd never seen me at my unvarnished worst.

"Bless you." I hugged Tang and gave him a loud kiss on the cheek. "And Brad, thank you so much for being a good sport."

"No problem," Brad replied, in his typical laid-back way, still staring at me as though he was trying to grasp what was going on.

I leaned toward him and whispered, "Forgive my appearance, but when you meet this guy, you'll understand."

Brad nodded. "Gotcha."

Mom came out of the kitchen, looking stunning in a silk kimono, her hair piled high atop her head in a perfectly executed messy bun.

"Tang, dear, how are you?" She gave him a hug and a kiss, acting as though it wasn't unusual at all to have two more dinner guests show up, unannounced.

"You look beautiful, as always," Tang replied, shooting me an amused glance.

I stuck my tongue out at him.

"And who is this handsome young man?" Mom moved on to Brad and held out her hand.

"This is Brad. I've been seeing him for quite a while now," I blurted before he could say anything.

He shot me a surprised look but got it under control, affecting a pleasantly neutral expression before my mother turned her sharp gaze back toward him. I wasn't exactly lying. It was true that I had seen Brad at least once a month for years…at his store, when I was shopping for my clients. But who needs to bother with those kinds of details? Desperate situations call for desperate measures. Mom whirled to face me, one eyebrow raised, then turned back to Brad.

"Oh yes, of course, how silly of me." She laughed, shaking his hand. "Well, welcome, gentlemen, you're in for a culinary treat."

"Come in and have a seat, boys," my dad invited.

"Sarisara, could you come help me in the kitchen for a second?" It wasn't a question, and I was in trouble.

"But we have guests…" I protested feebly.

Mom's reply was a direct look, which left nothing to interpretation.

"I'll be right back, you guys. Can I get you something to drink?" I asked hopefully.

"Don't you worry about it, honey. I'm the bartender tonight," Dad replied, heading to the small bar in the corner of the living room. Apparently, he'd stocked it earlier in the afternoon. With no remaining excuses or stall tactics, I went to the kitchen to face the music.

"You could've told me that you were seeing someone," Mom commented mildly, stirring some sort of spicy, yummy-smelling concoction on the stove.

"I…forgot. To tell you…I mean. Sorry." I didn't dare look at her, pretending instead to be transfixed by the bubbling substance in the pot.

"Well, you could have at least told me that you invited extra people. I'm going to have to add more noodles to the dish to make it serve five instead of three. It's a good thing I didn't make individual desserts," she groused, sending a reproving look in my direction. "And don't even get me started on your appearance. I'm all for natural beauty, as you well know, but…"

"Yeah. Sorry about that." I cringed when the doorbell rang.

Gabe.

"Now, you go answer that and make sure that you make this poor young man feel welcome." Mom waved a spatula in the general direction of the front door.

I trudged to the foyer and stood in front of the door, staring at it as though a writhing box of snakes was on the other side of it. I loathe snakes. Even photos of them make me shudder. Grasping the knob, I pasted on a smile and opened the door.

"Hey gorgeous, these are for you!" Gabe thrust a massive bouquet of red roses at me and started to move in for what looked terrifyingly like either a kiss or a hug.

I backpedaled immediately, and he sort of stumbled in, using the wall to catch himself.

"Thanks, Gabe, they're beautiful, but Mom is the one who is doing all the work tonight." I held the flowers up like a shield, still backing up. "Come on in, I want to introduce you to my boyfriend, Brad, and my friend, Tang," I called out, loudly enough for everyone to hear.

Gabe's face fell. He looked like a five-year-old who had just dropped his ice cream. I led him to the living room, introduced him to Tang and Brad, and disappeared into the kitchen to get a vase.

"Well, aren't those lovely...for a product commercially grown using unfair labor practices." Mom buried her nose in the roses and took a deep sniff when I went into the kitchen.

"Red roses? Does he not know what kind of message that sends?" I stood on my tiptoes to reach a vase in the top of my pantry.

I don't get flowers often enough to make my vases easily accessible. Sometimes Charla sends them on my birthday, or Tang might send some if I'm particularly in the dumps, but aside from that, nada.

"I'm sure he does." Mom glanced at me over the top of her reading glasses while expertly tossing something up into the air and catching it again in the frying pan. "And maybe you should stop pushing him away long enough to get to know him. He meditates, you know."

"Oh. Well, that changes everything." I rolled my eyes. "Do you have the herb scissors? I need to chop off these stems."

"They're by the sink. And don't think for a moment that I believe Brad is your boyfriend, young lady. I mean, he's cute, and he's obviously interested, but I know my little girl, and I can tell when she's fibbing." Mom smiled fondly, booping the tip of my nose with her forefinger.

"Just go with it for now, okay?" I pleaded, snipping the stems of the roses and arranging them in the vase. "There is not and will never be a universe in which I find Gabe attractive in the least."

"Fine, but you get out there and make him feel welcome, or I might slip and let the cat out of the bag."

"You put Safira in a bag?" I deadpanned, gazing down at the hairless animal who was resting against Mom's ankle while she cooked.

"You're incorrigible."

"You raised me," I shot back over my shoulder, carrying the roses out to the living room.

"Are those the flowers that I gave you?" Brad was so obviously acting that I cringed.

"No, sweetie, those are in my bedroom," I purred, setting the vase down on the coffee table and sitting next to him on the sofa.

"Pumpkin, we don't need to hear about what's in your bedroom," Dad suggested delicately, clearing his throat.

"I mean, I'm kinda interested, aren't you, Gabe?" Tang somehow managed to keep a straight face.

"Well, I mean…" Gabe blushed to the roots of his thinning hair.

Interesting. I thought the man had no shame.

Mom popped in from the kitchen. "Dinner is ready," she announced. "Everyone, have a seat in the dining room."

"Oh good, I'm starving." Gabe shot to his feet, relieved to be out of the spotlight.

"You're mean," I whispered, poking Tang in the ribs as we moved to the dining room.

"Oh honey, I'm just getting warmed up." He winked.

"Let's sit over here…my dear." Brad used his stage voice again, awkwardly slipping his arm over my shoulders and directing me to the table.

"Brad, did you forget that Sari always sits on the end, because she's left-handed?" Tang gave him an amused look.

"I totally did." Brad paled and looked over at Gabe, who had just sat in the end seat and tucked his napkin into his lap. "Gotta switch, my dude." He pointed Gabe to what would be the chair on my left, once I sat.

"That's my spot." Tang crossed his arms and grinned, enjoying the havoc that he was wreaking.

"I'll just sit over here," Gabe muttered, glancing at the spot that would be to my right.

"Oh, that's Brad's favorite spot," Tang said innocently.

"Come on down here, Gabe." My dad patted the spot to his left. "Best seat in the house, and I promise I won't tell you any embarrassing stories about Sari's childhood." He smiled, a wicked gleam in his eyes.

"You wouldn't." I narrowed my eyes at the man who had raised me and was now threatening to throw me under the bus.

"We'll just have to see, now, won't we?" Dad folded his arms.

"*I'd* like to hear those," Tang piped up.

"Yeah, I'd be on board with that, too," Brad added.

I shot both of them my cosmic death glare and was heartily disappointed when neither of them fell from their chairs, stunned into submission.

"Dinner is served." Mom brought a huge dish of vegan lasagna to the table and placed it on a lazy Susan in the center. "Don't start yet, though. It needs to rest, and I need to bring the salads out."

"You'd think being vegan, it wouldn't be tired and need to rest." Gabe tried to joke. Tang guffawed.

"Good one," Dad said, in that patronizing tone one uses with toddlers.

Brad seemed to be intensely interested in his dinner napkin.

Mom brought the mixed greens out, along with a glorious homemade dressing, and we all dug in, the sound of chewing seeming to underscore the excruciatingly awkward lack of conversation. I made eye contact with Tang, and the look on his face made an irrepressible urge to giggle rise up within me. I quickly looked away and pressed my napkin against my mouth to keep from bursting into laughter. Brad patted my knee, and when I raised an eyebrow at him, he snatched his hand away.

"So, about those embarrassing Sari stories..." Tang prompted, looking at my dad mischievously.

"You know, when she was five, she went on a clothing strike. She just decided that she didn't want to wear clothes." Mom gave me a sly glance and stood to serve the lasagna.

"Oh geez..." I closed my eyes, hearing titters of laughter around the table. "Anybody else need more wine?" I reached for the bottle.

"Aww...don't be embarrassed, Sari," Gabe counseled, his mouth full. "I walk around naked all the time. Makes me feel...free."

My mouth fell open, and I stared, while Tang and Brad burst into laughter.

"What?" Gabe protested. "Sometimes ya just gotta be free." He shrugged as Brad laughed into his napkin, and Tang wiped tears of mirth from his eyes.

"Indeed you do, Gabe," my dad agreed, raising his glass of lemon water. "A toast to freedom." He clinked his glass with Mom's.

"Hear, hear!" Tang raised his glass, laughing so hard that he couldn't even take a sip.

"I mean...I get naked on weekends," Brad offered.

I choked on my wine and nearly spit it out. Mom serenely plated six pieces of lasagna and handed them out, seeming all too pleased with the chaos that she'd wrought with her impulsive invitation. I was about to speak when the doorbell rang.

"I'll get it," I volunteered, shooting from my chair and practically running to the door as laughter erupted anew behind me. My eyes widened in shock when I saw who was standing on my porch.

"Detective Griff," I huffed. "Seriously?"

"Sarisara Samson, I need you to come with me—you're going to be held for questioning," Griff replied, not even bothering with a greeting.

"You've got to be joking," I said, making an effort to keep my voice even, despite my rising fury.

Mom suddenly appeared at my side. "On what grounds?" she demanded. Her normally pleasant expression was replaced by pure steel.

"Ma'am…" Griff raised a hand to stop her from continuing, clearly unaware of her thoughts on the patriarchy. "This doesn't concern you."

He turned his attention back to me. "Ms. Samson, we can do this the easy way or the hard way. I'll handcuff you if I need to."

"Are you kidding me? For what? I didn't do anything!" Now my fury was accompanied by stomach-churning terror, but I'd die before I'd let Griff see that.

"Sari, go with him for now. I'm going to be on the phone with our lawyer, and we'll have you out of there in no time." Mom's voice was like ice, her eyes locked on the detective.

"He's taking me to *jail*?" I whispered, my heart thudding in my chest as my mind conjured up scenes from every prison movie I'd ever seen. "I'll never survive."

"Can you actually do this, bro? Don't you need a warrant or something?" Amid the fanfare, Tang had joined us at the door.

"I'm not your bro," Griff said, "and you need to step back."

Next, Gabe joined the fray. "You're going to be an ex-con. That's kinda hot."

The detective stared at him for a moment.

"Come with me, Ms. Samson." He reached for my arm.

I jerked away from his grasp.

"I'm a law-abiding citizen. I'll come with you, but you keep your hands to yourself," I seethed.

"Hang in there, sweetie. We'll have you out in no time." Dad, too, glared at the detective.

Mom and Dad had their share of run-ins with the police at various protests, so they knew way more about the system than I did. I was terrified and defenseless; they were springing into action. Mom was on the phone with their attorney in California before Dad even closed the door behind me. I saw the look of determination on her face, but it didn't keep my insides from shaking like a bowl of Jello. Mom was a force with which to be reckoned, but I was clearly in trouble. I left the house hoping that I'd be seeing that warrior-woman again, sooner rather than later.

Chapter Fifteen

Riding in the back of a police car wasn't as terrifying, or as exciting, as I had imagined it might be, but my stomach still turned somersaults as I wondered what was coming next. The only thing that I knew of being detained and/or going to jail, was what I had seen in the TV crime shows. I imagined being thrown into a cage with street people, high on drugs, who were looking for someone to beat up. I might catch lice, for crying out loud!

My imagination worked me into such a state that by the time we got to the police station, my teeth were chattering, and I wondered if I was going to pass out or throw up. Thankfully, I hadn't eaten much of Mom's delicious dinner.

I tried to ask Griff questions a couple of times on the ride over, but my polite, and somewhat desperate-sounding, queries were met with stony silence. I didn't even attempt to use feminine wiles to sway the taciturn detective. That might work on ticket-issuing street cops, but I had a hunch that this guy would be impervious to even my boldest attempts to flirt. Why couldn't I be more like Charla, who could talk her way out of anything?

Griff opened the car door for me, after pulling into the police vehicle parking lot.

"Let's go," he ordered.

How rude. I got out of the car, and he made me walk in front of him, using nods of his head to steer me through various brightly lit hallways that weren't anything like the jails that I had seen on TV. We got to a secured area that looked like a waiting room, with molded plastic chairs bolted to the floor, in front of cubicles scattered throughout a warehouse-sized space. It was mostly quiet, with murmurings of official conversations barely audible in the background, and there were only two people in the chairs. One was a woman with a turquoise plastic mini-skirt and a bubblegum pink tube top, and the other looked and smelled like a homeless person who'd had too much to drink.

"Sit," Griff commanded, like I was a dog or something.

There were three rows of chairs. The homeless guy was in the back row, on the far left, the colorful woman was in the second row, on the far right, and I sat down in the middle of the front row. Griff went to one of the cubicles and spoke to someone. I felt naked and alone without my purse and phone, which he'd taken as we left the house and insisted that I couldn't have, and a chill went up my spine when the woman that I'd seen slid into the seat behind me and leaned forward to whisper in my ear.

"What'd they get you for?" Her voice was both sultry and weary.

She smelled like cheap perfume and cigarette smoke, which was oddly not unpleasant.

"Murder," I whispered back, thinking that I would stun her into silence.

I couldn't have been more wrong.

"Whoa, dang girl." She sounded impressed. "I woulda thought you were embezzling or counterfeiting or something. Who'd you ice? Your boss? Boyfriend? Mailman?"

"Nobody. I'm innocent. I've been trying to solve this case all along because this detective is just out to get me."

She laughed.

"We all innocent, child. I didn't do nothin' either." She cackled.

"But I really didn't do anything," I protested.

"Then you better find out who did. I'm Tesia, by the way." She held out a taloned hand, emblazoned with neon nail polish, and I shook it.

"Sari. Nice to meet you." My response was automatic.

"Don't be sorry, girl. Nice to meet you, too. It's almost always the squeeze," Tesia proclaimed, nodding sagely.

"Umm...what?" I blinked, confused.

"The squeeze. The boyfriend, baby daddy, whatever..." She waved a hand. "They the ones that kill. Love is a strange animal, girl."

"Come to think of it, the victim's son did say that his dad has a temper," I said, thinking back to my conversation with Byron.

"See? There you go. Just find out how he did it and why, and you'll be good to go."

"Totally makes sense." I nodded. "What are you in here for?"

Tesia gave me a strange look, then cracked up. "Embezzling," she said dryly.

* * *

I was summoned to Griff's office and sat stiffly facing him, clenching my teeth to keep them from chattering. He barked out a few questions that made me realize a couple of things. One, he didn't have anything on me. How could he? I hadn't done anything wrong. And, two, he kept mentioning the Lumpkins, which might just mean that he had the same thoughts about them that I did. The wonderful thing about that realization was that it alerted me to the fact that there was no way in Hades that he could keep me in jail. The thought made me bold, so when he asked his next question, I answered a bit more harshly than might've been prudent.

"Look, I already told you. I don't know anything. I was over there trying to figure out if they were the killers, and I found guns in their closet. Lots of guns. And ammo. It doesn't take a rocket scientist to figure out who might've killed the neighbor. And here's a hint: it's not the mild-mannered decorator; it's the surly, gun-loving couple next door." I huffed, insulted at being treated like a suspect.

Before Griff could open his mouth to reply, the phone on the desk in the cubicle buzzed, and he picked it up.

"Yeah," he barked into the phone. "Gotcha. Will do." He hung up after a very short conversation where he mostly listened.

"Apparently your attorney wanted to send someone down here to get you, so I'm going to save you some high-dollar legal fees and let you go. But I'm telling you right now, Ms. Samson, if you're poking your nose into this thing because of idle curiosity, you're in way over your head, and you may end up getting hurt if you don't back off."

"If you hadn't looked at me suspiciously in the first place, I wouldn't have even bothered to dig into it. I'm invested now, thanks to you. I'll prove to you that I'm innocent if it's the last thing that I do." I glared at him.

"Mess with the wrong people, and it just might be." Griff stared me down. "Come on, I'll take you home." He stood, looking at me expectantly.

I rose, not dropping my gaze, and snatched up the phone and purse that he took from a drawer and set in front of me on his desk.

"Don't trouble yourself, I'll take a cab."

"Suit yourself." He walked toward the exit.

I followed, far enough away to make it clear that I was done talking with him. I was able to hold my tears at bay until the cab had pulled away from the curb, and I could no longer see the police station. Detective Griff was insufferable. If he insisted on treating me like a criminal, I was going to double my efforts to prove him wrong.

I gave the cabbie Tang's address, then texted Tang to let him know that I was on my way. He and Brad left the dinner party shortly after the detective crashed it and Tang texted me to make sure that I told him every last detail as soon as I was available. My next move was to call Byron Bennett to schedule an appointment for a contract approval, making sure that his dad would be there. Tesia the Embezzler had said that the sweetheart is usually the culprit, so I needed to talk to Cliff Bennett to try and figure out whether the crotchety older man was just perpetually cranky, or whether he was indeed, a killer.

Chapter Sixteen

"Hey, girl," Tang greeted me, taking me in his arms after opening the door.

"Hey, girl," Leo, his cockatoo repeated.

"Hi, Leo." I burst into tears.

Tang held me while I had a great big ugly cry, patting my back, smoothing my hair, and making comforting sounds that Leo kept mocking. He drew back after the storm subsided a bit and brushed away the tears and mascara flakes that had cascaded down my cheeks. My breath hitched, and my nose leaked, as I tried to pull myself together.

"Oh geez, you need a tissue and some ice cream, stat." Tang kept his arm around me and led me to the sofa.

There was a white carton of takeout pork dumplings on the coffee table, with a pair of chopsticks and a container of dipping sauce. A pile of napkins was beside the carton, and I took one to blow my nose.

"Didn't you finish your dinner?" I tried to take deep breaths to calm down.

"Your mom gave us to-go boxes, but—no offense—I need more than grass and tofu lasagna for dinner." Tang chuckled. "Have some, they're delish. Oh, and I have some Crab Rangoons in the kitchen, too, if you'd like."

"Do you have wine?" I tore into a dumpling.

"Do ballerinas dance?" Tang went to the pantry and grabbed a bottle of red.

"Good, forget the ice cream, bring the Rangoons and the wine." I felt much more like myself as I dunked my dumpling in dipping sauce, leaving a rainbow-tinged oil slick on the top of the savory, coffee-colored liquid.

"Eat your feelings like a good girl and forget about all of that silly murder investigation stuff," Tang advised with a wry grin.

"I can't, Tang. This dude took me to jail, for crying out loud." I put a hand in front of my mouth so that I could chew and talk at the same time.

"Were you in a cell?"

"Well, no, but…"

"Were you in handcuffs at any time?"

"No…"

"Did anyone read you your rights?" Tang persisted.

"No, but I don't see what…"

"Then you weren't in jail. He took you in to intimidate you so that if you actually knew something, you would talk." Tang's frustration was evident.

"What makes you so sure? It's not like you've ever been arrested." I broke a Crab Rangoon in half and stuffed one of the halves into my mouth.

"Wow, slow down, tiger." Tang chuckled, watching me eat. "I watch *Law and Order* reruns before I go to sleep. It helps relax me. I learn all about the sordid world of criminals and the details of police procedure."

"And that relaxes you?" I mumbled, my mouth full of the most succulent Rangoon ever.

He shrugged. "Sure, the good guy always wins."

"The good guy always wins," Leo echoed, bobbing his head.

I had to laugh, and after the day I'd had, laughing felt good. Tang and I polished off the bottle of wine and all of the Chinese takeout while watching reruns of *Mission Makeover*, talking loudly to the television, and critiquing the fashion choices of the makeover subjects. Leo joined in on the fun and snuggled up in my lap while we watched. Yes, cockatoos snuggle.

I remember my eyelids getting heavy. I remember Tang gently lifting Leo from my lap and putting him in his cage for the evening. What I don't remember is how I stretched out and got covered up with a fuzzy beige blanket, which I discovered when I woke up the next morning, my head pounding and my mouth feeling like I'd been chewing on sawdust all night. Tang. Dear Tang had taken care of me. As usual.

"Coffee before you go?" he called out from the kitchen, apparently having heard me stirring.

"Coffee…coffee…coffee!" Leo squawked happily.

"Yes, please." I winced, sitting up and putting my hands on my temples.

"Yeah, you need to hydrate first if you're going to have that much wine." Tang handed me a steaming mug of liquid life.

"*Now* you tell me," I grumbled, sipping the elixir of the gods.

"Your mom texted me last night, and I told her that you and I were having a movie marathon." He held up his phone. "Your phone has been blowing up with notifications."

"Oh geez. Thanks, Tango." I breathed a sigh of relief.

I'd been so angry and shaken yesterday that I had completely forgotten to text Mom.

"You're welcome. She tried to convince me that I needed to marry you."

"It would make life easier. Although you'd always finish all my ice cream." I made a face.

"You're not organized enough for me, ironically." Tang chuckled, giving me a mischievous look over the top of his coffee mug.

"And I can't live on fast food, so I guess we're doomed from the start." I grinned. "Marriage is overrated anyway. What's the charm in seeing the same person day in and day out?"

"I see you almost every day," Tang reminded me.

"Well, yes, but that's because we want to see each other, not because a piece of paper says that we're obligated to be together. We have the freedom to say that we're not going to see each other for weeks at a time if we want to," I pointed out.

"Some married people do that too."

"Okay. Well, if you ever decide to propose, make sure that the ring is big, and you do it right after I get my nails done." I gave him a sly grin.

"Noted. What are you going to do today, besides recover?"

"Mom and Dad were talking about a day trip to Chicago, so I may just go with them. Get out of town, clear my head…"

"Great idea." Tang nodded. "So, you're going to leave the whole murder thing alone, right?"

"Not a chance."

"I'm telling your mom."

"I'll polish off your stash of pistachio parfait that's in my freezer," I threatened mildly, sipping my coffee with my eyes closed.

"You fiend."

"That's why we get along so well. Takes one to know one." I opened my eyes long enough to wink.

* * *

"That was such fun," my mother exclaimed when we got back to the house after a day of shopping and sightseeing in Chicago. She carried a purring Safira, and I had a squirming Foo in my arms, leaving Dad to bring in our shopping bags.

I'd been drinking water nonstop all day, and by the time we'd stopped at an Ethiopian restaurant across the street from the Green Mill, I was feeling well enough to tear off pieces of delightfully spongy bread and use it to scoop up mounds of some sort of delicious food with gusto. After lunch, I actually felt like I'd rejoined the world of the living.

"Yeah, I needed that, thanks you guys." I smiled at my parents, then focused on unlocking the front door, more than ready to just chill for the rest of the day.

I set Foo down once we were inside, and I immediately got goosebumps, feeling like something was off. Foo ran to the slider, so I let him out into the yard and had the strangest feeling that there was someone in the house, aside from the people who were supposed to be there. I wandered from room to room while Mom and Dad were in the guest room, looking for things that were out of place or missing, and I came up empty until I went into my office.

A couple of my desk drawers were slightly open. Had I left them that way? Open drawers drive me crazy, so I'm typically diligent about closing them, but yesterday wasn't exactly a normal day, so maybe I was just forgetful. Then I noticed something else, something alarming. The thumb drive that I use to back up my laptop every night was gone. I looked in every drawer. I got down on my hands and knees and crawled under the desk, I dug through the trash can. Nothing.

I was still under the desk when my mom came in, startling the daylights out of me.

"Sari, honey…"

"Huh?" I jumped, thunking my head on the underside of the desk. "Ow!"

"Careful, dear." Mom offered me a hand as I crawled out from under the desk. "Did you open the window in the guest room before we left?" She frowned.

"Why?" A feeling of dread began to build in the pit of my stomach.

"When we went in to drop off our things, the window was open, and there was a little smudge of dirt on the windowsill. Now, you know that we love fresh air, but honey, the air conditioner was on. That's such a waste of energy."

"I've been robbed." I wrapped my arms around my midsection, shivering.

"You…what? What makes you say that?" Mom took me by the upper arms and gave me a little shake.

"My desk drawers were open when I came in here, and my pink and green thumb drive is missing. It always sits in the Koa wood tray on my desk. I use it every night, and it's gone." I pointed at the tray.

"Did you check your purse?"

"It's never in my purse, Mom. It's always either in my computer, or on the Koa tray." I tried to be patient, despite my building panic. She was just trying to help.

"Then you need to call the police."

"I've had more than enough to do with the police lately, Mom. Definitely not going to do that. Why on earth would someone steal my thumb drive and not my computer, though? That makes no sense. There isn't anything on there that would be of use to anyone other than me."

"Maybe someone is trying to send you a message," Mom said quietly, making my blood run cold.

I paled and swayed a bit. Mom reached out to steady me.

"Call the police," she repeated. Her voice was quiet, but it was backed with steel. I called.

Less than ten minutes later, there was a knock at my front door. I opened it, expecting to see a uniformed officer, and my heart sank when I saw none other than Detective Marcus Griff glaring at me.

"They could've just sent a regular policeman." I stood back to let him in.

"Anything that has to do with you goes directly to me," Griff muttered.

"I'm flattered." I rolled my eyes.

"Don't be. Anyone who's on my alert list is usually in serious trouble."

I led him to the couch, where he interrogated me, then spoke kindly with my parents, before getting up to search the house, paying particular attention to my office and the guest room.

"What's on that drive?"

"My design work. Client files. Just business stuff."

"Anything else?"

"Nope. Nothing."

"Financials, credit card info, anything like that?"

"Definitely not. I don't retain that kind of information, other than whether a project has been paid or not, but that info isn't even on the flash drive, and the file cabinet that has it is locked."

Griff's eyes narrowed. "Now, will you leave the Bennett case alone? Have you gotten the message yet?"

"A message. That's what my mom said, too." I frowned, thinking.

"Then be a good girl and listen to your mother." The detective stalked from the room. "I'm going to talk to the neighbors. See if anybody saw anything or if anyone else had a break-in, but my assumption is that this is related to you meddling in the Bennett case."

"Oh, of course. I got robbed, but it's all my fault. Thanks for protecting and serving, Detective Griff."

"Are you always this stubborn?" he asked, his hand on the doorknob.

"Yes!" my mother called out from the guest room.

I looked at the ceiling and shook my head as Griff left. I thought he might have smiled, but I couldn't be sure.

Chapter Seventeen

"I can't believe that, between the two of us, *you're* the one who ended up in jail." Charla shook her head in amazement as she picked at her tuna tartare.

I had already devoured a salad and was slurping my way through a crock of lobster bisque, pausing now and again to dunk a hot, buttery roll into my soup.

"Right?" I agreed. "I wouldn't have placed a bet on those odds, that's for sure."

"Tell me all about it!" Her eyes went wide with excitement. "Was it gross? Did anyone talk to you? Did you have to take off your clothes in front of a policeman?"

"Whoa!" I nearly spit out my soup. "First of all, I don't think anyone ever has to take off their clothes, and if I did, I'm sure they'd have sent in a policewoman to supervise. I did meet this one woman who was in for embezzling, though. Her name was Tesia, and I was really surprised by her outfit. She must've been at a club or something when they arrested her. I didn't get put in a cell or anything. In hindsight, it really wasn't a huge deal." I took another bite of sweet, creamy bisque. It was sublime.

"Oh." Her face fell. "Well, that's disappointing. Tell me about the hot detective, though—did he flirt with you?"

I stared at her for a moment in disbelief.

"The detective is not the least bit hot, he's a jerk, and I don't know what you see in him. And no, he absolutely did not flirt with me. He *hates me*. Have you been reading romance novels again?" I accused, pointing my spoon at her.

"Yes. Every night. It's how I go to sleep and have sweet dreams." She winked at me.

"Well, detectives may be mysterious and handsome in romance novels, but in real life, they're just these normal-looking guys who are disillusioned with life."

"Ouch. That's a pretty deep analysis for someone you've only seen a handful of times." Charla's brows rose, and she crossed her fork and knife over the top of her plate to signal that she was done.

"Are you gonna eat that?" I eyed her plate hungrily.

"No, and you're not either." She gave me a stern look.

"But it'll go to waste. There are children starving all over the world, you know." I watched wistfully as the server removed her more than half-full plate.

"I'm sure the restaurant freeze-dries all the leftovers and mails them out to orphans." Charla rolled her eyes. "Do you have his number?"

"Whose?" I frowned, baffled at the sudden change of subject.

"The detective's. Just because you don't like him doesn't mean that I can't enjoy his company." She gave me a mischievous grin.

"Yes, I have it, and no, I'm not going to give it to you. If you want to talk to that insufferable man, you're going to have to do your own homework."

"Fine." She pretended to pout.

Thinking of the odious visit from Griff, I suddenly remembered what I wanted to tell her. "Oh, yeah, I forgot to tell you—my condo was robbed while I was in Chicago with my parents."

"*What?*" Charla's eyes went wide. "Oh my gosh, that's awful." She finally seemed to set all thoughts of Marcus Griff aside. "What did they take?"

"It looks like the only thing they took was my thumb drive." I scraped the dregs of bisque out of the bottom of the snowy-white bowl.

"Why on earth would anyone want that?"

"Mom figures that someone is trying to send me a message." I ate the last spoonful and sighed, putting the spoon down into the empty bowl.

"That's scary. But you have an alarm system, right?"

"Nope."

"Security cameras?"

"Negative."

"You live alone, and you have no home security?" She was astounded.

"It's a safe neighborhood." I shrugged.

"Until someone breaks in and robs you," Charla shot back, glancing at her watch. "Oh dangit, I'm late."

"Shocker." I smirked.

She gathered her handbag and tossed a fifty on the table. "Lunch is on me; can you wait for the check? I really have to run."

"Yeah, I've got this. Get outta here." I shooed her away. "And thanks for lunch!"

Charla planted a big, noisy kiss on top of my head on the way by, then ruffled my hair, totally messing it up. She knew it too because she turned around, giggled, and blew me a kiss as other patrons at the restaurant patio looked on in amusement. We are as different as night and day, Charla and I, but I don't know what I'd do without her.

* * *

I went for a walk with Mom after lunch to burn off some of the lobster bisque calories, and it felt good just to be outside, with the sun warming our backs. We chatted about everything and nothing, like we always do, and I got to bask in the glow of being with one of my favorite humans, who loves me no matter what. I was so refreshed when we got back to the house that I grabbed a glass of iced tea and my laptop and started on some designs for the Bennett house, feeling inspired.

I'd been happily working along for about an hour when the doorbell rang, causing an alarming burst of adrenaline to go shooting through my system. I hurried to the door and opened it, prepared to do battle if it happened to be Detective Griff. A man in navy trousers and a light blue polo stood there with a clipboard and a smile.

"Good afternoon. Ms. Samson?"

I found his cheery greeting suspicious. After what I'd been through since the Bennett murder, just about everything made me suspicious.

"Who wants to know?" I raised an eyebrow at him.

He seemed taken aback, his smile fading a bit, replaced by confusion.

"Uh...I do. I'm Robert Framden from ACE Alarms. I'm here to do a security assessment for you." He looked at me strangely.

"I didn't order an assessment," I said sharply, preparing to shut the door.

"I know you didn't. Ms. Beguile did, on your behalf. I would've thought that she'd notify you about it." Robert frowned, checking his clipboard.

"Well, she didn't, so I'm afraid I can't let you in. Have a good day." I stepped back so that I could close the door.

"Wait! What if I call her? You can talk to her, and she can confirm that I'm supposed to be here."

The door was only open six inches. I peered out at him.

"I guess that would be okay." I relented, not wanting to embarrass Charla if the assessment was a legit appointment that she'd made.

"Great, I'll put it on speakerphone."

He set his phone on top of his clipboard and called Charla, who seemed to think that my vigilance was hilarious. Once she confirmed that she actually *had* sent him, he hung up and I let the poor man in.

"Sorry about that." I led him into the house. "Things have just been a little weird around here lately, so I'm being extra careful."

"No worries, that's why I'm here."

"Do you need me for anything?"

"Nope, I'll just take a look around, make my assessment, and recommend some security solutions, if that's alright with you." He was already scanning the living room windows.

"Go for it. I'll be in the room down the hall and on the left if you need anything."

I got back to my office, and when I glanced out my window, I noticed that Mom and Dad were on the back patio doing yoga.

"Robert, The Security Man, is going to think this is the weirdest family ever," I muttered under my breath. "Speaking of weird..." I mused, closing out my design program and clicking over to browse the internet.

I entered Cliff Bennett's name into my search bar, convinced that Tesia the Embezzler may have been right. The spouse could've done it, and I was going to try my best to find out. I had to wade through pages of charity events, golf outing trophies, and country club news before I finally stumbled upon some items that gave me a bit more insight into the widower.

Byron, his own son, had mentioned that Cliff had a temper, and I found evidence to support that claim. He'd settled a lawsuit with his country club, after destroying one of the greens when he missed a putt, and he'd been ticketed for reckless driving after trying to run down a car that had cut him off in traffic. While those things were irresponsible, it was sort of a giant leap to go from there to murdering your wife, but maybe he was just smart enough to have hidden some very dark feelings. Hoping to find out, I called Byron and asked him to make sure that his father was present when we did the contract for renovations. I told him that involving his father in the process might help bring closure, and he didn't sound too enthusiastic about the idea, but said that he'd try. I hung up, feeling pleased with myself. I'd work on a list of questions to ask Cliff Bennett when we met. Questions that might just help me wangle a confession out of a killer.

The sound of voices in the backyard floated in through my window, and I peeked out to see Robert, the security guy, talking to Mom and Dad. They were all laughing and enjoying themselves, and I felt like a heel for thinking earlier that Robert would just think that my parents were weird. I mean, yes, they were into some things that most people found odd, but they were genuinely sweet people, and I'd do well to remember that.

I decided to go out and join them. It was a beautiful day, and I'd been hiding in my office, fixating on a murder case for far too long.

"So, what's the verdict? Do I have the least secure house you've ever visited?"

Robert laughed.

"Not at all, but I do think that you need an alarm system and better door and window closures. I can get someone out here as early as tomorrow morning if you'd like."

"Perfect." I returned his smile and signed on the dotted line.

"I'll feel so much better about you being out here by yourself once you have an alarm system, honey." Mom nodded her approval.

"Me too, actually." I surprised her by agreeing.

"Alright. I'll get this scheduled for you tomorrow. You'll recognize my team, they all have the same navy pants and polo shirt that I do, and they all have name tags. If you have any questions at all, just give me a call." Robert handed me his business card and left.

"Pleasure to meet you!" Mom called after him.

"You as well." He lifted a hand in farewell and disappeared around the side of the house.

"I wonder if he's single." Mom gave me a sly look.

Chapter Eighteen

"Hi, Mr. Bennett, I'm Sari Samson."

I offered my hand, and the older gentleman shook it, regarding me with more than a touch of suspicion, after Byron let me in.

"I don't see why we need someone to come in and redo the house. It functions perfectly fine as it is." Cliff turned and led me into the house, grumbling all the way.

"I'm sorry," Byron mouthed to me behind his father's back.

I shook my head slightly to let him know that I understood.

"Dad, try to be positive. Your blood pressure is going to be sky-high if you're sour all the time."

Byron's words were direct, but gentle.

"Sour. I'll show you sour."

Cliff took his place at the dining room table, looking as though he'd been recently sucking on a lemon. His arms were crossed over his chest, and his brow was furrowed.

"Let's make this quick," he ordered. "I've got things to do."

I looked at Cliff, hoping to get him to soften up a bit. "I want to make sure that the changes I suggest are okay with you," I said, "and I want you to feel free to share any ideas that you might have."

"Let's just get this over with." His voice sounded tired, and he raised a shaky hand to his brow for a moment. I looked over at Byron, whose concern was written all over his face. He nodded at me, and I sat down next to Cliff. I opened my laptop, clicking on their file, and brought up the 3-D rendering of the living room design. Cliff's face softened when he saw it.

"That's Rosalie's favorite color." He pointed at the screen to the soft green that I'd selected for the sofa.

"I figured that when I saw your closet. She had quite a few clothing pieces in that color, so I incorporated hints of it throughout the house."

"That's a new couch. We don't need a new couch." He frowned, crossing his arms again.

"We're not buying a new couch, Dad. We're just renting some furniture so that it'll look nice in here when people come to see the house," Byron explained.

"Renting furniture? That's appalling. Why on earth would we do that? We have perfectly good furniture already." Cliff glared at his son.

"We've been over this already. We have to sell almost all of your existing furniture because you'll be downsizing when you move."

Though Byron's tone was intentionally mild, his frustration was evident.

"You're not going to put me in some warehouse for old people." Cliff's face turned an alarming shade of red. "I'm an adult, and I can take care of myself. I don't need to live in some tiny condo with nosy neighbors checking in on me."

I squirmed in my chair. This was not a discussion that I needed to witness.

"We can talk more about this later, Dad. Nothing is set in stone with the condo in Florida yet, but even if you stay here in Champaign, this house is too big for one person." Byron's voice was quiet but firm, and Sari felt for him. He'd just lost his mother, and now he was having to help his dad make some difficult decisions. She wondered if Byron suspected his father at all.

"That's not your decision to make!" Cliff shouted, a vein throbbing in an alarming manner on his forehead. "This is my house, and I will decide when and what to do with it. You couldn't even manage to keep a wife; why on earth would I trust you to handle my affairs?" He stormed off, hobbling away with a slight limp.

"Oh man, I'm really sorry that you had to witness that." Byron shook his head, his expression pained. "He's not a horrible person. Anger is just how he deals with his emotions, particularly now that he's older."

"No worries. I had a friend whose grandmother was the same way, poor lady. Should I leave?" I asked, casting a worried glance in the direction that Cliff had taken.

"No, let's finish going through the design plan, and I'll sign off on it. I have temporary power of attorney, so I'm authorized to make these kinds of decisions, whether Dad is happy about it or not. Don't worry; he'll be fine once he sees how great the house looks afterward."

"Okay, not a problem." I said that with the highest hopes that Cliff wouldn't make a stink about things once we were in progress. I had also picked up on the fact that Byron was divorced. It might be worth my while to track down the ex-wife. She'd surely have insider info on the family, that might help me figure out if Cliff killed his wife or not.

After Byron signed off on the design presentation, I gathered the tools of my trade and stashed them in my bag, then headed for the door. I had just set foot on the last step coming down from the porch when I saw Buck Lumpkin's front door swing open. He spotted me and started speed walking in my direction. Thankful that I'd left my car unlocked, I tossed my presentation bag in the back seat and scrambled inside, locking the doors and pulling away from the curb just as Buck reached my car.

That man is out of his mind. I glanced in my rearview mirror and saw him standing where my car used to be, staring as I drove away. *But is he deranged enough to be a killer?*

My heart was pounding so hard from my short jog to the car, along with a huge burst of adrenaline, that I didn't want to go home right away. I headed for Tang's office. He's always been the best at talking me down from my figurative ledges and returning me to zen, as my mother would say. In my haste to see him, I rushed through the front door and into the reception area like a bull in a china shop, startling Tang's assistant, who smiled when he saw that it was just me crashing into his world.

"Hi, Lamont." I smiled at the handsome young man who dressed as though *GQ* might show up for a photo shoot at any moment. That's probably part of why Tang hired him.; he definitely projected an image.

"Hi yourself, Sarisara. Business or pleasure today?" Lamont asked. "I don't see you on the schedule." He tapped at his ultra-slim laptop.

"I don't have an appointment; I just need some Tang therapy. Is he here?" I asked, lifting the lid of the crystal candy dish where Lamont always kept gourmet chocolate for Tang's clients. I took a piece and popped it into my mouth. The explosion of flavor was sublime, and it reminded my stomach that I hadn't had lunch yet, so I took another piece to tide myself over.

"Yeah, he has clients in his office, but they've been in there for a while, so they should be out any minute now, if you want to hang out and wait." Lamont glanced at his watch and leaned forward conspiratorially. "I have a secret stash of Turkish tea that is just to die for."

"Oh, you know me too well." I grinned. "Hook me up."

Lamont went to the kitchen to brew my tea, and I sank down into one of the haute modern leather and chrome chairs in the waiting room. I'd complained about the extreme lack of comfort afforded by those chairs, and Tang had admitted that it was intentional. If there was someone who dropped by to see him, and he really didn't want to deal with them, they wouldn't hang out long in those chairs.

I finished one cup of Lamont's glorious tea and was halfway through the next when Tang's office door finally opened, and a well-dressed couple walked out, chattering excitedly as they left the building.

"Sari?" Tang enveloped me in a hug. "Everything okay?" he asked, leading me into his office.

"Yep, just had a weird appointment and needed a little boost before going home."

I plopped down into the much more comfortable sofa in his consultation area.

"I bet. Your mom reads you like a book." Tang chuckled. "So, what happened at your appointment?"

I gave him the basic rundown, and he listened intently, fingers tented under his chin, shaking his head.

"You know what I think? I think you need to drop every client that you have in that neighborhood and not go back to that area until the murder is solved. You literally could've been face to face with a murderer today, and I'm so not okay with that!" Tang was more animated than usual, and that was saying a lot.

"There's no way. That's one of my target neighborhoods, and I can't afford to lose that much business."

I shook my head, crossing my fingers behind my back. While what I'd said was absolutely true, the main reason that I wanted to keep going back was because I had every intention of solving the case myself, since the rude detective couldn't seem to do it.

"Look, just let me know what those clients are supposed to be paying you, and I'll pay it to keep you out of there. The Martins—that couple who just left—are building a mansion in the country, and they'll want to bring you on board in a few months, so you won't be hurting for money."

Tang's generosity brought tears to my eyes.

"You are seriously the best, but I'm going to do what I have to do. I don't need to be rescued, you big, strong man." I chuckled.

"It's the case, isn't it?" Tang's brows rose, and he folded his arms. Dangit. Was I that transparent?

"Yeah, and I'm not backing down." My mouth was set in a stubborn line.

"Why does my favorite sweet little decorator suddenly feel the urge to turn into Nancy Drew? If I have to take blood pressure medicine when I'm old, it'll be your fault."

"Of course it will. It'll have nothing to do with the copious amounts of junk food that you consume on a regular basis." I arched an eyebrow at him.

"That's what the gym is for, babe." He leaned back with a smile and patted his washboard abs. It so wasn't fair. Before I could reply, Lamont's voice came over the intercom.

"Mr. Feldman to see you."

"Looks like playtime is over for me." Tang sighed and stared at me. "You gonna be okay?"

"Always. I'll let you know if I need an ice cream break later." I rose and kissed his cheek when he hugged me goodbye. "Thanks for listening."

"You're welcome. I charge by the hour for therapy." He grinned.

"Put it on my tab." I laughed, waving on my way out. Tang was good for the soul.

Two pieces of gourmet chocolate didn't even begin to fill me up, and I knew that all that awaited me at home resembled someone's garden, so I made the impulsive decision to stop at Pandemonium, a donut shop just a couple of blocks from my house. I could grab a donut or two, wolf them down in the car, and dispose of the evidence before I headed home. Mom would probably smell the carbs and lard on my breath, but I'd deal with that when the time came.

Moments later, I walked in the front door of the donut shop, visions of lemon-filled joy dancing in my head, and like a sharp kick to the gut, the first person I saw standing in line was Detective Griff.

"Fancy meeting you here." I tried to be polite and felt the typical anti-authority flush rising in my cheeks. "Are you stalking me or just living out the stereotype of cops and donuts?" My lame joke fell so flat that even the guy behind the counter shook his head, which did nothing to help my flaming face situation. Griff merely grimaced and didn't deign to reply.

He ordered his donuts—a maple bacon, and a Bavarian, both respectable choices—paid and brushed past me on his way out.

"Gonna go stake out my house now that you have your snack?" I just couldn't keep my mouth shut, and I kicked myself as soon as the words left my lips.

"Why? Should I?" Griff turned around and gave me a death glare.

I had no words. I merely continued to flush scarlet and turned away. Mercifully, he left without another word. I consoled myself with lemon-filled donuts in the parking lot before heading home, glad that I saw no trace of Griff along my route.

Chapter Nineteen

I checked out the neighborhood unfolding in front of me as I drove with a bit of trepidation. It definitely wasn't the type of neighborhood that I typically worked in, but it did happen to be the neighborhood where Byron Bennett's ex-wife lives. I wasn't judging, I just found it incredibly odd that the ex-wife of someone who came from the Bennett family would be living so humbly. I never thought to ask Byron what he did for a living. I'd have to work that into the conversation the next time that I saw him. I triple-checked the address on my cell phone when I pulled up in front of the ramshackle cottage with a dead yard full of weeds.

Of course, it was correct. I'd found Shannon Kelpie's name in a public records check after searching for Byron's divorce. They'd split about three years ago, and Shannon had lived here ever since.

I probably sat in the car for a full minute trying to work up the nerve to actually get out and go to the door.

"Byron is nice, so his ex-wife probably is as well." I tried to convince myself, failing miserably. "I did not drive all the way out here to just turn around with no answers. I'm going in."

I knocked on the door, which had peeling, dingy white paint, holding my breath and halfway hoping that Shannon wouldn't be home.

"Hang on," a tired-sounding voice shouted from inside the house. She was home. Great.

A few seconds later, the door opened, and a thin woman with wispy brown hair and enormous brown eyes stared out at me.

"I'm not buying anything," she declared, her voice matter-of-fact.

"Well good, I'm not selling anything. My name is Sarisara Samson. Are you Shannon Kelpie?" I asked brightly, sticking out my hand.

She shook it limply, viewing me with suspicion.

"Why?" she asked.

"Well, this is going to sound a little bit odd, but I'm an interior decorator, and I want to make a special gift for one of my clients. I'm hoping you might be able to give me a bit of insight so that the gift can be extra special." That was true, at least...though my real motives were a bit more dramatic. I was hoping that Shannon would be happy to give me any dirt that might exist about her former in-laws.

Shannon frowned, confused. "How am I going to do that? I don't even know you."

"Well, if you're Shannon, you used to be...quite close to my client. Are you Shannon?" I knew she was, but for some reason I wanted her to say it.

"Yeah. Who's your client?"

"Cliff Bennett." I watched Shannon carefully for a reaction and wasn't disappointed.

"Oh, wow. There's a blast from the past. He used to be my father-in-law."

"Right. I wanted to get more insight into what might be a special gift that I could make for him and, after what happened, I didn't want to bother his son. You know, because it might be painful for him to talk about."

A strange look passed over her face when I mentioned Byron, which is understandable. Most people aren't exactly fond of their former spouses.

"I gotcha." Shannon nodded. "Yeah, come on in. Don't mind the mess. The maid doesn't come until next week." She snickered at her joke.

The house was sparsely furnished with worn and mismatched pieces, and though it was slightly cluttered, it had a homey vibe to it.

"Bet you don't go into houses like this, huh?" Shannon closed the door behind me.

"Sure I do. You've done a great job here."

"It's humble, but it's home." Shannon shrugged. "Have a seat." She gestured at the rust-colored floral print sofa. "You want some coffee? I was just about to make some."

"Coffee would be great, thanks."

Rapport was never built without food or drink. It was like a rule. The fact that Shannon had offered coffee was a good sign. She might actually open up and give me some info.

"So, what do you want to know?" she asked when she came back minutes later with two steaming mugs of fresh coffee. She sat down across the coffee table from me, on a striped recliner. I was thankful for her direct approach.

"So, I don't know Cliff very well, and he's really upset right now, so I'm hoping that you can give me ideas for something special that I can make to work into the new design for his house."

"That's a tough one. Cliff is nice, but I honestly think that Byron is probably suffering more than he is right now."

"Oh?" My heart rate accelerated, so I had to play it cool. I had no idea she'd get this personal so quickly. Ya gotta love people who get right to the point.

"Yeah, he was definitely his mama's precious boy, and I think it was mutual. I swear sometimes I felt like Byron loved Rosalie more than he loved me. After how things turned out, I guess he probably did." Shannon smiled wryly, but seemingly held no bitterness toward Byron. "Cliff is probably keeping his grief inside and trying to work it out on the golf course. He's sweet, but not a touchy-feely kinda guy, ya know? He used to tease Byron for being sensitive and a mama's boy. Byron handled it well. Usually, he just let it go and laughed."

"So, he didn't get upset when his dad teased him?" I couldn't help but ask. I was fascinated.

"Nope. He's a pretty confident guy. Got it from both his mom and dad."

"Gotcha. So, what do you think would be a good gift? I want something that will honor Rosalie without making Cliff or Byron too sad. It sounds like they both loved her so much."

Which took the crotchety old man directly off of my list of potential suspects. Looks like Tesia the Embezzler must've been wrong, at least with this case.

"Well, Cliff always called Rosalie the apple of his eye, so maybe something with apples would be good."

"Oh, that's perfect, actually. I'm using a ton of green in the house, so I can work in something with green apples," I thought aloud.

"That'd be great. Byron loves green apples. It's funny the silly things that I remember after three years of being divorced." Shannon smiled faintly. "He's a good guy. Things just didn't work out between us."

"I'm sorry," I said, feeling hugely uncomfortable. There were some things that I didn't want or need to know about my clients, and their failed marriages fell directly into that category.

"Yeah, well, water under the bridge." Shannon waved a hand, dismissing the topic. "You want some more coffee?" she asked when she noticed me finishing the dregs.

"No, I'm good, thanks. I actually need to run, but thank you so much for your time and insight. I think I'll be able to make a very nice gift for the Bennetts now."

I shook her hand, and she walked me to the door. I'd be focusing my efforts on Buck Lumpkin and the mystery electrician from here on out. Cliff might be cranky, but from what Shannon had described, he was no murderer. His wife had been the apple of his eye. I wonder if I'll ever be the apple of anyone's eye, aside from my mom and dad, that is.

I needed time to digest what I'd just learned, and to do some research in peace, so I decided to head to a coffee shop to mull things over and make plans to proceed with my impromptu investigation. And let's just be honest, a little more caffeine and perhaps a chocolate croissant might just help me think better. At least, that's what I told myself.

Armed with my laptop, two chocolate croissants, and a double-strength latte, I chose a small table in the back of the coffee shop and got to work.

"Oh, my, my, my..." I stopped in mid-chew, and my eyebrows rose as I stumbled upon Buck Lumpkin's criminal record.

Turns out that Buck had been convicted of several crimes before winning the lottery, including a failed attempt at counterfeiting money, check fraud, and theft. But, did a history of what amounted to small-time thievery mean that he was capable of murder? It seemed like a stretch, but he did seem to have a wicked temper and definitely wasn't a popular guy in the neighborhood. Maybe he'd had a disagreement with the victim that no one knew about.

Buck apparently also had a habit of pulling up stakes and moving rather frequently, both prior to his big jackpot, and later. It made me wonder what he might be running from. I made a note of the places that he'd lived before, along with the dates that he moved, to see if they coincided with suspicious deaths of sweet old ladies who lived near him. As I was feverishly jotting down details about Rosalie Bennett's surly neighbor, a flash of white outside the window of the coffee shop caught my attention.

My heart leapt to my throat when I saw a white van pulling into the coffee shop parking lot. It looked eerily like the one that I had seen at the scene of the crime, right before the lights and sirens filled Sally Edgerton's normally serene neighborhood. Did they know that I was looking into the murder? Was I being stalked by a killer? Was I next on his list? I swallowed hard, forcing down the last bite of my croissant, and watched as the vaguely familiar driver stepped out of the van and strode toward the coffee shop with a look of grim determination on his face. He'd found me. I was about to confront a killer, face-to-face.

Oddly, when the driver of the white van walked into the coffee shop, he didn't even glance in my direction. He filed in behind the last customer in line and stared up at the menu boards. Shaking off an epic case of the willies, I mustered my courage and marched to the spot directly behind him. In for a dollar, in for a dime. If I was going to investigate, why not go right to the source...errr...alleged source.

"Excuse me." I tapped the man on the shoulder, electric volts of adrenaline surging through me so violently that it made my ears ring.

He turned and gave me a head-to-toe once-over. His name, Rick, was embroidered on his shirt, and I made a mental note to etch that info into permanent memory.

"Yeah?" he replied, seeming semi-interested.

As always, in the face of male attention, I felt my face flush, but being a newly self-designated super-duper investigator, I shrugged off my discomfort and forged ahead.

"I think I might know you." I smiled brightly, feeling my lips twitch with anxiety. "Are you an electrician?"

"Nah, I'm a swimming pool maintenance professional." It seemed like an embarrassing admission for him.

We shuffled forward in the line, edging closer to the front counter. If he was a killer, at least there were several potential witnesses around. I tried to relax, as my heart still pounded out a tempo to beat the band.

"What a coincidence!" I blurted, feeling like I had to work to keep his attention. "I'm on my condo board, and we're looking for a new service. Do you have any clients in the Devonshire subdivision? For references, I mean."

His change in expression was abrupt and terrifying. A mask of indifference fell over his features, and his reply was cold and clipped.

"No."

He turned away and focused on the baked goods case in front of him, making it clear that he wasn't interested in continuing our conversation. It would've looked odd if I just went back to my laptop, so I stood in line, behind a man who may or may not have killed someone, intending to buy a cheese danish. I told myself that I could always eat it for breakfast the next day, but who am I kidding? Odds were pretty darn good that the danish wouldn't make it out the door of the coffee shop.

On the way back to my table, I took a longer route, one that brought me closer to the van that Rick had been driving. I pulled up beside it for a better look. GREAT WAVES POOL AND SPA was printed across its side panel—the same company that Byron Bennett said they used for their pool. Rick must have looked familiar because he was the man I saw on the day of the murder. As amazing as the cheese danish looked, I couldn't even bring myself to take a bite. My stomach was in knots, and I panicked, wondering what I should do.

"Okay, first, stop jumping to conclusions," I muttered under my breath. I rolled my head from side to side, trying to ease the growing tension, and took some deep breaths. I needed to be calm and think. I couldn't just accuse this guy. And I couldn't call the police on a hunch—that hadn't turned out well thus far. First, I needed facts to back up my suspicions.

"Alright, Ranger Rick…let's see who you are."

I went to the Great Waves website and found the staff listing. Rick's last name was Jervis, and he'd been with the company for five years. I typed his name into my search bar, along with "public records," and found his address. Curious, I navigated over to a street view maps app and saw his really nice lakefront home, on a decent-sized chunk of land.

"That's not suspicious at all." I made a face and looked up the salary for pool techs with five years of experience. The numbers just didn't add up. He should be living in a one-bedroom apartment, not a sizable home on a lake.

"Don't be judgy," I whispered, gazing at the screen. "Maybe he comes from a wealthy family. Or divorced a rich woman."

My searches for Rick's family or former wives were a complete bust, and I took a huge bite of my cheese danish out of sheer frustration.

"Oh man, this is so good," I groaned, my eyes nearly rolling back in my head.

I felt someone looking at me and turned my head slightly to the left to discover a woman about my age and size looking at me with amusement… and understanding. She raised her latte in tribute, and I nodded, blushing. Soul sisters of the coffee and danish realm.

Since looking for leads on Rick hadn't turned up much, other than a mystery property, I decided to do more research on the victim. Maybe there was a clue in Rosalie's life that would give me a hint as to who had wanted to kill her. Everything I'd heard about Rosalie Bennett had been glowing and positive—the woman was a veritable pillar of the community. And it had been my experience that sometimes the nicest people had the nastiest secrets. If that were the case, the clues to Rosalie's murder may have been right under my nose all along, if only I had thought to look for them a bit closer to home. Everyone has haters. Everyone. I was determined to find out who might have hated the dear woman who did so much for so many.

I was elbows deep in the society pages when a human tornado descended upon me in a cloud of expensive perfume.

"I knew you'd be here when you didn't answer the phone." Charla grinned triumphantly, easing gracefully into the chair across from me. "Parental avoidance maneuvers?"

I laughed. "Nah. I just needed to do some research and wanted coffee." I saw Charla glance down with disapproval at my half-eaten danish.

"Please tell me you didn't get that wicked syrup in your coffee." She shuddered, peering into my cup.

"Coconut *and* vanilla," I announced proudly, laughing when she cringed. My soul sister on the left grimaced and shook her head at Charla's obvious contempt for my lovely snack.

"Your funeral," Charla said.

"Bring flowers."

"So, what are you researching that you can't do at home with your mom peeking over your shoulder?" There's nothing that girl loves more than a juicy secret.

"You won't believe this." I lowered my voice and leaned toward her, checking the immediate area to make sure that no one was paying attention. "I found the pool guy that I saw at the murder scene."

"What?" Charla frowned. "What pool guy? I thought you saw an electrician."

"I thought so, too, but I didn't. It was a pool guy, and he came in here a little while ago." I was practically bouncing in my seat. Charla's mouth dropped open.

"Did you talk to him?" she asked, eyes wide.

"Yes, and before you ask, no, he wasn't cute."

"Oh, bummer." Her mouth twisted to the side in disappointment. "But, wait…do you think he might be…" She trailed off, the horror of the situation hitting her.

"I think there's a good chance, yeah, but when I did an internet search, the only thing I found out of place was that his house was way too big for what he makes as a pool guy."

"That doesn't mean anything." She waved a hand dismissively. "People buy houses that they can't actually afford all the time. But, why are you still messing with that case? I've told you a thousand times to walk away and let that hunky detective handle it."

"Yeah, sure, because he's doing such a great job." I rolled my eyes. "By the way, what can you tell me about potential enemies that Rosalie Bennett might have had? Like rivals or whatever."

Charla positively lit up.

"Well, for the record, I still think that you should mind your own beeswax. But since you asked...I have an idea."

The wicked glint in Charla's eye made me nod reflexively. Whatever plans she had, I was on board.

Chapter Twenty

"Tangie-poo, please...don't make me beg," I implored, hanging on to his hand with both of mine and batting my eyes.

"Your begging feeds my soul, but the answer is still no." Tang withdrew his hand and crossed his arms, gazing at me stubbornly.

"You could go with me. We'd look pretty together." I'd begun to wheedle. I hate wheedling. "Come on, you dated the activities director at the country club. You could totally get us in."

"It didn't end well. He made fun of my cuff link collection."

"Then he owes you, right?" I seized on the last thread of hope.

"Probably, but I don't want to go to the memorial service of a woman I didn't know so that you can snoop around casting suspicious glances at her friends."

"That's fair." I made a face, then brightened. "I can take Charla! She knows everyone. Come on, Tango, just get me an invitation for two, and we'll take care of the rest. Please? I'll get you a giant snowstorm from Custard Cup."

"Now you're manipulating my known weakness?" Tang raised an eyebrow.

"Is it working?"

"Yeah, kinda." He sighed. "Alright, fine. I'll get you two guest passes, but you have to keep a low profile and not do anything embarrassing."

"Cross my heart." I made the motion and beamed up at him, triumphant.

"And since you're taking that she-demon with you, you owe me *two* snowstorms."

"Deal," I agreed, kissing his cheek.

He unexpectedly pulled me into a hug.

"Just be careful, okay. You shouldn't be messing with all this, and I could kick myself for enabling you."

"That's what friends are for, silly. I'll tell you all about it over snowstorms on Sunday."

"Make mine peanut butter with brownie chunks," Tang ordered. "Double brownie chunks."

"You got it."

* * *

The women at the country club clearly paid more to get their hair done than I forked over to pay my mortgage on a monthly basis, and I couldn't feel more out of place if I tried, but there were perks to attending a memorial reception at the club.

"This is worth coming to just for the food," I whispered to Charla while munching on a bacon-wrapped scallop.

"How can you even put that fat-filled sodium bomb in your mouth?" Charla wrinkled her nose, scanning the crowd for familiar faces.

"Like this," I replied, sliding another luscious scallop off the toothpick and into my mouth.

She'd already been greeted like an old friend by half the people present at the very posh, post-memorial service reception. The woman knows everyone in town, I swear. I was on the receiving end of polite but vacant smiles when anyone chanced to notice me, and I was okay with that. I wouldn't be distracted by social interaction.

I washed down the delectable scallop with a gulp of Bloody Mary, yet another dietary choice that made Charla raise an eyebrow. I figured that I needed to get fueled up for my investigation, and I wasn't going to let my svelte bestie stand between me and my fuel.

"Gross. Don't you think it's a little odd that the husband and son aren't here?" Charla frowned, gazing around the room. I paused mid-chew, my eyes glancing toward the tribute to Rosalie Bennett at the end of the room.

"You're right." I swallowed my bite, continuing to scan the room for the Bennetts. I wondered if Byron's brother would show up since that relationship, or lack thereof, seemed to be a bone of contention for Cliff.

"Charla, darling, so good to see you. Isn't this just the saddest thing?" An older woman, dressed in a lavender designer suit that probably cost more than my car, came up to us and pressed her cheek to Charla's while making a little kissing sound.

"Oh, Pearl, it really is." Charla nodded, patting the matron's hand. "I wanted to express my condolences to the family, but I haven't seen them. Do you know if they plan to attend?"

Charla was on it. You go, girl.

"I understand that Cliff and Byron are quite distraught," Pearl said, then leaned in and lowered her voice. "As in needing medication distraught. Not that I blame them at all. This whole ordeal is such a shock, and they haven't even found the dastardly soul who did it yet."

"How awful for them." Charla's ersatz sympathy flowed like warm honey.

"I know. All the ladies at bridge club were devastated. When we had our first meeting after…we couldn't even play. We just shared stories about dear Rosalie and then went home." Pearl inhaled deeply and waved her hands, trying not to cry. "It was lovely seeing you, dear. If I see the family, I'll be sure to let you know."

"Thank you so much. You take care now." Charla gave the elderly woman a hug, then turned to me once Pearl was out of earshot. "Well, if there was anyone who might've been Rosalie's rival, it's Pearl, but clearly she's pretty broken up about the whole thing."

"Or she's really great at acting like she's broken up about it," I commented dryly, handing my empty plate and glass to a server.

"Come on, Sari, not everyone is a suspect."

"I just wish I had a better handle on who is the most likely suspect." I sighed, glancing about the well-appointed ballroom.

"Mmhmm…"

Something had distracted my bosom buddy and when I turned to see what…or rather, whom, my heart sank.

"Now, there's the kind of juicy hors d'oeuvre that I want to sink my teeth

153

into," Charla mused, already on the move toward Detective Marcus Griff. "Watch out, McGruff, here I come."

That's my cue to hit the road. I scoped out the nearest exit and hurried toward it.

Charla was so intent on her prey that she didn't notice my retreat. I was nearly to the door when I almost literally bumped into Shannon Kelpie, Byron Bennett's ex-wife.

"Oh, hi." Shannon stuck out a hand for me to shake when she saw me barreling toward the door. "You're Cliff's decorator, right?"

"Yes, Sari. Nice to see you again, even if it's under sad circumstances."

"No apologies. Good to see you, too. I was hoping to at least be able to hug Cliff and Byron, but I haven't seen either one of them." Shannon frowned. "I hope Cliff is okay."

"What do you mean?" I couldn't help but ask.

"I figured you'd know…Cliff has been in poor health. Some days, he can barely get out of bed from what I hear."

Shannon looked sad when she spoke of her former father-in-law, and I couldn't help but feel sorry for her. I've always thought it to be so unfair that when people get divorced, they often lose more than their mate; they lose the whole family.

"He may be bad enough now that Byron didn't want to leave him to come to this," she continued, waving a hand at the crowd in the ballroom. "Are you leaving?"

"Yes, I was just on my way out."

"Well, thanks for coming. I know that Cliff and Byron would appreciate it." Her smile was kind.

"Take care." I gave her a little wave, and off I went, my mind racing.

Had Cliff Bennett been so sick that he killed his wife so that she didn't have to face life without him? Had Rosalie's murder been a horrifically misguided act of love? For a fleeting moment, I wondered what that kind of love would feel like. I shuddered and shook it off, wondering if other people had morbid thoughts after memorial services.

I couldn't help but think that my friends were right. I was entirely out of my element. A high-society husband with anger issues had offed his much-loved wife, because of a twisted motive, and I still owed Tang two snowstorms. With extra brownie. I'd gotten this far on luck, with a little bit of chutzpah, and I wasn't about to give up now. When the whole ugly mess was finally resolved, I might just join Tang for an evening of custard-filled debauchery.

Chapter Twenty-One

My mom's eyes lit up when I came in the door after my entirely non-productive trip to the country club. "Oh, sweetie-pie, you look beautiful! Did you have a brunch date?"

"No, I just had a thing that I had to go to. Do you want to go for a walk after I change?" I asked, hoping that she wouldn't ask questions about where I'd been.

She stared at me, concern coloring her gaze. I swear the woman is psychic.

"Of course. I could always use some fresh air."

"Perfect. Can you grab my water bottle and fill it up while I get dressed?"

If she had a task, she'd be less likely to dwell on where I'd been.

"Oh, and please put Foo's leash on."

"Sure thing. Oh, I could bring Safira too!"

I stared at her. A cat...on a walk. Only my mother.

"Let's give Foo a little cat break and just take him."

Mom pretended not to pout at my suggestion.

"Whatever you want, Sarisara."

She stalked down the hall, and I headed for my room. It felt great to slip into a long-sleeved t-shirt, yoga pants, and running shoes, after being in hose and heels all morning. By the time I met Mom in the living room, she was over her disappointment and had my water bottle and Foo all ready to go.

"Let's have an adventure, shall we?" She grinned, handing me the water bottle, but not the leash. "You know, sweetie, I don't think that Foo would run off if we freed him from his bonds." She dangled the end of the leash between her forefinger and her thumb with a look of disdain.

"There are leash laws, Mom. I don't want to get fined by the condo board."

"Barbaric fascism," she muttered under her breath. I pretended not to hear and did my best not to giggle.

We hadn't even made it to the end of my driveway before Mom decided that it was heart-to-heart time.

"I'm worried about you, Sari."

"No need to worry, Mom. I'm just fine."

Foo trotted obediently beside Mom, who had tucked the end of his leash into the pocket of her linen capris.

"Your dad and I have discussed it for quite a while, Honeybear, and we want you to seriously consider coming back to California." She dropped her bombshell, and when I opened my mouth to protest, she held up a hand. "Now, hear me out. You're very good at what you do, and your opportunities are so limited in this small Midwestern town. You could become a sensation in Temecula, and you wouldn't be far from L.A., Hollywood, Bel Air, Beverly Hills. The sky would be the limit, and you'd be near your family."

I should've known that there was an ulterior motive for their "spur of the moment" visit.

"Mom, I have a life here. I have friends, I make a decent living, and I don't have to deal with the hustle and bustle of big cities. I like the slower pace. I love you and Dad, but I'm where I need to be right now. I am happy, Mom. Really."

"Well, then, we're happy too." She finally threw in the towel and wrapped an arm around my shoulders, giving me a little squeeze that felt like home. I leaned my head on her shoulder.

"Know what's not fair?" I asked.

"What?"

"That Foo-dog walks beside you so perfectly. The little turkey pulls on the leash when I walk him."

Mom laughed aloud and turned her head to kiss my forehead.

"That just means that the two of you need to work on your soul bond, dearest."

"I'll get right on that."

When we went back inside after a nice long walk, Dad rose from the couch to greet us.

"No, she didn't talk me into coming back to California," I said.

"I haven't the slightest idea what you're talking about," he said in a tone that clearly indicated he was fibbing. He wrapped me in his big bear hug and kissed the top of my head. "I know you're going to do your own thing, Sari. That's how we raised you." He released me, his eyes glowing with pride. "Oh, and before I forget, a package came for you while you were out. I put it on the table."

"That's weird. I'm not expecting anything." I frowned, heading toward the table. Mystery packages could be fun, and in this case, it was a great change of subject.

I spotted the package, which turned out to be a cellophane-wrapped box from a local florist, and slid it closer to the edge of the table so that I could open it. The bottom of the box left a trail of some sort of sticky substance that smelled a bit like a spoiled cabbage that had been left out in the sun to fester.

"What in the world?" Mom wrinkled her nose and waved a hand in front of her face. "Sweetie, you need to get some gloves on before you handle that and take it to the sink, so that it doesn't ruin your table. Steven, how is it possible that this dreadful smell escaped your notice?" she asked my dad, who was already back in his recliner.

Dad shrugged, his nose buried in a novel. "I just figured that Foo-dog had gas."

I grabbed a pair of disposable gloves and quickly moved the package to the sink. My curiosity was killing me as I tore through the cellophane wrapping. There was a note card taped to the top of the box, and when I read the message that looked like it had been scrawled by a kindergartener, I frowned, puzzled.

They'd still be swimming if they weren't in the wrong place at the wrong time.

"What does that even mean?" I muttered aloud.

"I don't like the sound of this, Sarisara." Mom peered down at the card.

"Something is off."

Her eyes went wide, and she paled. "It's death," she murmured, swallowing hard.

"What?" I frowned, glancing over my shoulder to see if the grim reaper had suddenly come to stand behind me.

"That smell. It's the smell of death. Don't open that box, Sari."

"Mom, that's ridiculous," I said, not feeling at all certain that she was wrong. "There's no way to know what this weird message means if I don't open the box."

I pulled back one of the flaps of the box before she could reply and gasped. Mom gagged and backpedaled, her hands flying up to cover her mouth and nose.

"What's wrong?" Dad sprang from his chair and hurried to the sink, where I stood staring in horror at the three fish heads that were gumming up the bottom of the box, their sightless eyes seeming to stare into the beyond.

"Fish heads?" Dad said incredulously. His brow furrowed.

"It's a threat." Mom's face was entirely drained of color. "Someone is trying to send you a message, Sari. I told you to stay away from that murder case. The killer knows who you are and where you live. You have to call the police, this instant."

"Mom, no. I'm sure it was just a prank." I wasn't fooling even myself. My shaking hands and pounding heart attested to that. "If we call the police, that awful detective will come over here again and will find a way to somehow blame this on me." I shook my head, unable to pry my gaze from the disgusting "gift."

"He wouldn't be entirely wrong, now would he, Sarisara?" Dad asked quietly.

"Huh?" I blinked at him. Dad was always on my side. What kind of world was this where he was siding with the surly detective?

"Where were you this morning? You were pretty vague about that earlier," he asked.

He gave me that look that went right through me. My dad had an uncanny way of detecting when I was stretching the truth a bit. There was no use in even trying to fib. He just knew.

"I went to Rosalie Bennett's memorial service at the country club." My eyes were downcast as I confessed, feeling about twelve years old.

"And why did you do that?" Dad raised an eyebrow.

"I suppose you won't believe me if I say that it was to pay my respects?" I sighed. "I wanted to talk to some of Rosalie's social acquaintances, to see if there might be someone who seemed...I don't know, jealous or vindictive."

"You do realize that sometimes murderers attend the services for the victim because it gives them a sense of satisfaction, right?" Mom's brows rose in a look that held both disapproval and concern.

"I watch *Law and Order.* Of course I know that." My face flushed.

"Your presence there may have alerted the killer that you're still digging into the case." Dad folded his arms, a haunted look in his eyes.

"Or...it could be just a prank." My protest sounded weak. "Maybe it was Gabe."

"Call the police right now, or I will," Mom said quietly.

Things had just become rather violently real. What on earth had I gotten myself into?

Chapter Twenty-Two

"How much more proof do you need that your meddling could get you killed?" Detective Griff asked, a muscle in his iron jaw flexing.

"She gets the point, Detective. That's why you're here." Mom's tone was light, but her glare sent its own message.

Griff didn't flinch nor drop his gaze. As dire as my situation had become, I had to admit, I was enjoying seeing my mother stand up to Griff. He needed to take his attitude down a notch, and if anyone could facilitate that, it was my mother.

"I was the one who received the package," Dad interjected. "Sari and her mom were out on a walk."

Griff glanced at me, and his eyes narrowed briefly before he turned back to my dad.

"Who delivered the package?"

"I don't know. He walked away after he rang the doorbell and set it on the welcome mat. Some kid—maybe fourteen or fifteen, shaggy brown hair. Had on a Lakers tank top and long black basketball shorts."

I had to stifle a gasp, because I didn't want Griff's laser beam eyes to focus on me again. Mom and I had walked by a kid who fit that description when we were on our walk. He was playing basketball with a couple of other guys at a park a few blocks away.

"So, this wasn't a professional delivery then." Griff made a note. "Did you see the kid get into a car or anything?"

"No, but I really wasn't paying too much attention. He just walked down the street, as far as I know," Dad replied.

"I'll be taking this." Griff nodded at the box, with the card sitting on top of it, and pulled what looked like a large, clear plastic trash bag, along with a pair of gloves like the ones that I had used, out of his jacket pocket.

He put the box into the bag and sealed it up, the foul stench of its contents wafting through the kitchen. Gagging again, Mom turned on the faucet and started scrubbing the sink.

Griff turned to me, bag in hand. "I'm going to tell you one last time…stay out of my case, before you get yourself killed. Got it?"

I nodded, not trusting myself to speak, as the reality of my situation descended upon me. The killer not only knew who I was, he knew where I lived. But what on earth did fish heads have to do with anything? Had he sent them just for the shock value? I had to find out, because the reasoning behind it might be some sort of clue as to why the murder was committed. Was I getting too close to the truth? I waited while Griff strode from the house and stashed the evidence in the trunk of his car, then watched him drive away until he turned the corner and his car disappeared from view. Grabbing my car keys, I headed for the door.

"And just where do you think you're going, young lady?" Mom eyed me suspiciously.

"There are these lemon-scented candles at the grocery store that are made to eliminate nasty kitchen odors. I'm going to go pick up a couple so that we can all breathe in here tonight." I made up a cover story on the fly, but this time, not even my seemingly psychic dad could refute it. I could actually go to the store and get the candles…after running a little errand first, of course. It's amazing and a little bit sad how confidently I can speak and not seem like I'm fibbing when I simply choose to leave out key bits of information. After the case was solved, I'd come clean and make it up to my parents somehow.

"That's a good idea. Do you want me to come with you?" Dad asked.

"No, it won't take but a minute. And honestly, I love you both, but I want a second to just drive with the windows down and process things." Again, not a lie. Not exactly the whole truth, but not a lie.

"Okay, sweetie," Mom relented. "But be careful, okay?"

I hugged her hard.

"I will, I promise."

I moved as casually as I could to grab my purse and even made sure that I backed slowly out of the driveway, but once I turned the corner, I drove a bit faster than normal, straight to the park where I'd seen the kid in the Lakers tank top. I didn't know if it was luck or just good timing but when I got to the park, the basketball game had just broken up, and the kids who had been playing, Laker boy included, were beginning to head for home. Parking quickly on the side of the road, I hurried toward the kid, who tilted his head and looked at me curiously through a tangle of bangs.

"Hi!" I smiled when I approached him, trying my best to diminish any potential creepiness involved in an adult stopping her car and running toward him. "Can I talk to you for a sec?"

"What's up?" He had a well-worn basketball tucked under one arm and took occasional sips from a sports bottle in his other hand.

"Can you tell me if you delivered a box to a house down there and around the corner?" I pointed.

"Yeah, I did, why?"

I couldn't believe he just openly admitted it. It threw me for a second, and I took a breath so that I wouldn't sound too animated when I replied.

"Who gave you that box?" My heart sped up.

He shrugged. "I don't know. We were all playing basketball, and when I came off the court to get a drink, this dude came up and gave me some money to take it to that house."

"What did the, uh, dude look like?" I asked, a plastic smile hurting my face.

"I don't really remember." The kid gave me a look.

"Will twenty bucks help you remember?"

"The dude gave me fifty."

"I don't have fifty." I stared him down, then dug in my purse and gave him my last twenty.

"Oh yeah, now I remember." He grinned, pocketing the money. "He had a bushy mustache and like...lightish hair."

"Tall? Short? Heavy? Muscular?" I now understood Detective Griff's frustration with vague descriptions, which still hadn't given him the right to be rude.

"I don't really remember. Honest." The kid shrugged again. "Anyway, I gotta get home for supper."

"Wait!" I called out as he started to walk away. "Did you happen to see a car that he was driving?"

The kid shook his head.

"Nope, wasn't looking. Said he wanted to surprise his friend with a present. It sure stunk, though. Had to wash my hands when I got back here."

"Okay, thanks."

I watched him go, and a horrible realization hit me. Bushy mustache? Both Buck Lumpkin and Rick, the pool guy, had them. So did Gabe, for that matter, though I didn't believe for a moment that he had a cruel bone in his body. Awkward, yes. Creepy, sure. But cruel? Nope, I just couldn't buy into that. I obviously had more digging to do, but at the moment, I needed to hurry to the store and buy a boatload of lemon candles.

* * *

"How do you eat this stuff, Mom? It's like sawdust with raisins in it." I took several gulps of coffee to wash down one of the bran muffins that she'd made for breakfast.

"Don't be rude, dear. They're good for your colon and it's never too early to be looking out for your colon health." She gave me a warning glance.

"You're so right. I think about it every day."

Mom shook her head, Dad hid his amusement behind the sports page, and I slipped the rest of my muffin under my napkin when she got up to refill her carrot juice, wadding it up to disguise the shape. I cleared my place, burying the offensive muffin deep in the trash, then washed my hands and grabbed my purse.

"And where are you headed off to so bright and early?" Dad lowered his paper and gave me a pointed look.

"Don't worry, Dad. I'm going to have coffee with Tang."

CHAPTER TWENTY-TWO

I kissed his cheek on the way to the door.

"You know, Honeybear, if you spent as much time with a straight man as you do with darling Tang, you'd be married by now," Mom commented dryly.

"That's what you think." I grinned and shut the door behind me before she could reply.

I hadn't even thought about marriage for a very long time—since my last breakup actually. Licking my wounds after Tristan, I had come to the conclusion that maybe marriage and kids and the whole happily-ever-after thing just wasn't in the cards for me, and I was okay with that. Or, at least most of the time, I could convince myself that I'm okay with that. I have a great job, friends who love me, and the best parents ever. Surely that's enough, isn't it?

"I'm still waiting for my snowstorms." Tang answered the door, looking and smelling fabulous, as usual, and wrapped me in a bear hug.

"Me too." I set my purse down on his foyer table and sighed. "I've been eating so much vegan food that I feel like a rabbit."

"Meh, it's good for you." Tang waved a hand. "Besides, I went to Pandemonium this morning." He shot me a devilish grin.

"You didn't! Please tell me they had the Cereal Killer." My eyes went wide at the thought of fluffy, sweet, gorgeous donuts.

"Odd that you'd make that choice under your current circumstances, but yes, they did, and I got two for you. You're welcome."

Tang led me by the hand to the dining room table, which was all tricked out with coffee and a spread of donuts that was so beautiful I could have cried.

"Oh, you've outdone yourself." I stood, mouth watering, staring at the festive red and white checked tablecloth, white cloth napkins, and porcelain plates and cups for the donuts and coffee. A large bouquet of stunning white flowers formed the centerpiece for our feast.

"Natch. I haven't had a chance to entertain much lately, and I didn't want to get out of practice." He grinned and pulled out my chair. "Now sit and tell me any and all drama that's been going on in your life."

"What makes you think that I have drama going on in my life?" I asked, my voice muffled by a colossal bite of my first Cereal Killer.

"Oh honey…you can play innocent with Mommy and Daddy, but Tang knows just by looking at you." He touched the tip of my nose with his forefinger. "Now, spill it, girl, or I'll snarf down your other donut." The way he eyed the pastry made me think that he was serious, so I grabbed my fork, ready to defend my donut if necessary.

"Tools down, sister, and speak." He looked at the fork, then at me.

"Fine." I put down the fork and sighed, telling him about the fish head incident.

Tang set down his caramel apple fritter and gazed at me with an expression that clued me in to the fact that I was about to get a lecture.

"Sari, I'm worried about you."

"Oh, here we go." I rolled my eyes.

"Now you stop it. Maybe no one else in your life has the chutzpah to call you out on this stuff, but I'm sure going to. You're tempting fates all over the place, and I have to wonder why." He eyed me speculatively.

"I told you, Tango…I refuse to let that detective look at me like a criminal. I'm going to prove him wrong, or—"

"Die trying?" Tang finished my sentence, raising an eyebrow.

"Well, hopefully not. Besides, it'll be good for Rosalie's family to have closure too."

"What a humanitarian," Tang said dryly. "I think the police are far more qualified to bring Rosalie's family closure than you are."

"Clearly they're not, if they're still looking at me as a suspect."

I washed down a bite of donut with fresh, hot coffee and felt it warm me the whole way down. Bless Tang. Even if he meddled in my whole life entirely too much, I loved him for it.

"I've seen you like this before." He shook his head. "There's absolutely nothing that I can say to deter you from this, is there?"

"Nope." I stuffed a huge bite of donut into my mouth.

Tang glared at me, arms folded, and neither of us spoke for a bit. Me, because my mouth was full, and him because I think he was contemplating hog-tying me and holding me hostage until the case was solved.

"Fine," he said, finally. "When do you have to go to Rosalie's neighborhood again?"

"Tomorrow. I have some appointments stacked up over there. Why?"

"Because I can't go with you—I have clients of my own stacked up—but I'm going to send Lamont with you."

"Tang, Lamont is your assistant, not mine. I don't need an assistant and couldn't afford one if I did."

"He's not going to be helping you with your work; he's going to help keep you safe," Tang said firmly, his mouth set.

I recognized that look. There was no changing his mind when he was making that face. It was a lost cause.

"So, Lamont is going to be my bodyguard?" I chuckled at the thought.

"Until this mess blows over, I don't want you to go anywhere near that neighborhood without him."

"Guess that means I'm a rock star now." I giggled. "Are you sending me in a limo too?"

Tang's response was a quirked eyebrow.

"What would I do without you?" I asked, standing and giving him a loud kiss on the forehead.

"Girl, I don't even want to contemplate." He brushed imaginary crumbs away from his forehead and refilled my coffee.

We finished our donuts and chatted for more than an hour about anything and everything, aside from murder, before I finally headed for the door. It had been great to just be normal and catch up for a while, but now I needed to get back to investigating, and my first stop was a logical one that I hoped might finally yield some results. I neglected to mention that to Tang, of course.

I pulled up and parked in front of Fleur de Lis, one of my absolute favorite local florists, because the box that the fish heads had been in came from there. The young woman behind the counter smiled when I came in, and I was relieved that I wouldn't have to deal with a sourpuss.

"I have an odd question." I beamed as I reached the counter.

"I've heard lots of those, so go for it."

"Is it possible to buy one of the boxes that the flowers come in from you?"

"You mean, like, a delivery box?" She frowned.

"Yes, exactly. Do you sell those?"

"No, ma'am." She shook her head. "I don't think any of the florists in town sell them."

"So, no one could've come here and purchased one from you then?" Now, *I* was the one who was confused. How did the killer get the box?

"Nope."

I thought fast. Maybe someone who had received flowers had reused the box that they'd come in.

"Can you tell me if you delivered flowers to a certain address in the past few days?"

"Umm…sure, I guess so. Is everything okay?" She frowned again.

"Yes, I'm just trying to figure out who my secret admirer might be."

"Oh wow. Is that a good thing, or are you creeped out by it?" the woman behind the counter asked, eyes wide.

"Little of both." I shrugged.

"I bet. What address are you asking about?"

I gave her Rosalie's address, as well as Buck Lumpkin's and Rick Jervis'. She tapped at her computer and squinted at the screen.

"There were a few deliveries at the Bennett house, but none that would have a box with it. They were either wreaths or vase arrangements."

"None at the other places?" I asked, baffled.

"Nope, not a one. At least not from our shop."

"Okay, thanks."

"No problem, have a nice day. I hope it works out with you and your secret admirer."

"Me too."

I left, dejected, head down, but a sound caught my attention. A floral delivery truck had just started its engine in the parking lot as I approached my car, so I got in quickly. When the truck left the parking lot behind the florist, I stayed with it, a couple of car lengths behind so that I didn't look suspicious. I had a hunch that the driver might just be someone that I'd recognize. Like, maybe Rick the Pool Guy had a second job. Not gonna lie. I felt like a bit of a superhero, following my hunches and chasing bad guys. We'd see how that worked out. Things tended to go astray whenever I started feeling saucy and acted before thinking. I brushed aside all thoughts of the wrath that would surely rain down upon my head if my mother and Tang knew what I was up to and kept following the floral truck.

It stopped in a neighborhood about a mile from my house, and I parked roughly half a block away, where I could see the truck, but wouldn't catch the attention of the driver. When he stepped out of the truck and walked to the back for the delivery, I could see him. It wasn't anyone I knew. He opened the back of the truck and left the doors wide open while he went to the front door with a lovely vase filled with daisies and sunflowers. If that was a common procedure, anyone who walked by could've stolen the box that was used for fish heads.

Frustrated and ready to spit nails, I pulled away from the curb, wondering whether or not I'd ever solve this stupid case. I hadn't gotten more than a block away when I saw red, white, and blue lights flashing in my rearview mirror, which instantly sent adrenaline rocketing through my system. I'd gone from feeling like a superhero to feeling like a fugitive in the space of about twenty seconds. Awesome. Pulling over, I fished my registration out of the glove box and dug in my purse for my wallet. When the cop got out and walked up to the car, things took a turn for the worse. It was Detective Griff, of course.

Chapter Twenty-Three

"On a stakeout, Ms. Samson?" Detective Griff peered into the car. "I don't know what you're talking about." I could feel my cheeks burning. Darn it, I really needed to practice preventing that.

"Imagine my surprise when I went to talk to the woman in the floral shop where the box that you said you received came from, and I find you there. Were you paying her off so that she wouldn't tell me that you'd sent the fish heads to yourself?" he asked. "Very clever. Nice try anyway."

"Are you seriously accusing me of staging that? How dare you?" My eyes blazed, and I wanted to jump out of the car and throttle the boorish detective with my own hands. Thankfully, I thought better of it.

"Well, that's one way to make yourself look like a victim, rather than a perpetrator." Griff's tone was blasé as he made the accusation.

And that, folks, was the straw that broke the camel's back. I flung my car door open, not caring when it slammed against his upper thighs, making him grunt.

"Now you listen to me, *Detective...*" I was furious and didn't care if he knew it. In fact, I hoped that he could see the depth of my fury. "I have been doing nothing but trying to help since this whole ugly mess started, and you've accused me at every turn. I'm done with you looking at me like a criminal and implying that I had something to do with Rosalie Bennett's death. I saw some kind of technician when I looked out of Sally Edgerton's window. That's it. If I hadn't been trying to be a good citizen and help, you never would have even known that, and you've been throwing accusations in my face ever since. I'm done with it; do you hear me? I've discovered a few things that you may not know yet, and I'm going to make darn sure that I follow up on them, because I WILL prove my innocence, if it's the last thing I do!"

I was red-faced and out of breath by the end of my tirade, but man did it feel great to let that anger fly. Detective Griff deserved it, and if he arrested me, so be it. I'd had my say. He didn't speak, but just stood there, eyebrows raised, apparently trying to decide what crimes he could charge me with. When he finally replied, you could have knocked me over with a feather.

"My apologies," he said quietly. "I haven't actually thought of you as a suspect for quite a while. I was just hoping that you might slip and tell me something that you discovered along the way."

My mouth dropped open. I gaped at him, not knowing whether to laugh, cry, or hit him with the car door again.

"Are. You. Serious?" I went with anger, while I was at it. It went well the first time, so why reinvent the wheel?

"It could really help me to know what you've found out."

"Help you? You want me to help you when all you've done is harass and demean me at every turn? I'd be crazy to do that." I shook my head, appalled at his audacity.

"I could arrest you for hindering an investigation."

I didn't dignify that with a reply, but merely stared at him defiantly. My parents had great attorneys, and this guy had just admitted that he'd been intentionally harassing me.

"Look...I know this great coffee shop that's not far from here," he said. "Can we just go have a cup of coffee and talk about this?" He sounded almost human.

"Coffee." I was dumbstruck. Was he kidding?

"Yes. My treat."

I stood, gawking at him, arms folded. This was a curve ball that I hadn't been expecting, and I didn't quite know what to do with it.

"You want to be a good citizen, don't you?" he dared ask.

"I've been a good citizen *all along*, and look what I've gotten for my trouble."

"Like I said, I'm sorry. I could really use your help here. I'll get back in

171

my car, and you can follow me to the coffee shop, whaddya say?" He didn't smile, but he at least looked like smiling might be a possible function for him.

"And you'll leave me alone forevermore?" I asked, eyes narrowed.

"Cross my heart." He made the motion.

"I can't be sure that you have one, but fine. I'll follow you. And there had better be pastries involved, too."

"Whatever you want." Griff jangled his keys and headed toward his car, which still had the red, white, and blue portable light flashing on the roof.

"You sure about that?" I couldn't resist another shot before he sauntered back to his car.

He didn't turn around.

To his credit, Detective Marcus Griff didn't protest a bit that I had two lattes and a cake pop while we talked. The more of my experiences that I shared, the more he seemed to warm up, and it didn't take terribly long before I forgot my abject hatred of him and actually started enjoying his company, though I didn't divulge everything I knew about the case. Some cards were meant to be kept close to the vest. We were just about to wrap up our conversation when I heard a loud gasp from the front door of the shop.

I looked up and saw Charla staring at us, mouth agape. The look on her face as she strode toward our table was nothing short of frightening. To a stranger I'm sure she appeared calm and sweet, but I saw an expression that clearly indicated that she was madder than a hornet and that there would be heck to pay at some point.

"Well, lookie here," she trilled, a bitter edge to her voice as she approached the table. "You two aren't here discussing where Marc and I should go to dinner, are you?" She followed the question with a laugh so plastic that I could've used it to wrap up my leftover cake pop.

"No. It's a business meeting." Griff's manner was curt and dismissive, which infuriated Charla to her foundations. She was not a woman who was accustomed to getting brushed off.

"Then I'll just get my coffee and leave you to it." Her smile was sweet, but venomous. "I'll be waiting for your call, Marc." She brushed the back of her hand across Griff's cheek and didn't even glance in my direction.

"Lunch tomorrow?" I called after her when she headed for the counter.

She pretended not to hear me. Oh boy. I knew her I'm-mad-at-you routine. She'd ignore all calls and texts for a few days, then call me like nothing had ever happened. Predictable. She just needed some time to cool off…though I hadn't seen her this angry in quite some time, if ever.

After a few minutes of wrapping up our conversation, Detective Griff stood to go.

"I appreciate you taking the time to fill me in." He extended his hand, and I shook it, astonished at the about-face that he'd done with his attitude. If I'd known that it would have this kind of effect, I'd have told him off eons ago. When he left, I immediately tried to call Charla. It went to voicemail in a split second. Yep, I was on the naughty list.

I put my phone in my purse, and it rang. Shocked that she had actually called me back, I pulled it out, only to see Tang's smiling face on my screen.

"Miss me already?" I inquired in my best Southern belle voice.

"More than anything." He answered without missing a beat. "Hey, I need a favor when you get a chance."

"Oh?"

I held the phone to my ear with my shoulder and unwrapped a stick of gum on my way to the car. Coffee is divine, but coffee breath definitely is not.

"Yeah…I have a buddy who is out of work right now, and he's feeling really down. I was thinking a room makeover might cheer him up, so if you're willing, I'll pay for it."

"Is he cute?" I just had to give Tang a dose of his own medicine.

"Yeah, totally, but not my type. Plays for the other team."

"So, you want me to hang out with a cute guy, and you'll pay for it? Throw in an ice cream sandwich, and you've got yourself a deal."

"Consider it done."

"Cool, email me his info and I'll give him a call."

"Thank you, Sari-licious." I could practically hear Tang's smile over the phone.

"Don't forget my ice cream sandwich."

"Says the girl who owes me two snowstorms."

"Anticipation increases the pleasure ultimately," I teased.

"So they tell me. Be careful out there."

"You know it."

As always, I hung up with a silly grin on my face. Tang is the best guy ever. When we fight, which doesn't happen hardly at all, he doesn't ghost me like Charla does; he will talk me to death until we resolve whatever it is. And I love him for it. Doing a project for a friend of his would be fun. Any friend of Tang's is a friend of mine, and it won't matter at all how cute he is. Not at all.

Chapter Twenty-Four

Lamont was standing outside of Tang's office, waiting for me, because I had to return to the literal scene of the crime to check in with Cliff and Byron and see how their makeover was going.

"Hi, Lamont." My tone was apologetic when he slid into the passenger seat.

"Hey, Sari. Stop looking at me like that. I'm fine. In fact, since Tang is paying me for the day, and I don't have to put up with him...I'm great," he joked. "I even have his credit card in case we need lunch, or shopping, or whatever."

"Well, since you put it like that, welcome to my world. You're probably going to learn more about colors and patterns than you ever wanted to."

"Nope, actually, I won't. I might be okay with some of the patterns, but I'm colorblind." Lamont shrugged.

I don't know why, but it felt like my heart was being squeezed when he said that. Color is such a huge part of my life. I couldn't imagine what it must be like to live without it.

"Why the sad face? It's no big deal. I have no idea what I'm missing, so I don't miss it."

"I never thought about it that way. How do you choose your clothes? You always look great." I was fascinated.

"I made friends with one of the salesgirls in Macy's. I have a furniture girl, too, for when I need something for my apartment."

"Smart." I nodded. "Did Tang tell you that the house we're going to today is the one where a woman was murdered?"

Lamont's mouth fell open, and his eyes went wide.

"Uh…no. He failed to mention that part." Lamont licked his lips and shook his head. "I'm not going in that house, no way."

"I thought you were supposed to be protecting me?" I reminded him.

"I'll protect your sweet, sassy self from the car."

"It's okay," I reassured him. "I think Tang's just being overprotective by making you my bodyguard anyway."

"I'm taking it seriously, but no way am I going in that house."

"No worries. I have a stop to make before I even head over there, and you'll love this house. The owner has a pet iguana."

"Iguana?" Lamont said. "Do you ever work with anyone normal?"

"What is normal anyway? We'll only be in there for a few minutes. I need to check on her closet installation. It was planned out months ago, but the contractor had an emergency and couldn't get to it until this week."

Kit Rathbone was a hoot. A world traveler, she had expensive taste and wasn't afraid to shell out the money when it came to reinventing her sanctuary. I thought that she and Lamont would get along well, and I was right. Once he got past the embarrassment of shrieking like a schoolgirl when Chester, Kit's iguana, came strolling out of the bedroom to greet us, Lamont and Kit hit it off, chatting like old friends while I checked in with the installers. By the time I left, Lamont had convinced her to redo her den. I had to chuckle to myself. Tang's assistant was promoting my business more than I was. Lamont was definitely a welcome addition.

Our next stop was to check in with Agnes Hackles on her closet project, which was also going well. She had insisted that the cabinetmakers use purpleheart wood for her closet shelves, even when I told her that the wood would eventually turn brown like every other species. Lamont gasped when he saw the closet with its vibrant purple shelves. I had to agree; it was stunning.

"See, Sari! That reaction right there…" Agnes pointed at Lamont. "That's why I had to have the purpleheart wood. Even though it changes eventually, I'm going to enjoy the majesty of it while it lasts. You bet your sweet bippy." She folded her arms, gazing at the closet with a smile.

Purpleheart *is* stunning. It's also expensive, and Agnes hadn't cared one bit. Her closet cost more than most kitchen renovations that I've done. Agnes forced a dozen cookies, each, upon us before we left, and Lamont and I were munching on them before we left her front stoop.

"That woman can bake." Lamont sunk his teeth into the gooey, crunchy perfection that Agnes had created with her chocolate toffee cookies.

"I swear my clients make me gain weight." I groaned, enjoying my cookie as much as he was enjoying his.

"Good problem to have." He grinned and plucked another cookie from the giant ziplock baggie that Agnes had given him.

"Heck, yes. Also, the murder house is our next stop, and it's right there." I pointed as Lamont practically leaped into the car.

"You didn't tell me that we were right next door to it!" The whites of his eyes stood out prominently against his skin as he locked the car door.

"I forgot." I stifled a smile. Truth be told, I was more than a bit edgy about going in there myself, but it was part of the job, and I was determined to be a professional. I only hoped that Cliff was in a better mood this time around. And that I made it out alive.

True to form, Cliff was glowering over Byron's shoulder when they opened the door after I rang the bell. He returned my greeting with a stiff nod and strode through the house like he couldn't wait to get me out of it.

"You know, since we're doing all this useless work to the house, we might as well redo the patio, too," Cliff said, as I followed him about, checking on the progress that had been made thus far.

"Dad, that will set your move date back by months." Byron reminded him, his eyes sad.

"I'm not in any hurry to leave this place, and I want the patio done. It's not like I've got any place to go anyway." Cliff's tone was aggressive, and I got the impression that he was accustomed to getting his way in every situation.

"Fine, lead the way." Byron gestured toward the door that led to the back yard.

As we paced around the patio that led to the sparkling pool, talking about improvements, I noticed a small, empty pond liner, under a tree in the corner of the yard.

"Oh, how pretty. That would make a perfect koi pond." I stepped to the edge and peered down. The pond liner was surrounded by stone and plants to make it look like an oasis in a forest. It was so charming.

"It was a koi pond, but every single one of the fish died recently." Cliff stood beside me, hands in his pockets, seeming to ponder. "We'd had some of them shipped in from Thailand years ago. Rosalie liked the colors. Thought the fins were graceful."

A wave of nausea washed over me. I realized that the fish heads in the box had been koi fish heads. Apparently, whomever was threatening me was still angry at the Bennetts for some reason and had killed their fish. I swallowed hard.

"Oh, how sad." I turned to Byron and spoke quietly while Cliff wandered around the pool area, seeming to take stock of the changes he'd like to do. "What do you do with fish when they die like that?" I asked, affecting innocence. "I mean, they're too big to flush, like you do with goldfish."

"I just threw them in the trash." Byron shrugged.

"Oh my, they must be making the garage smell awful."

"We don't keep our trash cans in the garage; they're by the side of the house, near the air conditioner, but the trash was taken away the same day that I put them in there anyway."

"Well, that was good timing."

Whoever had sent the fish heads must've known the Bennetts' trash schedule and picked through it, hoping that they could find something that would threaten both me and the remaining Bennetts. I wondered if they had received a nasty package as well. I nearly jumped out of my skin when the back gate suddenly swung open, and in walked Rick Jervis. He clearly recognized me from the coffee shop and wiped his hands nervously on his pants when he approached us.

"It's...uh...maintenance day, but I can come back later if you have something else going on." The way he stammered and the speed at which his eyes darted around, never quite meeting our gazes, made me suspicious.

"Absolutely not," Cliff insisted. "We have a schedule, and we will stick to it."

"Yes, sir." Rick nodded, shooting me a scathing glance before he turned away to check the pool filters.

"You two know each other?" Byron asked, noticing the odd interaction.

"Nope." I managed to keep my voice steady, though I was shaken to my core from the encounter with the man who was looking more and more like Rosalie Bennett's killer. "So, if you can get the pond going again, that would be a plus, but if not, you'll want to fill it in. Should we go back inside?"

"Sure, of course. Dad can tell you what he'd like to have done to the patio without having to stand outside." Byron looked at me sympathetically. Had he read my mind? Once we got inside, I had to share some honesty with him. He deserved that much.

"Byron, I was thinking about something..." I gestured for him to follow me so that our conversation didn't upset his dad. "The pool guy comes on Tuesdays, right?"

"Yeah, like clockwork, why?"

"Your mom...that all happened on a Tuesday. Today is Wednesday. Don't you think it's a little odd that your pool tech showed up today?"

"Yeah, now that you mention it, that *is* strange, because he was just here yesterday." Byron frowned.

"Maybe you should talk to the police about the pool guy," I whispered, darting furtive glances out the window. "I mean, they'd probably appreciate any help they can get, right?"

Byron slowly turned his head to stare out the window at Rick, who was testing the PH of the water. Muscles in his jaw flexed, and his hands clenched into fists, then he took a deep breath, closed his eyes, and released it.

"I'll definitely mention it to the detective. Thanks for picking up on that, Sari. I've been so distracted that I can hardly put two thoughts together."

"Completely understandable. Should we invite your dad to join us on the rest of the tour? He can talk about patio ideas while I check on the installations," I suggested, relieved to have finally discovered who really might be the killer.

We finished up the house tour, more than pleased with the project, and

Cliff nodded politely to me before retreating to his den. The home would be an absolute masterpiece when it was completed, and I had no doubt that Charla would get them top dollar for it. I told Byron as much, and he seemed relieved.

"Thank you so much for all you've done, Sari. I'm going to have someone come out and redo the pond, as well as the patio, now that we've talked about it." Byron walked me to the door.

"That'll be great. I'll give you a call next week to see how things are progressing," I promised.

"Perfect. Have a good day."

Byron waved from the front porch, and Lamont, watching from the passenger seat while I got in the car, averted his gaze.

"How did it go?" he asked, clicking a game app closed on his phone.

"I think I know who the killer is, Lamont, and he's in the back yard right now." I felt numb.

"Wait, what? The killer was the husband?" Lamont gasped.

"No. The pool guy. Things are starting to add up. Rick Jervis was there when Rosalie was murdered, he was there the day that the fish heads showed up at my house, and he's there today, while I'm there, even though he isn't supposed to be." I stared out the front window, dazed.

"That him?" Lamont inclined his head toward Rick when the tech came to get something from his white van.

Unable to speak, I nodded.

"Want me to go mess him up?" Lamont blustered, as if he'd do anything that would get his immaculate outfit dirty.

I shook my head. "No. We have to do this the right way. I'll tell Detective Griff about it as soon as I have a chance."

"Then…can we just get out of here right now?" Lamont asked, giving me a pointed look.

"Yeah. Yeah, we can." I nodded and turned the key in the ignition.

Rick stood by the back door of his van and stared at me until I turned the corner.

Chapter Twenty-Five

"Hi, are you Dustin?" I asked when Tang's buddy answered the door. His house was a relatively small ranch that was very humbly furnished, but it had striking art on the walls.

"Yep, I'm Dustin. You must be Sari." He stuck out his hand a bit awkwardly, and I shook it.

He was absolutely adorable. Dark curly hair, deep brown eyes, and a smile that melted me a little bit from the first time that I saw it. He was tall and lean but had nice definition in his arms. They flexed a bit when he folded them shyly and invited me in.

"Yep, nice to meet you."

"Same. Wanna come in and take a look?" Dustin held the door wide open and invited me inside.

I was excited because the house was an entirely blank canvas, aside from some epic landscape art that I could literally plan the room to match. I had promised Tang that I'd try to economize, and he had waved off my budget suggestions, which was even more exciting.

"The art is amazing." I stood in the living room, doing a 360-degree slow turn, taking it all in.

"Thanks." He gave a little cough and stuffed his hands in the pockets of his artfully worn jeans. His blush gave me a clue that made me look at him with even more admiration.

"Are these yours?" My brows rose.

"Yeah. I'm an artist; that's how Tang and I met. He went to a show where some of my work was featured and bought paintings for some clients and a sculpture for himself."

"Which sculpture is yours?" I asked. I knew Tang's swanky abode from top to bottom.

"You know the niche with the light in his hallway?"

My mouth dropped open.

"Holy moly, the glass wave with the sand beach is your work?"

Dustin nodded. "Yep, that was me." He gave me a shy smile that warmed me from head to toe.

"That's literally one of my all-time favorite sculptures...ever."

My eyes were wide as I stared at the humble artistic genius in front of me.

"Really? That's cool. I moved here from California, and I missed the ocean, so..." He shrugged.

"Get outta town! Where in California?" I blurted, all thoughts of my interior decorating task momentarily fleeing.

"Umm...it's in SoCal. Fallbrook. You've probably never heard of it."

"This is crazy. We were practically neighbors. I'm from Temecula. I miss the ocean, too; that's probably part of why I think that piece is to die for."

"Temecula, wow, that's cool. What are you doing out here?"

"My mother would say that I'm running from commitment, but the truth is, I just needed to get away and become my own person, you know?" The honesty flowed from my mouth in front of this total stranger with no effort whatsoever. What on earth was happening to me?

"Same." Dustin's eyes widened. "My mom owns a health food store, and my dad is a sound therapist. I found it ironic that they wanted me to do the whole traditional nine-to-five thing. I suffered through getting my MBA, but art is my love, so...here I am."

"Wow. It's like we have parallel lives or something. My parents are lovely people, but a little..."

"Out there?" Dustin supplied.

"Exactly. They don't mind what I do, but they want me to do it in a bigger market."

"California."

"Of course."

"Well, we showed them, huh?" Dustin laughed, and it was the sexiest thing I'd heard in a very long time.

"Yes, we did." My thoughts were making me blush, so I changed the subject back to work to rein in my wayward mind. "So, what were you wanting to do in here?" I asked. I tore my eyes away from the ridiculously handsome man in front of me and focused on his pathetic drapes.

"If possible, I'd like to have my art as the focus." He shrugged. "Beyond that, I'm pretty open."

"Oh, your art will absolutely be the focus. You have great natural light coming in the house, so that will help tremendously." I started making notes. "I'm thinking a gallery feel, with pale grey on all of the walls, contemporary trim, all in white, chrome accents...maybe a marble coffee table, and furnishings in leather, neutral colors. What do you think?"

"I think that you made that sound way easier than it actually is." Dustin chuckled. "I think I'd like an area rug too. I like something soft underfoot, you know?"

"Definitely part of my plan. I'll be using your artwork as a color palette for things like the area rugs, lampshades, and throws."

"Wow, you're really good at this, aren't you?" There was admiration in his smile, and it made my stomach do a little flip.

"I try. Is there somewhere that I can set up my computer and show you a few design ideas?"

"Sure, let's go to the dining room. It needs work, too, and so does the kitchen. Tang doesn't know it, but there's a painting of mine that a collector in New York is considering, and if she buys it, I'll be able to pay him back all at once, so I want to get all of the major rooms in the house done."

"You know that if he offered you a gift, he's not going to let you pay a dime, right?" I quirked an eyebrow at him.

"Oh, I'm aware. He can't stop me from gifting him with paintings, though." Dustin winked at me.

"Well, aren't you clever?" I grinned, utterly charmed. Who even *am* I right now? Was I actually...flirting? I'd forgotten what it felt like.

"Not clever enough to decorate my own place, apparently." He spread his arms wide and gestured to the horribly outdated dining room.

"Never fear, we can fix this."

I opened up my laptop, and we got to work. Four hours later, I closed the computer and rubbed my shoulders. They were a bit stiff from leaning over the keyboard for so long. Dustin had moved one of the dining chairs next to mine and sat so close that his knee often rubbed against mine under the table when he shifted forward to see the designs more closely. I didn't mind in the least, and there were so many butterflies fluttering in my stomach that it was hard to concentrate.

"You're amazing." Dustin stared at me with a delicious look of awe.

Before I could respond, beyond my ever-recurring blush, my stomach growled loud and proud, turning my light pink blush into a full-on bonfire.

"And hungry," I said with a giggle born of humiliation.

"I'm ordering pizza for dinner, and I have a full-bodied Cabernet to go with it. Would you want to stay and…eat with me?" Dustin smiled. Perfect teeth. I'm a sucker for a man with good teeth.

I nodded. "I love pizza."

"Perfect!" He seemed relieved. Did a guy like that honestly think that a fluffy girl like me was going to turn down free pizza and wine? "What's your favorite kind?"

"Pepperoni and mushroom."

"No way! Mine too." His grin grew.

"You know what that means." I gave him a pointed look.

"What?"

"It's a battle to the death for the last piece."

"Bring it, decorator girl."

"Be careful what you ask for, art boy."

Pizza and wine turned into watching a movie and having cookies delivered. I finally made it back home just after midnight, and Mom was sitting in the recliner that Dad usually occupied, doing a crossword puzzle.

"You're up late." I could hear the giddiness in my own voice and knew that Mom would begin an inquisition.

"So are you, and it looks like you've had a wonderful time. Please tell me it was a date." Mom grinned, setting her book of puzzles aside.

"Well, it started out as work, but then...yeah, I guess it did kind of turn into a date." I felt like a dolt, but I couldn't keep a silly grin from lighting up my face.

"Mixing business and pleasure? That doesn't sound like you, Sarisara. He must be something pretty special. Or she, if that's what happened."

"*He's* adorable." I plunked down onto the sofa and flopped back against the cushions. "It was so much fun, just talking and hanging out."

"And what does this fascinating man do for a living?" Mom tried to sound casual, but the way that she peered at me over the top of her reading glasses was a dead giveaway.

"He's an artist." I cringed inwardly, waiting for her reaction.

"Interesting. For whom?"

"What do you mean, for whom?" I frowned.

"What company does he work for? Disney? Marvel?"

"He's an independent artist." I waited for the disapproval.

"Meaning he doesn't have a job?" *And there it was.*

"Tang has one of his pieces in his art niche, and it's literally the most beautiful sculpture I've ever seen. He also has one of his pieces being considered by a collector in New York."

"Uh-huh. And how is he paying you?"

"He's not. The makeover is a gift from Tang, but Dustin plans to repay Tang with a painting."

"Mmhmm. And what kind of date did this...artist take you on?" Mom arched a brow at me.

"We had pizza and cookies delivered and watched a movie. It was perfect." Even I could tell how defensive I sounded.

"Oh, Sarisara, honey...We raised you to have good self-esteem, and I just want you to be happy. Are you having issues with insecurity?"

Every. Day. But that absolutely was not what had spurred my attraction to Dustin.

"No, I'm fine, Mom. It wasn't a big deal. I was there. We got hungry and enjoyed each other's company over some delicious food. That's it."

"Did he kiss you?"

"Mother!" My mouth fell open.

"It's a valid question." Mom blinked at me, unfazed.

"No, he did not, and I'm a strong, independent woman. If I had wanted a kiss, I would've taken one." I folded my arms.

"Of course, honey. Are you going to see him again?"

"I'm doing a makeover on his house; it would be hard not to see him again," I replied dryly.

"You know that's not what I meant."

"I have no idea. If he asks me out, I'll probably go."

My phone chimed, indicating that a text had come in, and I looked down, seeing a message from Dustin.

Hey Cali girl—I am SO glad that I met you. Gonna buy Tang a beer for that.

I grinned down at my phone and started texting back, forgetting that my mom was even in the room.

"Well, judging by the smile on your face, I don't have to guess who that text is from." She rose from the recliner and chuckled, heading for the bedroom.

"Yeah. G'night, Mom."

"Goodnight, Sarisara."

I knew that despite Mom's protests, she'd love anyone who was important to me. I wasn't getting ahead of myself and thinking that Dustin might be that person, but…if he was, she'd come around. She'd see that he had a good aura, I'm sure.

Chapter Twenty-Six

I f someone had told me that I'd be having coffee with Detective Marcus
Griff not once, but twice, in less than a week, I'd have laughed at them,
yet here I sat, across from the perpetually grim detective. It earned me
free caffeine the first time. I'd have been a fool to turn it down. The second
time, I was feeling so smug about my discovery of the killer, that I bought
Griff an Americano.

"I know who killed Rosalie Bennett." I leaned across the table, keeping my
voice low when I made my announcement. Griff was unimpressed.

"Do tell," he drawled, taking a sip of his Americano. This guy was so
hardcore that he didn't have cream or sugar in his Americano. He drank it
straight. The very thought made my toenails curl.

"Rick Jervis."

"Nope." Another sip.

"What do you mean, nope? He had access to the koi pond, which is where
he got the fish heads to scare me to death, and he acted super-nervous when
he was over at the Bennett's yesterday, on a non-scheduled day." I stared at
Griff as though he'd lost his mind.

"He wasn't scheduled to be at the Bennett's the day that the fish died, and
he has a rock-solid alibi for the day of Mrs. Bennett's murder. Would you
like me to tell you why he was so nervous yesterday?" Griff asked, his tone
more patronizing than I could muster.

"Sure, why not." I stared him down and folded my hands in my lap.

"Rick Jervis has been overcharging his clients for years and pockets the
difference between what their bill should be and what he charges them.

When I questioned him after the fish head incident, he started blubbering and proclaimed his innocence regarding the fish heads but confessed to the thefts. His employer, when I asked if they wanted to bring charges, decided to cover for him and call the overage 'tips.' I believe Rick Jervis is terrified that his clients will discover his little scheme and press charges themselves."

"But…he was there yesterday when he wasn't supposed to be, and he was there on the day that Rosalie died. I saw him."

"Yes, and I'm sure he's probably making extra stops at most of his client's homes so that he can justify the overages if the company does decide to press charges. The logs in his daily tracking show no room for him to be able to take time out to commit murder, and the clients that I've questioned who were scheduled before and after the Bennetts confirmed that he was right on time, as usual. They all seem to love the guy who has bilked them out of thousands of dollars every year. Besides, the neighbor who lives behind the Bennetts showed me security camera footage that showed Rick arriving, doing his job, and then leaving. Pretty solid evidence that he didn't do the crime."

"Overcharges. That's how he afforded that big house." The words were out of my mouth before I could think about them.

"Yes, that's correct, and how did you know about that?" Griff's eyes narrowed.

"Real estate thing." I waved my hand vaguely. "So, if he's not the killer… who is?" I thought aloud. "It's gotta be Buck Lumpkin. I knew it the moment I saw the guns and ammo in their closet."

"Let's not get ahead of ourselves here," Griff warned. "Thanks for the coffee, and stay out of the investigation." He rose and headed for the door. I had to wonder, why is it that every time I try to do the right thing…it's never the right thing?

After a quick glance at my watch, I took the rest of my latte with me and hurried out the door. I didn't want to be late. I had to go check out Agnes Hackles's new closet, now that installation was finally finished. It was such a quick trip that I didn't bother to ask Lamont to come with me. If Tang found out that I went without him, I'd just buy him off with ice cream. I know what makes that man tick.

"It's absolutely beautiful." I nodded my approval when Agnes showed me the finished closet. She'd already restocked it with her...interesting wardrobe, and it looked spectacular.

"Yes, it is, and while the closet guys were here, I had them measure the rest of the closets in the house. They'll send them to you so you can do the designs." Agnes was positively beaming.

"Perfect. Well, I'll just be on my way then." I edged away from the closet, hoping that I could get out the door before she tried to feed me. Again.

"Oh honey, don't rush off just yet. I made some amazing banana bread. You should sit down and have a slice with me so I can tell you what I heard yesterday about the murder."

That was the one thing that she could've said to make me stay and eat banana bread with her. It's not that I have anything at all against banana bread, but I certainly didn't need the extra carbs. Agnes loves a captive audience and might take my staying as her cue to talk all day, but if she had worthwhile info about the murder, it might be a good investment of my time.

"Oooohh...I love banana bread." I smiled and headed for the dining room while Agnes puttered in the kitchen. "So, what did you hear?" I asked, trying to sound casual before the poor dear even had a chance to seat herself.

"Have you met Nico Karagiorgis yet?" Agnes sat down and took a bite of banana bread.

"Doesn't sound familiar, so I don't think so." I frowned.

"He and his wife and two kids live right behind Buck and Vikki Lumpkin, poor things. Anyway, do you know what Nico was doing, right when the murder happened?"

My hand, holding a delightfully moist slab of banana bread, froze, halfway to my mouth. My heart rate accelerated.

"What?" My voice was a bit breathless.

"He was arguing over the fence with Buck Lumpkin. Buck's maple tree had grown over the fence and was dropping those little propeller seed pod things into Nico's lawn, so Nico cut down one of the branches, and Buck lost his mind. The two of them had been going at it for at least half an hour when the lights and sirens came down the street. Which means…"

"That Buck Lumpkin isn't the killer." I finished her sentence, now more confused than ever. "Has Nico talked to the police and told them that?"

Rick had been eliminated as a suspect, so if Buck wasn't the killer…who was?

"Nope. Nico doesn't trust law enforcement for some reason. He seems to me like the type that might have done drugs at some point, so maybe that's why." Agnes gave me a meaningful look over the brim of her teacup, and I had to exercise a great deal of willpower to refrain from rolling my eyes.

"Makes sense." I swallowed a piece of banana bread and got a hare-brained idea that I just had to follow up on. I'd go talk to Nico myself. Maybe he might've seen something else if he was out in the yard trimming his tree when the murder was taking place. I scarfed up the banana bread, downed my tea in a single gulp, thanked Agnes again, and headed for the door. There was work to be done, and of course, I didn't escape empty-handed. Agnes foisted an entire loaf of banana bread on me. Tang would love it.

* * *

The Karagiorgis family lived in a white Cape Cod with black shutters, and when I rang the doorbell, Nico answered. He looked like he was in his early forties and had a kind smile.

"Hi, are you Nico?" I asked, using my most professional smile.

"Yes, how can I help you?" His slight accent was delightful.

"I understand that you have a living room that's in dire need of a makeover." I made up the fib on the spot, and I didn't have a clue as to how I'd follow up on it.

"I'm sorry? I don't understand. Who are you?"

"My name is Sari Samson, and I do interior decorating for some of your neighbors. When I talked to Buck Lumpkin, he gave me a referral for you." I crossed my fingers behind my back, taking note that just the sound of Buck's name kindled a fierce fire in Nico's eyes.

"There must have been a mistake. I do not need your services." Nico moved to shut the door.

"I knew it!" I blurted, making a desperate attempt to keep him from closing the door on our conversation.

"What?" He hesitated.

"He sent me over here just to mess with you, didn't he?" I shook my head, acting appalled. "I'm so sorry to have bothered you. I suppose the story that he told me about a fight over the maple tree was a fib, too, huh?" I asked, then held my breath.

"No. That was real. Our beautiful neighbor lady was getting murdered, and we didn't see anything helpful to the police because I was bickering with that awful man."

"So, you knew Rosalie?"

"Not much. She helped my wife revive her rose bushes when they were dying. Nice lady. She didn't deserve to die, and if I hadn't been arguing with Buck Lumpkin, I would've suspected him right away. Something is not right with him."

"Yeah, it's too bad that nobody saw anything, like before the murder, that might be helpful." I put on my best mourning expression.

"Such a shame." Nico nodded. "I'm sorry I was so abrupt before. That man makes me, you know…" Nico moved his finger in a circle by his ear.

"Crazy? Yeah, he has that effect on people." I chuckled. "Have a nice day, Mr. Karagiorgis."

"You too, Ms. Samson." He shut the door, and I felt utterly deflated. He'd been telling the truth; I was certain of that. Rick hadn't done it, and now Buck hadn't done it. I was back at square one.

* * *

"This banana bread is the bomb," Tang said, his mouth full. "I know you didn't make it, and there's no way it's vegan. I can taste the butter, so your mom didn't make it either. Where did you get it?"

"Agnes Hackles."

He nearly choked and quickly took two huge gulps of piping-hot coffee.

"You gave me banana bread made by someone in that neighborhood? What if she's the killer?"

I stared at him.

"Agnes? Interesting. I never thought of that angle, but no. She has the capacity to be seriously annoying, but she's not a killer unless she complained someone to death. Besides, I had banana bread at her house, and I'm not dead." I shrugged.

"Well, she's not going to give you the poisoned stuff while you're there. She'd send it home with you so you'd die, and when the police found the banana bread, they wouldn't know where it came from. I should throw this down the disposal." Tang eyed the bread like it was a snake about to strike.

"Don't you dare. That poor old lady worked hard on that, and it's some of the best that I've ever tasted."

"Yet you're not eating it…"

"I had a piece at her house."

"Right. Didn't we just go over this?" Tang's eyebrows rose.

"Yes, and we concluded that you're being paranoid."

"I don't remember reaching that conclusion."

"You're a little slow, but you'll catch up." I shot him a mischievous grin, and he made pantomime choking motions in my direction.

"Seriously though, love. You're in that neighborhood more often than the people who live there."

"Oh, stop it, Tang. You're supposed to be my best friend, and now you're sounding more and more like my mother."

"Are we both wrong?" Tang put his hands on his hips and stared at me.

"So…Dustin is nice…" I smiled, trying to throw him off track.

"Girl, don't think I don't know what you're trying to do." He pursed his lips. "But it's working. Tell me everything." He plunked down on the couch and patted the cushion beside him.

Chapter Twenty-Seven

After telling Tang all about my impromptu date with Dustin, which garnered squeals of joy from my dramatic matchmaking friend, I drove home, the events of the day replaying in my mind. I was so distracted that I barely heard my phone ringing in my purse. I pulled over to the curb to answer it, not recognizing the number, and was practically rendered speechless when I heard Shannon Kelpie's voice on the line. Why on earth would Byron Bennett's ex-wife be calling me?

"I just had to make sure that you were okay."

"I'm fine…why do you ask?" I frowned, baffled.

"I just…Cliff Bennett has been way more agitated and angrier than usual, and… on the off chance that he might be the murderer, I just wanted to warn you to be careful, that's all."

My eyebrows rose, and my pulse accelerated. I suddenly felt very alone and vulnerable in my car, and I hit the door locks.

"Do you really think he could've done it?"

"He loved her so much that I think he may have done it so that she didn't have to put up with him and his nastiness anymore…if that makes sense?"

"Yeah, I've definitely seen that side of him."

My mind raced. Rick wasn't the killer. Buck wasn't the killer. Could Cliff Bennett be the killer? Had Tesia the Embezzler been right after all?

"Please don't tell anyone that I called you. I don't want that family to hate me. They're not people that anyone wants to have as an enemy."

Shannon Kelpie sounded genuinely afraid, and I had to wonder what prompted that comment. *They're not people that anyone wants to have as an enemy.* Could she sound more ominous? I shivered but hid it well.

"No worries, I won't tell a soul. Thanks for the warning."

Mom could tell the minute that I came in the door that something was off and demanded to know what it was. I was so tired of deceiving her about absolutely everything regarding the case that I told her about what I'd discovered about Rick and Buck and that Shannon had called me out of concern.

"Okay." Mom nodded, thinking. "What do we need to do?"

"Just be on the lookout for anything weird, and don't let Foo out of our sight, even when he's outside. Anyone who knows me knows that the one way to hurt me, outside of hurting my family or friends, is Foo-dog."

"You should probably call Charla and let her know, too, then."

I sighed. "She's still not talking to me just yet, but I'll leave a voicemail."

"Why isn't she talking to you?"

"Long story. She'll be fine, and we'll be fine. She just needs to pout for a while."

"Some people are pouters." Mom nodded sagely.

My head hitting the pillow at bedtime brought sweet relief. Nothing weird had happened, and I'd been able to just hang out with Mom and Dad, laughing and talking. It was everything that I'd hoped their visit would be, their hidden motives for coming notwithstanding, and I fell asleep immediately after.

My peaceful slumber was shattered by Foo's piercing, insistent, there's-something-wrong bark. That sound sent a tidal wave of adrenaline coursing through me. Foo only used it when there was an emergency that needed my attention. What happened next, however, made that adrenaline jolt seem like a walk in the park. I got Foo settled down and heard a light tap on my window. That wasn't rain; it wasn't a plant blowing in the wind, it was a tap. Someone was out there.

"I'm done being scared, and I'm done being a potential victim," I muttered.

Setting my distraught doggie down on the bed, I slid my feet into the nearest pair of flip-flops and hurried outside, grabbing a flashlight from the kitchen on the way.

"What's going on?" Dad appeared behind me like a ghost, startling the heck out of me.

"Someone tapped on my window. I'm going to go check it out." I whispered as though the killer would be eavesdropping outside the kitchen window.

"Not alone, you're not."

"What if Mom wakes up and you're missing? She'll freak out."

"Your mother has her ear plugs in and meditation mask on. There's no way she'll wake up."

Dad grabbed a second flashlight from my junk drawer and led the way out of the back sliding doors after popping on the porch light, which would hopefully scare away anyone with ill intent. There was a rustle in the bushes at the far side of the yard and Dad and I exchanged a glance.

"Probably a rabbit," he said softly.

I knew better and kept an eye on the bushes, even as we crept toward my window, where Foo, from the inside, was causing a cacophony to beat the band. I looked at my window and gasped.

"What the…" My father's jaw went slack.

Written on the window, in mud, was a single word.

NEXT

As I tried to process the moment, my gaze dropped to a spot beneath the window.

"Dad, look! Footprints!" I pointed to a large footprint that was directly below the word NEXT. I hadn't heard just a tap; I'd heard a killer sending me a message that was pretty darn clear.

"Sarisara, you're going to call the police, and you will not argue with me about that." Dad's voice was hoarse, but his vehemence was undeniable.

Dad and I hustled back into the house and locked the doors and windows, then he went in to wake Mom and let her know what had happened, while I made the dreaded call to Detective Griff.

Griff appeared at my door, looking as fresh as a daisy. It was the middle of the night for goodness sake. "You look like you always do," I said. "Don't you sleep?"

"I was still at the office. Crime isn't nine-to-five," he remarked dryly.

"I'm sorry. Please, come in."

My relationship with the detective was much more cordial since I'd started to cooperate with him. Funny how that works.

I told him what had happened, from the time that Foo woke me up until the time that I'd called him, and he listened intently, taking it all in. My dad stayed with us, still in his pajamas and zoris. I was thankful that at least while they were visiting me, they used pajamas. Mom chose to get dressed, but she came out to join us as well, Foo under one arm, Safira under the other.

Griff looked down at Dad's feet. I doubt that he'd ever seen a man in zoris before.

"Mr. Samson, I'm going to need to see all of your shoes and slippers, please."

"What? Why?" Mom frowned at the detective.

"Because when I make a cast of the footprint, I'm going to need to make sure that it wasn't made days ago, by someone who has every right to be in the back yard."

"Seems like a waste of time, but fine." Dad shrugged and went to gather his shoes. When he came back, dumping them in a pile on the floor, Griff had more questions.

"Mr. and Mrs. Samson, what were you doing when this incident took place?"

"It's the middle of the night, Detective. We were sleeping." Mom gave him a look.

"So, you weren't able to witness what was happening until the dog's bark woke you up, is that correct?"

"Obviously." Mom's brows rose. I wondered briefly if the detective had picked up on the fact that my mom was not someone who would be trifled with. I had to intervene, before her temper landed us all in jail.

"Maybe it was Agnes Hackles!" I blurted out the first name that came to mind.

"Excuse me?" Griff stared at me.

"I mean, she may have been jealous. Rosalie had everything that Agnes wanted. A loving husband and family, looks, money. She belonged to the society set. It's possible." I shrugged, making it up as I went along.

"Then why would you be next?" Griff asked. "She likes you for some reason."

I gasped, and my face went white. In the midst of my desperate manufactured suggestion, I started to wonder. Wonder turned to terror in a heartbeat. The banana bread! I texted Tang immediately, and when he didn't answer right away, I called.

The phone rang once. Twice. Three times.

"Hello?" I heard Tang's very groggy voice on the other end of the line and nearly fainted with relief.

"Tang, are you feeling okay?"

"You seriously called me in the middle of the night to ask if I'm okay? You are losing it, girl."

"Fine. I'm losing it. But…are you okay?"

"I'm fine, and I'm going back to sleep. And you owe me more ice cream. You're lucky I love you. Good night, my sweet weirdo friend."

"Oh, I'm the weirdo now?" I laughed with sheer relief and heard a click as Tang hung up and went back to sleep.

"Is there something you'd like to tell me?" Griff asked when I hung up the phone.

I bit my lip, trying to decide just how much to share, then finally caved and told him about the phone call from Shannon Kelpie. I really didn't want to point fingers at an elderly widower if he wasn't indeed the guilty party, but it was looking more and more like he might be.

"And how is it that Byron Bennett's ex-wife knew who you were and had your phone number?" Griff was riled again.

"I talked to her when I was first investigating the murder," I said in a small voice.

"Investigating. Okay, Nancy Drew. Is this enough? Is the threat of murder enough to make you mind your own business and leave this alone?"

"There's no need to be snitty." Mom's eyes flashed as she confronted the detective. "If someone was threatening your life, wouldn't you be the least bit curious about who was doing it and why?" She stepped closer, hands on hips.

"Yes, I would be. And I would trust the trained professionals with years of experience to find some answers for me."

Griff's phone buzzed, and he looked at it. "The evidence techs are here. They'll be here for about an hour or less. After they leave, I want you to make sure all of your windows and doors are locked and stay put. Whoever is doing this is escalating, so you need to be certain that you don't make yourself vulnerable. When the dog needs to go out, at least two of you should take him."

"Wow. Okay." I nodded, my mind racing. I felt numb and queasy. I needed sleep, but I knew that wasn't in the cards for me without pharmaceuticals, and I wasn't about to do that.

Mom waited until Griff closed the front door behind him before she spoke her mind.

"Is it evident to you yet that you need to come home to California, where you'll be safe?"

Seriously?

"I love you guys. Try to get some sleep," I said.

Picking up Foo, I went down the hall. I couldn't sleep, but I could read. No true crime for me tonight. I disappeared into the magical world of Hallmark until the first rays of the sun shone through my window. My eyes were grainy, my throat was parched, and I had a headache that would kill a horse, but I was still alive, and nothing weird had happened after the techs left. So there's that.

Despite Griff's stark warning, I was more determined than ever to get to the bottom of things.

Now, it was personal.

Chapter Twenty-Eight

I took a nap after breakfast, sleeping soundly with Mom and Dad on guard, and woke up four hours later, groggy, but feeling much better. Not quite ready to face the real world yet, I sat up in bed and decided to play on social media for a bit. I hadn't scrolled for very long when I saw pictures of Charla celebrating the basketball team's win...with another friend. From what I'd heard, that game had been epic, and she'd taken someone else. All because she'd seen me having coffee with a detective that I have no romantic interest in whatsoever. I immediately sent a text.

"I see I've been replaced as your basketball date."

I figured that I wouldn't hear back for a few days, but she surprised me by answering right away.

"I see you've decided to get together with the guy that you hated."

I rolled my eyes so hard that I think I saw my brain.

"Oh puhleeze...totally not my type. Ew. Strictly business, but I put in the good word for you."

"... Fine. See you at Esquire at 12:30 for lunch tomorrow."

"Make it 11:30, so they don't sell out of meatball subs."

"You are so pushing it with me..."

"You love me anyway." I giggled when I sent that one.

"Lucky for you."

"See you then."

Once Charla and I had lunch, all would be right in our world. It felt so wonderfully...normal to sit across from her and watch her pick through a plateful of plants.

"You have the craziest life of anyone I know, right now, and that's saying a lot." Charla poked at her salad while I wolfed down my meatball sub. "So, you think Captain Lantern Jaw is going to catch the guy?"

I shrugged. "Hope so. It's looking more and more like the husband did it."

"Well, he does have anger issues." She sipped at her club soda with lime. "And are you sure you're not interested in Markie-poo?"

I shuddered. "Not in the slightest. Not in any possible way. Not a chance in this lifetime."

"Geez...tell me how you really feel." Charla laughed at my vehement reply.

"But...I did meet someone who unexpectedly made my little grinchy heart go pitter-patter." I grinned, keeping her in suspense. She nearly dropped her fork, and her eyes went so wide I thought she might get mascara in her bangs.

"Whaaaaat? And it took you this long to tell me?" She threw a cherry tomato at me, and I caught it, popping it into my mouth with glee. "You'd better spill it, sister."

"Well, I'll just point out that someone wasn't responding to my texts." I blinked at her.

"I've been busy." She gave a faux-haughty sniff. "Besides, you deserved it. Having coffee with the man that I haven't yet conquered."

"Ugh." I grimaced. "I can't even think of him in those terms. Gross."

"You, my dear, have a problem with authority. Now spill it, before I stab you with my fork."

"I think your nails are probably more lethal, but fine. His name is Dustin..."

Just then, my phone dinged with a new text. I looked at the screen, grinned, and blushed at the same time.

"Oh my, it's him, isn't it? It's been far too long since I've seen you gaga over a guy. You answer him right this minute! What's he saying?" Charla put down her fork.

"He wants to take me to dinner and an art show." If I smiled any bigger, my face would hurt.

"Tell him yes!"

"I will, hold on. Geez." I laughed and texted him back, then waited for a response before putting my phone back on the table. "Okay, we're all set. We're going out on Saturday night."

"Wow, you didn't even play hard to get." Charla gave me a wicked grin.

"You told me to tell him yes." I threw a French fry at her, and she dodged it, making a face. "Besides, I don't play those kinds of games."

"I know, silly. I was messing with you. You *will* tell me all about it afterward."

"Yeah, and now that I've cast aside the dastardly detective, you can go out with him."

"Nah, actually, I met a guy at the basketball game the other night, and I'm going to see where that goes...for a while anyway."

"Please tell me he has good season tickets," I breathed.

"Courtside, baby!"

We high-fived across the table.

"Oh, holy moly, you need to keep him at least for the rest of basketball season."

"I'll try my best. I haven't given him a test drive yet, but he's taking me out on Saturday, so we'll see." She waggled her eyebrows.

"Does that mean I can have your season tickets?"

"If I'm sitting courtside, yes, you'll be more than welcome to my sixth-row tickets, and you can bring your new little friend. What's he do anyway?"

"He's an artist."

Charla's brows rose.

"Oh, so he's unemployed."

"Are you, like, actually sharing a brain with my mother?" I shook my head.

"He must be hot. Is he hot?"

I nodded, a dreamy grin on my face. "Totally hot."

"Nice. So, no long-term potential, but good short-term material. Artists are interesting and fun, and then you move on."

"Are you always this calculating?" I asked.

"How long have you known me?" She picked up her fork again and gave me a look.

"You're right, dumb question." I laughed. "Oh hey, before I forget...do you know Shannon Kelpie?"

"Remind me who she is again?" Charla frowned.

"Byron Bennett's ex-wife."

"Oh, yeah. I mean, I don't *know* her, but she seems nice enough. The divorce was pretty ugly, from what I heard. She took him to the cleaners, but the lawyer's fees were so high that they both ended up with nothing. Why?"

"She called to warn me about Cliff Bennett's anger problem. She thinks he killed his wife."

"She may be right." Charla shrugged, nibbling at a cucumber slice. "Oh, hey, does Cliff have a realtor yet?"

"I don't think so. You should stop by and tell them I sent you, but talk to Byron if you can. He's way nicer than Cliff."

"I will. So, where is Cliff moving to?"

"A condo in Florida, apparently, but last I heard, they hadn't even looked for one yet."

Charla cocked her head and frowned. "That's strange."

"What?"

"Most of the senior living communities down there have waiting lists. It's really odd that he's getting ready to sell his house, but he doesn't have another home to go to yet, don't you think?"

I hadn't even thought about that.

"Well, he doesn't seem too keen about the idea of moving."

"He still needs someplace to go. It's not like he can share his son's studio apartment."

"Byron has a studio apartment?" What on earth was the son of a very wealthy man doing living in a studio apartment?

"Yep, and it's not even a very nice one. I don't think he was Daddy's favorite."

"From what I understand, he was his mother's favorite. And I have no idea whether or not their other son, Broderick, ever even came to town."

"I'm so glad my life is mostly business. Who needs the drama?" Charla shook her head and pushed her plate away. "Wow, girl, you ate that whole thing." She looked pointedly at my empty plate.

"It was delicious."

"So is salad. I've gotta run. I may have time to swing by the Bennett house on my way to my next appointment." Charla glanced at her watch, panicking. "Can you...?" She gave me a desperate look.

"No worries, I've got this." I shooed her away, fully accustomed to her having to dash out in the middle of a conversation.

"You're a peach." She kissed the top of my head on her way by, her perfume wafting along behind her.

"Remember that when you're giving your season tickets away!" I called after her.

She waved without turning around.

Chapter Twenty-Nine

It was so cute and flattering, Dustin was already seated when I got to the sushi place, but he stood and pulled out my chair for me. It made me sort of glow, which, I have to admit, wasn't a bad way to start our evening. The food was amazing, and Dustin kept me entertained with stories of a backpacking trip through Europe and a roommate in London who had a bad habit of stealing his socks.

I tried to insist upon paying half of the dinner bill, because that's standard policy for me on first dates—it levels the playing field—but he absolutely refused and paid the check when I was in the bathroom. I pretended to be a bit pouty, but truthfully, it made me all warm and fuzzy inside. How was it that this guy, whom I'd just recently met, had the ability to make me feel so special?

"We can just take my car to the show, if you'd like, and leave your car here," Dustin suggested.

"Great idea. No sense in both of us driving when we're going to the same place."

That would work perfectly, because I'd had two glasses of wine during dinner and shouldn't drive anyway. Charla calls me a lightweight, and it's absolutely true.

As fate would have it, the art show that he took me to was an invitation-only event...at Sally Edgerton's house, and Dustin was the featured artist.

Sally gasped when she opened the door and saw us there together. Clapping her hands and reaching out to hug each of us, she began gushing before we even got into the house.

"I didn't know the two of you knew each other, but oh my goodness, it makes so much sense. You're both so talented and creative and just dear, dear people," she chattered on, leading us inside. "Matt, darling, look who showed up here *together*." She waggled her eyebrows in a manner that made Dustin smile and made me want to disappear into the wide-plank floor.

Dustin's talent was astonishing, and I wandered around Sally's stylish home with my mouth hanging open half the time. Dustin had been immediately swarmed by fans shortly after we entered, so I had plenty of time alone to check out his work. Did I say astonishing? The man is an artistic genius. I wanted to buy one of his paintings—an abstract seascape—but he told me that it had already sold. I looked at the prices and counted my lucky stars. Though I loved the painting, it would've put quite a balance on my credit card, and that's generally not how I roll.

Just before we left, with Sally proudly taking the lead, I showed Dustin her newly renovated guest room, and he was kind enough to act very impressed.

"Wow, I never imagined that pink could be used so perfectly. It's tasteful, inviting, warm," he said, smiling that smile that makes me warm from head to toe.

"Right?" Sally agreed enthusiastically. "Sari made magic happen, and we both just love this room now."

"I'm glad I could help," I told Sally, who then proceeded to drag us down to the kitchen. This time, as we were leaving, instead of cookies, she foisted two bottles of wine and a gift basket filled with all sorts of exotic goodies.

"You know what this means," Dustin said, holding up the basket when we left the house.

"Movie night?" I boldly suggested.

"Amazing. She's beautiful and can read minds, too."

He opened the car door for me, and I was thankful that he couldn't see the depth of my blush in the dark.

When we pulled into the restaurant parking lot to get my car, it was such a letdown. I'd had so much fun that I didn't want the night to end. Sally had been a delightful hostess, of course, and I think, the way things looked when we left, that Dustin might just sell his entire collection by the time all was said and done.

"I had a great time..." I smiled shyly when he killed the engine and turned to look at me.

"Oh no!" Dustin's eyes went wide as he glanced over my shoulder.

"What?"

"Your car." He pointed at the window beside me.

"You've got to be kidding me." A slow fury burned in the pit of my stomach when I turned around and saw, under the dim light of the parking lamps, that someone had slashed my tires.

Dustin got a flashlight out of his glove box and hurried around the car to open my door. I glanced around to make sure I didn't see someone lurking in the shadows as we went to check the damage.

"That's weird." He frowned, crouched down, inspecting the tires.

"What?"

"It looks like whoever slit your tires used a fish knife. There are scales in the cuts. Look." He trained the flashlight along one of the gashes in my right rear tire. The fish scales shimmered in the beam. Mocking me. I took pictures of it on my phone and had an inner debate about whether or not to tell Detective Griff about the whole incident.

"Let's call a tow truck to take it to a tire shop, and I'll drive you home." Dustin's voice was warm with compassion, and I was shocked when tears suddenly welled in my eyes.

Not trusting myself to speak, I didn't dare look at him. I merely nodded, wrapping my arms around my midsection. He opened the passenger door of his car, and after I notified my insurance company that I needed a tow truck, we sat for a while, in silence, waiting.

"Oh, shoot." I closed my eyes and sighed.

"What?" Dustin asked, apparently startled from his thoughts by my exclamation.

"I need to get my work bags out of the car. I have to have those with me."

"No worries. Just tell me what all you need, and I'll put them in the back seat for you."

"You are the best date ever." I sighed. "I'm really sorry about all of this."

"Don't be sorry, it's not your fault. I'm kind of worried about you, if you want to know the truth. And by the way, I'm not the best date ever. You are."

He flashed his amazing smile, making butterflies flutter madly in my stomach, and I told him what to grab from my car. This guy. I didn't even want to think about how much I was beginning to like him. I'm the one who's avoiding relationships.

Once the tow truck driver hitched up my little car and drove it away after swiping my credit card and making me sign on the dotted line, of course, we buckled up and followed him out of the parking lot.

On the ride home, Dustin and I talked about the pieces that I had liked best from his collection and why. It was so great talking to someone who actually spoke my language when it came to color and style and mood. I have that with Tang, too, of course, that's probably a huge part of why they're friends, but I don't swoon when Tang grins at me. We chatted about how we both love Sally's sense of humor, and I just felt warm and safe, despite the mess that I was dealing with.

"Well, this is me," I said when he pulled up in front of my condo. "Thank you for taking me home. What a night."

"You're so welcome. It was a great night. I'm sorry about your tires, though."

"Yeah." I sighed. "I'd totally invite you in, but my mom and dad are visiting, and I'm just not prepared for the inquisition that you'd receive."

"I hear ya. I'm turning in early anyway. There's always next time."

That look in his eyes. Oh, my goodness. Does he practice oozing warmth with those magical eyes?

"I mean, that is…if you want to go out again," he added.

"I'd love to." I replied, my heart quickening.

He glanced in the back seat. "Do you want me to help you with your bags?"

"Nah. I'm used to toting them around like a pack mule." I laughed.

"Well, at least let me get the door for you."

He got out and trotted around to my side of the door to open it for me, then reached into the back seat and handed me my bags.

"You're a delightful person, Sari. I'm so glad we met." He gave me a hug, bags and all, then brushed his lips across my forehead before getting back in the car.

"Me too."

It was utterly mystifying how a kind gesture that was just barely a kiss sent my pulse skyward. I walked, dazed, to the front door and opened it with my key.

"Sari?" Mom frowned from her spot on the couch. "Why did you use the front door?"

And here we go.

"When Dustin and I got back to the restaurant to pick up my car after the art show, the tires were slashed. And get this, it was obviously done by the same person who sent the fish heads."

"Now, how could you possibly know that?" Mom asked as Dad perked up and set his book aside.

There was something about the way that they shared a look that made me wonder if I'd interrupted something or if they had some sort of secret. Maybe I was just being paranoid because everything was a bit weird in my life.

"Look." I tapped my phone, pulled up the pictures of the fish scales in the tire cut, and handed it to Mom. She looked, then gave the phone to Dad, who nodded.

"Yep, looks like you're right about that," he agreed, handing me the phone. "Have you called the detective yet?"

"No, and I don't plan to. It seems like something is up with you guys... Is anything wrong?"

They exchanged another glance. Foo came trotting out from the kitchen and I scooped him up, hugging his little body and kissing his head.

"Your mom is a bit worried about Safira..." Dad began, an odd look on his face.

"Oh no! Did she and Foo get in a fight or something?" I gave Foo a preemptive warning look.

"Sarisara! Those two lovely creatures would not create that kind of disturbance in the group dynamic. Safira is probably just out exploring."

CHAPTER TWENTY-NINE

Mom scolded, casting a loving glance in Foo's direction.

"Did you look under beds and stuff?" I clutched Foo to my chest, realizing the potential implications of the missing cat and growing alarmed.

The fiendish person who sent fish heads and slashed tires probably wouldn't be above catnapping...or worse. Mom and Dad didn't seem overly concerned, so I just kept that dark little thought to myself.

"Of course we did. I'm sure she's fine, and she'll come back in her own time." Mom sounded like she was trying to convince herself as much as us. "But you really need to call the detective about your tires."

"I'm tired. I had a good night, and I'm going to have to organize a search party for a cat tomorrow. The last thing I need is a cranky detective looking at me suspiciously. I'm going to bed, and we can regroup in the morning." I kissed Mom's cheek and got a hug from Dad.

Foo rested his furry head on my shoulder as we walked down the hall, and I inhaled deeply, enjoying the fresh, clean scent of his fur. Foo, and bed. That's all I needed. I'd deal with the rest of the drama and issues tomorrow.

* * *

"Sari, honey, I'm out of kale." That was Mom's greeting when I emerged from my room in dire need of coffee after a decent night's sleep.

"Good morning to you, too. You eat kale for breakfast?" I blinked at her, still groggy.

"No, I blend it into our smoothie. You should try it. The fiber is out of this world. Seriously, it'll change your life."

"I like my life, thanks. Do you want me to go get you some kale?" I offered, hoping to be spared a first thing in the morning lecture on my regularity and how I should improve it. I love that she cares, but I'm not capable of participating in that conversation before coffee. Or maybe ever.

"That would be lovely, Honeybear. I'll make you some coffee while you're gone."

I nodded. "Sounds like a deal. I'll need to borrow your rental car, though, since mine is at the tire place."

"I think your dad put the keys on the table in the foyer."

"Cool. See you in a few."

I put my unruly hair into a messier-than-usual bun, slipped into yoga pants and a ratty t-shirt, donned my drugstore rubber flip-flops, and out the door I went. I hoped against hope that it was early enough in the morning that I wouldn't run into anyone I knew.

I was standing in the organic foods section, contemplating the kale, when I heard a rough voice just over my left shoulder.

"You're the decorator." Cliff Bennett made it sound like an accusation.

I turned, startled. The poor man looked like he was knocking on death's door. His movements were slow and labored, and his skin was a strange greyish-yellow color. I nodded. "Yes, Sari."

"Don't apologize. At least you have a job."

"Doing your grocery shopping?" I glanced at his empty cart, wondering if I was standing face-to-face with Rosalie's murderer.

"Byron usually does all the cooking, but I wanted to make something for myself, so I came to the store before he got up. Figured I wouldn't see anybody I knew that way."

"Yeah, me too." I reached up self-consciously and tried to pat down my wayward tresses.

So, Cliff was trying to lay low. Interesting. He coughed into his sleeve, and it took him a few seconds to recover, as he stood in the produce section, a shaky hand over his eyes.

"Mr. Bennett, are you okay?"

My life had been weird lately, and I definitely did not want to deal with a potential murderer keeling over in the organic foods. To my surprise, he shook his head, and tears welled in his eyes.

"I haven't been okay since I lost my Rosalie. I was in my den sleeping when she was murdered. Byron had to shake me awake to tell me what was happening. I should have been with her. I should have been awake. I could have stopped it...somehow. She was my world. My love. And now she's just...gone."

Cliff took in a long shuddering breath, and I couldn't determine whether he was the best actor ever, or if he really was mourning. He looked so lost. Had he killed her and regretted it?

"Don't be so hard on yourself, Mr. Bennett. Byron was there, and he was awake, but he didn't see the murderer either."

"He wasn't there. He didn't arrive until after the police did."

I stared at the elderly man, whose memory was obviously out of whack. I could've sworn that I'd seen both him and Byron come out of the house to greet the ambulance and police. And, if Byron hadn't been there yet...who called the police? And why?

"Are you sure about that?" I couldn't help myself.

"I'm not sure about anything anymore. It's all a blur. Everything has been a blur since my Rosie died. I can't remember anything, can't seem to stay awake for more than a few hours at a time, can't eat. Byron was tired of me complaining about the food, so I figured I'd make my own breakfast today. Now that I'm here at the store, I can't remember what I wanted to get." His shoulders drooped. Cliff Bennett was a sickly shell of his former self. A tickle of fear formed in the pit of my stomach.

"Have you talked to a doctor about how you've been feeling?" I asked.

"Why would I? I'm just old, and I know it. Don't need some hack to charge me a bundle just to tell me what I already know. And there's only one cure for old age." His eyes were haunted. He was a man who saw the handwriting on the wall. Did he want to die so that he could escape the guilt of killing his wife? There's no way that he could have slept through all of those lights and sirens. He wasn't sleeping...he was a killer. And maybe he was smart enough to know that he shouldn't look like a man who was capable of murder. Was his conscience really killing him, or was he just playing victim to throw off the police? I wasn't about to take the chance of him even guessing at the direction of my thoughts, and since everything I feel tends to show on my face, I had to get out of there, and fast.

"Well, I've gotta run." I smiled as best I could and grabbed a random bunch of kale. "My mother is waiting for me. I'll stop by your house tomorrow to see the finished design. I have a gift for you."

"Gift?" He made a face. "Not necessary."

He turned away and shuffled off before I could form a response. Yeah, buddy, I'm not too thrilled with the idea of giving a thoughtful gift to a murderer, either.

Entirely spooked, I headed for the checkout line. When I got home and pulled into the driveway, I thought I saw the bushes by my front porch rustling a bit. There was no breeze, so I found that more than curious, and an ominous feeling of dread gave me shivers. I grabbed the bag of kale and got out of the car, moving cautiously toward the bushes. They rustled again, and I almost screamed.

The closer I got to those bushes, the more quickly my fear evolved into anger. Someone had been tormenting me, and it wasn't fair. I was done ducking from shadows, and I was done dealing with chasing killers. Whoever was in those bushes was going to get a piece of my mind. It was broad daylight, after all. What could go wrong?

I set my purse and the kale down on the top step and crept closer, fully prepared to do battle. Closer. Closer still. The bushes rustled again, and I saw that the source had to be down low. It was the lower branches that were moving. Was there seriously someone lying under my bushes?

"Come out of there!" I used my most authoritative voice. I heard a faint sound in response but couldn't identify it. As long as it wasn't the sound of a gun being cocked, or a knife being unsheathed, I would probably be fine out there in broad daylight, so I stepped closer and darted behind the bushes.

"Ha!" I yelled, holding my hands out to the sides, my fingers bent like claws to appear bigger…and scared the daylights out of poor Safira, who gave me a pouty look and mewed softly.

I dropped to my knees, hoping that the poor girl wasn't hurt.

"Oh, thank goodness," I gasped, my heart thundering. "So, this is where you disappeared to. You okay, pretty kitty?"

I crept closer and saw more movement under the bush. Safira stood and stretched, revealing three naked little kittens, their eyes still closed. I yelped with delight.

"Safira! You're a mommy."

Motherhood must've suited her, because she rubbed her head against my knee and purred when I stroked the wrinkled spot between her ears.

"Mom is going to be over the moon. Do you want to come in with me, or should I bring her out here?" I asked.

I figured if she understood whenever Mom spoke to her, she'd probably understand me, too. Safira butted her head against my knee one last time, then went back to her precious babies.

"Okay, sweetie. You stay there for now, and I'll bring Mom out to you."

As always, even on the weirdest of days, there were moments of joy to appreciate. Cliff Bennett, a likely killer, looked as though he was near death. Safira, my mom's beloved kitty, had just brought new life into the world. Balance.

Chapter Thirty

There's just something about the feel of driving on new tires. The ride is smoother, and you feel somehow more secure knowing that you once again have traction and dependability. I had to keep thinking those positive thoughts to keep my mind from the pain of spending $500 for tires to replace a set that had only been used for one year. I was trying to take my cues from Mom, who always advised me to roll with the flow of nature and events.

My gift for the Bennetts, a hand-sculpted ceramic apple pie filled with apple cinnamon potpourri, sat in its gift bag on the seat beside me. I'd been vague when Mom and Dad asked me where I was going, and since they were so enraptured with Safira's kittens, they'd accepted my non-answer response. Detective Griff's response to the fish-scaled slashes in my tires had been lukewarm at best, and I figured that they thought if he wasn't worried, maybe we didn't have to be. I had my own ideas about that.

My plan was to drop the gift off at the Bennetts, do my final walk-through to make certain that the design had been fully executed—no pun intended—and then leave, washing my hands of the Bennetts and Rosalie's murder case forever. Mom, Charla, and Tang were right. Things had gotten too dangerous, and though I'm loathe to admit when I've been bested, I finally recognized that I was in over my head.

A fish head delivery was bad, NEXT written in mud on my window was worse, and slashed tires were the last straw. The situation had escalated out of control, and I didn't want anything to do with it. It would be quite nice to just go back to being Sari-not-sorry, decorator extraordinaire, who might even settle down enough to think about having a cute, artsy boyfriend. When I arrived at the Bennetts, I checked my look in the rearview mirror, took a deep breath, and strode with confidence to the door.

"Hi, Byron. I'm here to do my final walk-through, and this is for you and your dad." I handed him the gift bag and noticed his pale, drawn look. He was fidgeting and seemed somehow off. Poor guy—he'd just lost his mother, and you didn't have to be a doctor to see the handwriting on the wall as far as his dad's health.

"Is everything okay? Should I come back at a better time?" I asked, hoping that he didn't say yes. I was more than ready to be done with the Bennetts once and for all. My plan was to get in, inspect, and get out.

"No, please, come in. Thank you for the gift. You didn't have to do that." He tried to smile, but it withered before it reached his eyes.

"I always bring a special gift for my clients. It's a privilege to partner with someone in working on their home." Somehow, I managed to make my pat response sound authentic.

"That's very sweet. Look, Sari...I'm sorry if I seem out of sorts. My dad went into the hospital last night and..." He swallowed hard, blinking fast. "...and they don't know if he'll..." Byron pressed his lips together and shook his head, tears welling in his eyes.

"Oh, Byron, I'm so sorry. I had no idea. I saw him in the grocery store, and he really didn't look well." I bit my lip, uncertain as to what I should do.

Byron raised his head, looking confused. He wiped his eyes with the back of his hand.

"The grocery store? Are you sure that it was him?"

"Yes, he spoke to me when I was looking for kale. Said he wanted to make himself something to eat. I think he felt guilty about you having to do all of the cooking."

"Did he say anything else?" Byron raised a brow.

"Just that he missed your mom."

Byron nodded, his lower lip trembling.

"I'm so sorry. I can't imagine how you're holding up. Both of your parents in such a short time. Are you sure that you want me to do the walk-through right now?"

Lips tightly compressed, he nodded. "I want everything to do with this house to be done as soon as possible." His voice quavered.

"I understand. I'll be as quick as I can. I'll check everything and go. You don't even need to accompany me. Why don't you go rest, or maybe get some air? I'd be happy to lock up on my way out."

I was more than willing to work alone. Being a decorator isn't supposed to be a job that makes one cry on a regular basis. Or call the police, for that matter. Stick a fork in me; I am done with that nonsense.

"Thank you, Sari. I will. It's been a pleasure working with you on making the house presentable. Thank you for your effort and for putting up with all the drama."

"It's been no trouble at all." I had no issue with fibbing to a grieving son. His emotions should be respected, even if his father is a stone-cold killer. Maybe especially so.

Byron let me in, then turned and strode to the back door and out onto the patio by the pool. I moved through the living room. Everything was in place and looked stunning, so I went to the kitchen, which also checked out. I breezed through the rest of the common area rooms, checking them off of my list, then headed down the hall toward the bedrooms and bathrooms. Two guest rooms and two guest baths, check. Hobby room, check.

When I entered the home office, I saw something that nearly made my heart stop. Sitting on the desk, just beneath the edge of the multi-line telephone, was a thumb drive. My hot pink and neon green thumb drive. My heart pounded so heavily in my chest that I swore I could hear it, and my stomach rolled. How I moved one foot in front of the other to retrieve the thumb drive, I have no idea, but reach it I did. I told myself before I picked it up that surely it must just be a lookalike. It could be the same style and colors without being mine, but I turned it over and saw my initials. I shuddered, swallowing the bile that tried to creep up the back of my throat.

Cliff Bennett was a murderer, there was no doubt in my mind now. Being a sick old man was the perfect cover if you think about it. No one would suspect him. He'd stolen the thumb drive and had no doubt made all of the arrangements for the rest of the scare tactics. It was probably pretty easy for him to pay people to make those things happen. Pocket change for a guy like him. I slipped the thumb drive into my purse and kept going, feeling like a zombie, moving along on autopilot, while my mind whirled with fear and disbelief. If I could just maintain my composure and act as though nothing was out of the ordinary, I could do what I needed to do and then get the heck out, with no one the wiser.

I entered the master bedroom as though it was a death chamber, because in a certain sense, it probably was. My skin crawled, and the hair on the back of my neck rose in a primitive self-preservation response. I so badly wanted to run screaming from the house, but something pushed me forward—something more than just the sheer determination to see the job through to the very end. I think, in the deep, dark corners of my psyche, I knew that there was more to find...and that I was about to find it.

Master bedroom, check. Master closet, check. I entered Rosalie's dressing room. It was connected to the bedroom by a short hall and contained another closet, display cases for her jewelry, and a long marble vanity with a lighted mirror above it. One of the drawers was slightly ajar, and I couldn't help myself. The semi-open drawer was practically beckoning me to come open it and explore.

I knew full well that Byron could walk in at any minute. The thick, plush, wall-to-wall carpet that I'd selected would muffle his footsteps to a degree that I wouldn't even know if he was standing right behind me. As soon as that thought crossed my mind, I slowly turned, half-expecting to see Cliff wielding a knife or something. No one was there. I rubbed the goosebumps that had risen on my upper arms, and moved swiftly to the drawer that drew me like a moth to a flame.

There was something sticking out of it. Something that caused alarm bells to ring in my mind, though I couldn't quite figure out why just yet. The doorbell rang, taking several years from my life, and I knew that if I was going to snoop, I had to do it quickly. I yanked the drawer open and gasped. There was a light-colored man's wig, and a matching fake mustache in the drawer.

The basketball boy in the Lakers tank top had said that the man who paid him to deliver the box with fish heads in it had light hair and a bushy mustache. Cliff Bennett wouldn't have needed a light-colored wig and mustache, because he had them naturally. Someone had used these to frame him, but who?

I swayed on my feet as the realization dawned on me.

Byron.

He had access to the fish heads, and he could've gotten the florist's box out of the van when sympathy flowers were delivered.

I had to get out of the house as fast as my shaking legs would take me. And worse…I had to play it cool so that Byron would have no idea that I suspected anything. Easier said than done.

I shoved the drawer shut, wincing when it made a dull thud, and hurried out of the room, nearly colliding with Shannon Kelpie in the hallway.

"Oh!" I yelped, stumbling backward into the master bedroom.

"Fancy meeting you here." Shannon's smile was dark, sinister…predatory.

At this point, it wouldn't have surprised me at all if she suddenly sprouted fangs, but what on earth was she doing here, in her ex-father-in-law's house?

"Shannon!" I squawked, sounding like a pubescent teen. I cleared my throat and tried again, clutched my clipboard to keep my hands from shaking. "Nice to see you. You must be so worried about Cliff."

I didn't bother to even attempt a smile; I just pulled my face into an expression of sympathy so patently fake that I felt like one of those clowns who looks pathetic when their makeup starts to run.

"Nice try, Sari." Byron spoke from behind Shannon, and they both slowly advanced toward me. I wanted to stand my ground, I really did, but the looks on their faces promised trouble, so I backpedaled.

Now, I was trapped. There was no way to get out of the master bedroom, aside from the door that they now blocked. Sweet, mild-mannered, doting-on-his-mother-until-he-killed-her Byron was smirking in a manner that terrified me, and Shannon's grin was savage. Apparently, she'd been in on Byron's evildoing.

Byron opened his mouth to speak, and everyone in the room jumped when a loud booming thundered at the front door.

"Help me!" I screeched at the top of my lungs. "Master bedroom! Please help!!"

There was a loud crash and the sound of splintering wood as the door frame gave way to the police battering ram. Stunned, I froze in place, and Shannon dove at me, screaming like a banshee. Her teeth were bared, and in the split second of terror before impact, I absently hoped she didn't have sharp nails.

"You should have minded your own business." She tackled me to the ground and yelled in my face, spittle flying from her lips. Her knees held my arms down, and her hands went to my throat. Just as her grip tightened and my vision swam with black flecks, a uniformed police officer took Byron down, and none other than Detective Marcus Griff himself roughly dragged Shannon off of me. I scrabbled backward, away from Shannon, as Griff quickly subdued her. My hands went to my throat, and I coughed, a searing pain ripping through my windpipe as I sucked in life-giving air.

"You alright, ma'am?" Another uniformed officer hurried over to check on me.

I couldn't speak but I nodded, my horrified gaze firmly fixed on what was happening in front of me. Byron and Shannon were taken into custody, both of them shouting vile things as they went. The officer helped me stand up, and when he saw how shaky my legs were, he seated me in a chair near that closet, then disappeared for a moment. When he came back with a bottle of water, the cool liquid felt amazing on my raw and abused throat. The officer stayed with me until Griff appeared a few minutes later.

"You okay, Sari?" he asked. For once, his tone was neither hostile nor aggressive. He'd never called me by name before, either. Oddly, I liked the sound of it when he said it.

"I'm fine," I whispered, glad that I could at least speak quietly. "I've heard huge dumps of adrenaline are good for the skin."

Griff stared at me for a moment before speaking. I think trying to assess whether or not I'd lost my grip on reality. He apparently decided to give me the benefit of the doubt.

"Byron and Shannon were arrested for murder, conspiracy, attempted murder, and a whole host of other charges related to this case, but you probably already guessed that."

I nodded and pointed toward the dressing room, trembling as I realized how close to death I'd come.

"The wig and mustache that he used when he gave the fish heads to the kid in my neighborhood are in a drawer in the vanity." I couldn't speak very well, but Griff had obviously heard enough to send someone in.

"Munson." He inclined his head toward the officer in uniform. "Grab an evidence bag and go check it out."

"Hey, Detective." Another officer entered the room carrying something. He held up the evidence bag, which contained a knife that still had dried blood and fish scales on it. "Found this in the shed by the pool."

Griff acknowledged the find with a nod, and the officer left.

"Is that how he did it?" I rasped, my throat still on fire.

"Did what?" Griff frowned.

"Is that how Byron killed his mother? With the knife that he used on the fish?" My eyes were like saucers, and a fierce nausea gripped me. It hurt to speak, but I had to know.

"No. Her autopsy showed that she'd been systematically poisoned for months, but that wasn't her cause of death either. Cliff Bennett's lab work showed evidence of systematic poisoning, too. My guess is that Byron and his ex-wife were trying to kill them both so that they could split the inheritance."

"Poisoned?" I made the connection and realized that must've been why Cliff looked so bad in the grocery store. "With what?"

"He was mixing chlorine, in high doses, into their food and drink and disguising it with strong flavors. It eventually made his mother weak enough that he easily smothered her with a pillow. There are certain...indicators that show up when a person is smothered. If we hadn't seen those, we would've suspected death from natural causes rather than foul play. Cliff would most likely have suffered the same fate if he hadn't collapsed in the front yard. Agnes Hackles called an ambulance and most likely saved his life."

"Oh wow. So, he's alive then?" The muscles in my gut that had been clenched with anxiety suddenly relaxed, and I felt as though a weight had been lifted.

"He is. And when he regained consciousness, he told us his suspicions about his son. He caught him in the act of putting chlorine into the food and ran out into the front yard to get away. Unfortunately, he didn't make it to his car before he collapsed."

"That poor guy. No wonder he was so cranky all the time. He's been ill for months, and his wife had been too."

"And their son was the cause." A muscle in Griff's jaw flexed. "There's a search for his brother right now. No one has heard from him in weeks, and we're hoping that there's been no foul play there."

I shook my head and carefully took a sip of water. "I'm so glad I have a normal, boring life. This whole thing is awful."

Griff nodded, eyeing me closely. "It is. And now that you can go back to your normal, boring life, I suggest you refrain from meddling in murder investigations. You got lucky this time, but you could've been seriously hurt...or worse."

"Oh man, my mom's gonna kill me when she hears about this." I closed my eyes briefly, wincing at the image of my mother's face that flashed through my brain.

"Well, if she does, I'll be sure to arrange for organic food when she goes into custody."

And in that odd moment...Detective Marcus Griff actually smiled.

Chapter Thirty-One

"Oh, my baby!" My mom grabbed me the second that I walked in the door, enveloping me in a fierce hug, the scent of patchouli and home filling my senses. There was a comfort so profound in that scent that tears that I hadn't known I'd been containing flowed freely. "Yes, sweetie, let it out," Mom murmured, gently swaying back and forth with me in her arms while she stroked my hair like she'd always done when I was a child. At some point, Dad came and joined us, handing me a tissue before wrapping us both in his arms.

"I'm so sorry that I made you worry," I croaked, tears further clouding my already weak voice. I had texted them both from the car once Griff released me to leave the scene. I told them that the murder had been solved and that I was fine, but I hadn't provided any details.

Mom pulled back, her arms on my shoulders, and surveyed me from head to toe, her eyes locking on the red marks that Shannon had made on my neck. Her mouth dropped open, and she looked up at my dad, who inclined his head toward the couch. This was a first. I had never, in my entire life, seen my mother speechless.

"Sarisara, why don't you go sit down and tell us what happened," Dad suggested, placing a hand on the small of Mom's back and leading her to an easy chair. She plopped into it and just stared at me, her eyes brimming with tears.

Wiping my nose, which already felt raw, I nodded and curled my legs under me in a corner of the overstuffed couch, grabbing my favorite thick-weave blanket and clutching it. We were all silent for a moment, until my mother regained her voice.

"Who did this to you?" She touched her neck, her eyes filled with Mama Bear fire as a lone tear rolled, untouched, down her cheek.

"One of the killers," I whispered, the reality of it finally hitting me. I trembled, my breath still hitching from my crying jag.

"You could have been killed." My mother paled, and my dad stood, patting her hand.

"Let's try to remember, our darling girl is alive and well," he reminded her gently, shooting me a tender look. "I'm going to go get us some tea, and then Sari can tell us what happened." He turned to me. "Are you up to that?" he asked, his voice a bit hoarse.

His simple expression of love made my throat clog with unshed tears again, so I just nodded and tried to take a few deep breaths. Mom stared at me, transfixed, and Foo jumped up to snuggle in my lap. Dad returned in minutes with a fragrant lavender tea that eased the pain in my throat and soothed my soul. After a few sips, I was beginning to feel much more like my old self.

Recounting the horror show that I had lived through was cathartic. Out of necessity, I had buried my terror, doing what needed to be done—giving a statement to the police, submitting to an examination by the EMTs, and finally driving home, ignoring the concern in Agnes Hackles' eyes as she waved goodbye.

Dad placed a box of tissues at my side and refilled my tea twice before I was done talking and my mom was done interrogating and at the end of it, we all sat quietly in my living room. I felt drained, but better, and it seemed like talking it out had helped Mom process as well.

"So do you still feel like Champaign is safer than Temecula?" she joked weakly, clearly hoping that I'd suddenly change my mind, pack up Foo, and move back home.

"I feel like maybe I helped make it a safer place." Our eyes met, and she nodded.

"I don't know about you guys, but I'm starving. Should we go out?" Dad asked, effectively pulling the plug on the tension in the room.

A slow smile spread across my mom's face, and a much-needed chuckle erupted from me. "I could use a pizza."

"Pizza it is," Dad agreed.

"And I'm sure Mr. Tang will be up for ice cream later, under the circumstances," Mom added.

"Oh geez." I put a hand to my forehead. "I'm never going to hear the end of this."

"Absolutely not. Tang and I will make sure of that." Mom threatened with a smile.

Chapter Thirty-Two

Dustin showed up at my doorstep with a box from Fleur de Lis. I took one look and shuddered, the still-fresh memory of the smell of slimy fish heads roiling through my brain.

"What's wrong? Are you allergic to roses?" He frowned, quickly moving the box behind him.

"No. Killers. The last time I saw one of those boxes, it had fish heads in it, sent to me by a deranged killer." The words came out of my mouth with an ease that I hadn't imagined was possible. I had lived that—it still blew my mind.

"Oh, geez. I'm sorry, should I throw it out?"

"You're not Sari, *I'm* Sari, and don't you dare throw that out. Come in here. I have some surprises for you." I grabbed his arm and practically dragged him inside.

"Okay, but first, open the flowers. Please?" Dustin's request was so sweet that I couldn't deny it.

I opened the box of flowers and inside were the sweetest miniature peach and yellow roses that I'd ever seen.

"Oh my gosh, they're so beautiful."

Butterflies tickled in my midsection. It had been a long time since I'd received flowers, and the thought that they were from Dustin made my pulse flutter. Impulsively, I stood on my tiptoes and kissed him quickly on the cheek. We hadn't progressed past that...yet. He wrapped me in a warm hug, and I felt...safe. After what I'd just been through, that was the best feeling in the world.

"Thank you," I said, gazing into his eyes like a lovesick puppy. I could feel the silly grin that split my face in two and I didn't care in the least. I was totally fine with letting him know how delighted I was.

"You're welcome." It was funny how he seemed to have that same grin. "So, what's my surprise?" He bent down and picked up his new best friend, Foo. I've always said that dogs are great judges of character, so it was no surprise that the furry emperor of my home would adore Dustin.

"Well, you might want to put him down before I give them to you."

"Them? As in plural? Wow, okay. Sorry, buddy." He kissed Foo on the top of his head, which made my heart melt, and gently set him down.

"Okay, surprise number one…" I paused dramatically and reached into the pocket of my jeans, pulling out a pair of season tickets that Charla had given me for the game tonight. She'd be there with her new beau, courtside, of course. "Ta-da!"

"Oh wow, basketball tickets!" His eyes lit up, and I considered the possibility that I just might be able to fall in love again, before quickly dismissing the idea as being much too risky. I mean…maybe…

"My favorite sport!" we said in unison. It was as if the stars had aligned, as Mom would say.

"This is an amazing surprise; thank you, Sari. What could possibly be better than this?" He gazed at the tickets as though they were holy relics.

"Oh, just wait," I said, giving him a sly smile. "Go sit on the couch and close your eyes. I'll be right back."

"Close my eyes?"

"Yes, close your eyes!"

"I'll be sitting there by myself with my eyes closed. Isn't that a little weird?"

"Do you want your surprise or not?" I stood in front of him, hands on hips.

"Closing my eyes." Dustin chuckled, holding up his hands in surrender.

I hurried down the hall and grabbed his other surprise.

"Are they closed?" I called out before turning the corner into the living room.

"Yes, ma'am."

"Okay, stay very still, and don't open your eyes until I tell you to."

"I hear and obey." He laughed.

I set his present carefully on his lap and knelt in front of him, my knees popping embarrassingly loudly.

"Okay, open 'em," I said softly, hoping that I hadn't made a huge mistake. If he was who I thought he was, he would love my gift. If not, I guess I'd know all that I needed to know.

"Whoa!" Dustin's eyes went wide. "What is that?" His mouth dropped open, and his brows rose, a smile twitching at the corners of his lips.

"That is a hairless kitten, courtesy of my mom's beloved Safira. She's nine weeks old and is the pick of the litter."

"Look at those blue eyes. She looks like a little alien." He chuckled, shaking his head in what looked like wonder. "Wow, she's the second most beautiful thing I've ever seen."

Dustin gently picked up the tiny kitten and held her to his cheek, cuddling her close.

"Second? What's the first?" I whispered.

"Don't you know?" he asked, his gaze locking with mine.

I closed my eyes, feeling like I might just pass out, as he inclined his head toward me. Kisses, kittens, and basketball. It had been a rough few weeks, but man, what a happy ending.

Acknowledgements

Special thanks to my incredible agent, Cindy Bullard, for easing me out of my comfort zone and into the realm of traditional publishing—her ongoing support is phenomenal.

A hearty thank you to my Editor, Shawn Reilly Simmons, and the rest of the Level Best Books gang—this book wouldn't be a reality without all of you.

And finally, my heartfelt thanks to my family, friends, and colleagues who have believed in me and cheered me on. I couldn't do what I do, without all of you.

About the Author

Summer Prescott is a *USA Today* and *Wall Street Journal* bestselling author, who has penned nearly one hundred-fifty books in the cozy mystery, thriller, romantic suspense, sweet romance, and women's fiction genres.

Her books have the distinction of having risen to top ten rankings in their categories on Amazon, showcasing her work next to names like Janet Evanovich, Agatha Christie, and James Patterson.

As owner of Summer Prescott Books Publishing, Summer is responsible for a combined catalog of nearly five hundred cozy mysteries and thrillers. Mentoring and assisting new cozy writers in launching their careers has long been a passion of Summer's, and she has played a key role in the incredible success of cozy writers such as Patti Benning, Gretchen Allen, Thea Cambert, Emma Ainsley, Maggie Benton, and Carolyn Q. Hunter.

Summer enjoys travel and was honored to be a featured speaker at the International Writer's Conference in Cuenca, Ecuador, in 2018. The event draws writers from all over the world.

A doting mother to four grown children, Summer lives in Champaign, Illinois, with her Standard Poodles, Elvis and Chubby.

SOCIAL MEDIA HANDLES:
https://www.facebook.com/summer.prescott.58/

https://www.facebook.com/groups/summerprescottcozymysteries
https://twitter.com/SummerPrescott1
https://www.amazon.com/stores/Summer-Prescott/author/B00M2IE
APE
https://www.instagram.com/summer.prescott.cozies/
https://www.youtube.com/@summerprescott2806
https://www.bookbub.com/authors/summer-prescott

AUTHOR WEBSITE:
www.summerprescottbooks.com

Also by Summer Prescott

Frosted Love Series

A Murder Moist Foul (2015)

A Pinch of Murder (2015)

Murder So Sweet (2015)

A Mouthful of Murder (2015)

Cupcakes and Murder (2015)

Black Bottom Murder (2015)

Buttercream Murder (2015)

Rum Cake Murder (2015)

Pink Velvet Murder (2015)

Devil's Food Murder (2015)

Creamsicle Murder (2015)

Plain Vanilla Murder (2015)

Strawberry Murder (2015)

Raspberry Creme Murder (2015)

Mango Madness Murder (2015)

Chocolate Filled Murder (2015)

Pumpkin Spice Murder (2015)

Apple Cider Murder (2015)

S'more Murder (2015)

Chocolate Fudge Murder (2015)

Gingerbread Murder (2015)

Peppermint Murder (2015)

Eggnog Murder (2015)

Sugar Cookies and Murder (2015)

Peanut Brittle Murder (2015)

Fruitcake Murder (2015)

Champagne Murder (2016)

Hot Chocolate Murder (2016)

Cranberry Orange Murder (2016)

Apple Crisp Murder (2016)
White Chocolate Murder (2016)
Red Hot Velvet Murder (2016)

New England Series
New England Clam Murder (2015)
Clam Bake Murder (2015)

Key Lime Cozy Mysteries Series
A Lime To Kill (2015)
Key Lime Die (2015)
The Lime and the Dead (2015)
Murder By Lime (2015)
Death By Lime (2015)
A Deadly Slice of Lime (2015)
Death, Limes and Videotape (2015)
Live and Lime Die (2015)

Hawg Heaven Cozy Mysteries
Patriot's Passing (2016)
Baby Back Murder (2016)
Nacho Usual Murder (2017)
Hawgs, Dogs, and Murder (2017)
Twists and Tears (2017)
Entitled to Murder (2017)
Bittersweet Murder (2017)
Burnt Endz (2019)

INNcredibly Sweet Series
Irish Creme Killer (2016)
Coconut Creme Killer (2016)
Caramel Creme Killer (2016)
Chai Cupcake Killer (2016)

Streusel Creme Killer (2016)

Peaches and Creme Killer (2016)

Marshmallow Creme Killer (2016)

Boston Cream Killer (2016)

Bourbon Creme Killer (2016)

Spiced Latte Killer (2016)

Toffee Apple Killer (2016)

Peppermint Mocha Killer (2017)

Sweetheart Killer (2017)

Killer Me Green (2017)

Blue Suede Killer (2017)

Cupcakes in Paradise Series

Vanilla Bean Killer (2017)

Star Spangled Killer (2017)

Salted Caramel Killer (2017)

Caramel Pretzel Killer (2017)

Southern Pecan Killer (2017)

Creamy Pumpkin Killer (2017)

Butterscotch Dream Killer (2017)

Frostycake Murder (2017)

Cookie Dough Killer (2018)

Butter Pecan Killer (2018)

German Chocolate Killer (2018)

Tropical Punch Killer (2018)

Chocolate Cherry Killer (2018)

Sweet Strawberry Killer (2018)

Killer Gingerbread Cupcakes (2018)

You Can't Kill A Cupcake (2019)

The Dark Hobby Trilogy

The Quiet Type (2017)

The Killing Girl (2019)

Standalone Novels
Christmas Reunion Killer (2018)
Criminals and Coral (2019)
Cookies and Crime (2019)
Hitting the Jackpot (2019)

Calgon Chronicles Series
Kidnappers and Killers (2019)
Books and Bodies (2019)
Homicide and Holidays (2019)
Questions and Quarantine (2020)
Feasting and Felonies (2020)
The Paths We Take (2021)

Appleton Farms Cozy Mysteries
Homicide and Honeycrisps (2020)
Felonies and Fujis (2020)
Perpetrators and Pumpkins (2020)

Stand Alone Novel
Cozy Conspiracy (2020)

Tea Series
Tempest in a Tea Room (2021)
Hot Tea and a Cold Case (2021)
Teas, Keys, and Mysteries

Standalones (Some are series related)
A Match Made in Murder (2017)
Home for the Holidays (2018)
A Blush of Murder (2018)
A Slippery Slope of Murder (2018)
A Twinkle of Murder (2019)

A Blossom of Murder (2019)
Spellstruck (2019)
Puppy Loves (2019)
Chas by Choice (2020)
Echoes of Murder (2020)
Christmas Songbird (2021)

Novellas
Charming Chalice (2021)
Mewy Christmas (2021)
Hang Out the Stalkings (2021)

33rd Street Roastery Series – 8 books